BLOODTIDE

By Bill Knox

BLOODTIDE

BILL KNOX

PUBLISHED FOR THE CRIME CLUB BY
DOUBLEDAY & COMPANY, INC.
GARDEN CITY, NEW YORK
1983

All of the characters in this book
are fictitious, and any resemblance
to actual persons, living or dead,
is purely coincidental.

Library of Congress Cataloging in Publication Data

Knox, Bill, 1928–
Bloodtide.

I. Title.
PR6061.N6B5   1982   823′.914
ISBN 0-385-18452-2
Library of Congress Catalog Card Number 82-45622

For Debbie

PRELUDE

A weather satellite photograph first caught the birth of a new, deep depression off Iceland. Three days later, on a Sunday in midsummer, the depression became a storm which raged out of the Atlantic to hit the Scottish northwest coast. A force-eight hell of wind, rain and mountainous seas, it first hit the long chain of the Hebrides Islands. Then it swung and raved in fury down the sea men called the Minch, between the Hebrides and the mainland coast.

Shipping fled. Fishing fleets huddled in shelter. Giant waves hammered continuously against stone breakwaters at a score of tiny harbours. White spray drenched far inland.

Things stayed that way for thirty-six hours as the storm used the Minch like a giant funnel. Lighthouse keepers reported sixty-foot waves near the Butt of Lewis. Six men died when a Dutch coaster went down off Barra Head. Two were swept overboard and lost from a navy supply ship which made Oban with her superstructure reduced to twisted metal. A Campbeltown lifeboat somehow rescued two men and a girl from a yacht which overturned and sank within sight of harbour. Another girl aboard drowned. When they found her body later, it was lying in a field, well above high-water mark.

All were only incidents in a trail of fury.

Then, at last, on the second night, the storm moved away. First the wind's incessant howling gradually eased, then faded. The rain stopped. Last of all, the sea began to quieten.

Big Gibby MacNeil didn't know about it.

He was dying. He had reached the stage where there was only an occasional confused, half-formed tendril of thought still left in his mind.

He didn't know if he was comfortable or uncomfortable. He was tired and he wanted to sleep. Where he was and how he'd got there were vague uncertainties. Once, lapsing in and out of his dreamlike state, he was vaguely conscious of a swaying motion and a steady vibration which might have been an engine.

Maybe he was on a boat. Not that it mattered, not that anything
really mattered.

Big Gibby MacNeil slipped into death.

He didn't even know he had been murdered.

By dawn, the storm had gone. The wind had become a slight
breeze, the sea had quietened to a greasy swell and the weather out-
look was good. The coastline might be strewn with torn weed and
broken flotsam and, to the sensitive, the very air still seemed damp
and bruised and quivering. But, in practical terms, that was incidental.

The fishing fleets were heading out again. They had lost two days'
work and there was no time to lose—not when there was mackerel in
the Minch. Vast shoals of the silver-grey fish, a harvest as rich as any
fisherman could remember.

And when the mackerel came like that, every man and every boat
worked to the twin limits of endurance and capacity. The mackerel
only stayed so long, then moved on. Days or weeks, no one could be
certain how long the harvest might last.

It had always been that way.

Hugh Campbell was skipper aboard the *Cailinn,* a fifty-foot boat
with a crew of five. She was one of the first fishing boats to leave the
little harbour at Port Ard, and as soon as she was clear of the breakwater the *Cailinn* swung on a southwest course with the sun still rising astern.

It was the kind of morning when Hugh Campbell let instinct rule.
He kept the *Cailinn* on that one course for over an hour, until that
same instinct made him steer north for a few minutes. Then, suddenly, the sea around the fishing boat was alive with mackerel. Her
crew could see them, layer upon layer in the steel-blue water. A mul-
titude of gulls and other seabirds dived and plunged all around, attacking from above while every now and again some other, unseen
predators, attacking from below, sent fish fleeing upward, breaking
the surface briefly as they tried to escape.

By midmorning, the *Cailinn*'s nets were out for the third time. The
sun was high in a cloudless blue sky, the sea glinted, metal fittings
were hot to touch, and the fishing boat's crew worked stripped to the
waist. As before, the nets bulged with wriggling fish as they were
hauled in, and the water which drenched along the deck dried away
almost as quickly as it landed.

Once again, mackerel by the hundreds began to spill into the fishhold. Down there, the youngest member of the *Cailinn*'s crew had little chance of rest as he wielded a shovel, sending a cascade of crushed ice from the boat's ice bunker over each new basket of fish that was filled and stowed.

The boy paused, wiped sweat from his forehead, and raised the shovel again. Then he stopped, work forgotten, staring in disbelief at the bunker. At the spot where he'd taken the last swing at the crushed ice, a man's hand now protruded.

Work stopped. Using the shovel and their hands, more of the crew helped the boy and uncovered the dead man. Big Gibby MacNeil lay as if sleeping, his lined, leathery face still powdered with ice dust. More ice caked his blue wool jersey and waterproof jacket, or clung to his dark serge trousers and short yellow seaboots.

They all knew him. Everyone knew Big Gibby.

Curious, one of the crew tried to move an outstretched arm. An elbow joint, frozen stiff, cracked in loud protest. The movement disturbed the dead man's jacket and an almost empty half-bottle of cheap whisky rolled from one of the pockets.

A fisherman clambered out of the hold and went aft to the wheelhouse. As skipper, Hugh Campbell had stayed at the wheel while cursing his luck and keeping the *Cailinn*'s blunt bow to the swell.

"Well?" asked Campbell curtly.

The fisherman told him.

"Bloody hell," said Campbell, talking to the world in general.

It seemed totally typical that Gibby MacNeil could have got himself frozen to death on what looked like the warmest day of the year. But it didn't need a genius to imagine how it had happened. The *Cailinn* had spent the storm tied in tight against the quay at Port Ard. Big Gibby MacNeil in drink was always unpredictable, but more than once he'd been found curled up in some corner of anybody's boat, sleeping it off.

It had just been his bad luck if he'd crawled into the empty ice bunker. Then, when the storm had ended, it had still been dark, and the only thing that had mattered to any fisherman was getting his boat ready for sea. Like the rest of the Port Ard boats, the *Cailinn* had taken on her ice in a hurry.

"What do we do about it, Skipper?" asked the fisherman. He glanced at the radio-telephone on the bulkhead. "I mean—well, will you let them know ashore?"

"There's no rush." Hugh Campbell frowned for'ard, at the great bulge of fish still waiting in his nets. He was a civilised man, the kind who went to church with his wife most Sundays. But he was the *Cailinn*'s owner as well as skipper. Priorities mattered. "Cover him up with something, then get the lads back to work."

"And the ice?"

Campbell blinked. "Use it, man. What else?"

"Aye." The fisherman nodded his understanding, then grimaced. "It's a pity. When Big Gibby was sober he played the best damned fiddle music I've ever heard."

"Then he shouldn't be too bad on a harp, if he gets the chance." Hugh Campbell thumbed at the net. "Get them moving."

It was noon before the last of the mackerel were aboard. By then the *Cailinn* was on a new course, the thumping beat of her engine pushing her through the low swell towards Loch Armach.

That was where the big Russian factory ship lay at anchor, her vast processing plant greedily waiting for fish, two refrigerated carrier ships flying the hammer and sickle tied one on either side of her and still only half-loaded.

The Russians bought all the fish they could get.

A rogue sea emerged from the swell, hit the *Cailinn* along the port quarter, and creamed white along her deck. As the boat heaved, then settled, Hugh Campbell braced himself in the wheelhouse. Then, humming under his breath, he eased the engine throttle another notch forward.

The wheelhouse door opened.

"Coffee, Skipper?" asked the boy.

Campbell took the steaming half-pint mug in one hand. He peered towards the gap in the distant coastline, which was the mouth of Loch Armach. He could make out two dark specks ahead of him, other boats, heading in the same direction.

That didn't matter. The Russians paid a guaranteed price, no more and no less.

Still, a thought crossed his mind. He'd better tell the lads to keep their mouths shut about Gibby MacNeil until they'd unloaded at the factory ship. He didn't believe the Russians would be particularly sensitive about a dead man having shared the fishhold with their catch, but why take chances?

Another swell lumped towards the *Cailinn* and Hugh Campbell fined the helm a shade to meet it. He turned his mind to a problem waiting him ashore. His wife had been making more noises about needing a new washing machine. His share of the day's catch could go in that direction.

The machine she wanted was an American make. He chuckled. That's what she'd get—with the Russians paying for it.

Man, life could be complicated.

CHAPTER 1

It was three days after the storm. Hunched in the command chair aboard Her Majesty's Fisheries Protection Service cruiser *Marlin,* Captain James Shannon peered dispassionately ahead through the bridge glass.

"She's an ugly big brute," he decided aloud. "Probably handles like a cow, even in a flat calm."

For once, First Mate Webb Carrick found it hard to disagree with his commander. It was also a warm day, particularly in the enclosed bridge area. He eased his cap slightly back from his forehead and was glad he wore an open-necked white shirt in place of his usual roll-neck sweater.

"Maybe they're sold on 'big is beautiful,'" he suggested, a twinkle in his dark-brown eyes. "Mother Russia seems to go for size."

"So do elephants, mister." Shannon, a small, stout man with a greying beard and moon-shaped face, looked hot but refused to discard his uniform jacket or even loosen his tie. He gave a snort. "Just look at her."

The fourteen-thousand-ton Soviet factory ship *Zarakov* lay at anchor half a mile ahead, white hammer-and-sickle emblems prominent on her tall twin funnels. She had an ungainly, almost top-heavy superstructure liberally festooned with aerials and radar masts, flanked fore and aft by a small forest of derrick booms. Long black hull liberally streaked with rust, she looked exactly what she was—more floating production line than ship. She already had company. Two west coast fishing boats, big purse-netters, were unloading their catches on her port side.

Shannon stirred again. "Come down to two hundred revolutions, mister. We'll let them have a good look at us first."

"Two hundred—slow ahead both, sir." Carrick flicked the telegraph levers and the throb of *Marlin*'s twin diesels eased to a new, lazier note. One thing puzzled him. "Wasn't she supposed to have company, a couple of refrigerated carriers?"

"Must have taken their cargo aboard and started for home," shrugged Shannon. "Another will probably arrive tomorrow. That's the way they work." He glanced at the duty helmsman, a tall Stornoway man who hadn't bothered to put in his teeth that morning. The sight brought a faint grimace of disgust from Shannon; then he barked, "Andy, give me five degrees port rudder."

"Five degrees port." The helmsman spun the wheel. "How close in are we goin', Captain?"

"Spitting distance." Shannon eyed the shrinking gap. "Then we'll come round tight by her stern. But remember those fishing boats." Switching his attention to Carrick, he nodded towards the *Zarakov*. "Met up with her before, mister?"

"Not till now," admitted Carrick.

Though there had been others. A string of East European factory ships made an annual visit to Scottish waters for the mackerel season, the few short weeks each year when vast shoals of the silvergrey fish came boiling into the waters of the Minch. For these few weeks, working to a tight quota system, the fishing boats involved could net and land well over one hundred thousand tons in a brief, hectic harvest.

British law banned the East Europeans from joining in. But the factory ships could still buy and process and send back home.

There was an East German ship to the south, near Loch Broom. The Poles were off Ullapool. Another Russian had become part of the scenery near Stornoway. There were others scattered along the coast. All buying catches from Scottish boats, all scheduled to move on the day the mackerel season ended.

But the Russian anchored at Loch Armach, that deep mainland bay to the north of the Summer Isles, was the biggest of them all.

Carrick smiled to himself. He wasn't the only one aboard *Marlin* who thought the black hull ahead different and interesting. Several of the fishery cruiser's crew had found a reason to be on deck. Some were making a pretence of checking the for'ard derrick boom used to swing out *Marlin*'s high-speed launch. Others, including the cook and a couple of the engine-room squad, were simply leaning on the foredeck rail and spectating.

"I hate disturbing you, mister," said Shannon with sarcasm. "But do you mind coming awake?"

"Sir?" Carrick ignored the helmsman's sideways grin, an alarming display of empty pink gums.

"Make sure those two up top are ready." Shannon included the helmsman in his glare. "And you—watch your damned heading. Tighten up."

The helmsman scowled indignantly. The compass needle had barely quivered. But he didn't argue.

Leaving them, Carrick went to the door on the starboard side and went out onto the open bridge wing. The fishery cruiser's big twenty-one-inch searchlight was mounted on a platform above the bridge, covered daytime style by a canvas hood. Two men were on the platform, one young and worried-looking, festooned with camera gear. The other, bulky, red-haired and wearing overalls, saw Carrick and waved a greeting.

"Everything okay?" asked Carrick.

"Don't ask me." Chief Petty Officer William "Clapper" Bell scratched his thigh through his overalls. *Marlin*'s bo'sun, a tough Glasgow-Irishman, had a face that might have been shaped with a blunt axe. Pointing at his companion, he winked. "Ask the expert."

"Well?" demanded Carrick.

"One problem," came the sad admission. Young, freckle-faced and overweight, Jumbo Wills was Second Mate and lived partly in awe of Shannon and partly wondering what minor disaster would next come his way. He licked his lips. "Webb, it's this damned telephoto lens. I'm not sure how to handle it."

"Or where to put it," suggested Clapper Bell.

"Shut up," said Carrick, glad Wills wasn't alone up there. "Jumbo, just point the thing and keep clicking."

He turned away but stayed on the bridge wing for a moment. Fleet Support wanted photographs of the Russian, photographs that would probably end up on some Ministry of Defence desk. If Wills had remembered to load film in the cameras.

Carrick sighed and watched a large black-backed gull plane across *Marlin*'s bow, then bank round and stay overhead. It was early afternoon, the sun high in an almost cloudless blue sky and, now they were in the shelter of the sea-loch, there was only a light swell running. *Marlin*'s course had become a slow curve, her wake a milky ribbon over the sparkling water. A light breeze was just enough to ripple the blue ensign with the gold badge of the Scottish Fisheries Protection Service flying at her stern.

On ahead, where the *Zarakov* was anchored, Loch Armach was still more than two miles wide. He could see a sprinkling of cottages along either shore, and small shapes moving in a handkerchief-sized field were cattle. There were sheep on the hills beyond the fields, heather-covered hills which ran back to meet a distant range of mountain peaks.

It made a beautiful, peacefully normal picture except for that long, black, twin-funnelled hull ahead, which intruded like an unwelcome centrepiece—a centrepiece which also reduced *Marlin*'s one-hundred-eighty-foot length to almost midget proportions.

But *Marlin,* with her squat single funnel and the sleek grey lines of a cut-down destroyer, regularly dealt with visiting problems of all sizes. Four hundred tons of Clyde-built steel, her twin two-thousand-horsepower diesels could produce a thirty-knot speed when required. To man her, Shannon had a crew of thirty, plus three watch-keeping officers and the engineering team. Every last one, even Jumbo Wills, was a hand-picked professional.

The Russians on the *Zarakov* might find it amusing that ships in the Protection Squadron didn't carry as much as a deck gun for armament.

But the fishery cruisers represented the law around the Scottish coast out to the two-hundred-mile sea limit. In *Marlin*'s case, any fisherman unlucky enough to tangle with her knew she carried something as potent as any weapon.

His name was Shannon. He ran his ship with a blend of skill, cunning and tight efficiency that had earned him the description "a hangman in seaboots." Which had delighted Shannon when he'd heard.

Carrick grimaced. Shannon was nearing the age when compulsory retirement lay ahead, though God help anyone who suggested he was getting too old for the job.

It just happened that Carrick had a problem. Without knowing it, his captain was part of it.

Marlin came in towards the *Zarakov*'s bow on what looked a few degrees short of a collision course. Then she idled her way down the Russian's starboard side, the sea lapping nervously in the gap between the two hulls, a shimmer of exhaust coming from the fishery cruiser's funnel. The top of that funnel was several feet lower than the Russian's main deck, which had suddenly become lined with spectators.

"Like I said, an ugly big brute," murmured Shannon. He was on his feet now, most of his attention devoted to an apparently casual consideration of the gap between the two ships. "Bow-thrust, mister?"

"Standing by," confirmed Carrick. He had the bridge intercom

phone in his hand, ready to pass the order which would bring the
bow-thrust auxiliary machinery into play, one of the reasons *Marlin*
could almost turn on the legendary and now obsolete sixpence. He
spared a glance at the other ship's deck. "We're drawing a crowd."

"Some o' them women," said the helmsman helpfully.

"Then you should have put your teeth in," snapped Shannon.
"Steer fine."

But the man was right. Carrick stole another quick glance. Several
of the figures lining the Russian's rails were unmistakably female, despite the rubber aprons and overalls. A few were waving at the
seamen on *Marlin*'s deck, and one, a woman of vast proportions,
added a gesture which needed no translation and which had nothing
to do with workers' solidarity.

"What do you make of her?" asked Shannon unexpectedly.

"Not much," said Carrick. As a ship—and he presumed Shannon
meant the ship—the rust streaks on the *Zarakov*'s hull combined with
blistered paintwork and a shabby air of neglect. She couldn't be more
than a few years old. But though most Russian ships were well main-
tained, she already looked worn out. From a lifeboat which seemed
to have jammed at a drunken angle in its falls, to the way in which
several unemptied trash buckets were lying in the open, under attack
by gulls, the *Zarakov* lacked basic shipkeeping. Even the hammer-
and-sickle crests on her funnel needed a repaint. "They can have
her."

Shannon grunted, hands touching the bridge rail, short legs wide
apart on the thick rubber vibration mats, for the moment more part
of his ship than anything else.

"That's a damned floating fish market," he said curtly. "She'll gut
and freeze a ton of fish in minutes and do it twenty-four hours a day
if necessary."

"Busy." Carrick hoped Wills and Clapper Bell, up above them,
were using their cameras—if only in self-defence. Two of the *Zarakov*'s crew were hurrying along her deck, keeping pace with them,
taking pictures all the time. In addition, someone up on the Russian's
bridge was using a telescopic lens which looked more like a gun
barrel. "What else does she do? Spyship?"

"Don't they all?" Shannon pointed at the Russian's proliferation
of aerials and radar. "That's not for music while they work."

Gradually, first *Marlin*'s bow and then her bridge drew level with
the Russian flag flapping at the *Zarakov*'s stern. Blue water showed
beyond the black hull.

"Full starboard helm," ordered Shannon. As the wheel began to spin, he nodded to Carrick. "Starboard bow-thrust. Main engines half-ahead port, slow astern starboard." Then, for the helmsman's benefit, he added, "Remember those fishing boats. They've got lawyers and they sue."

The deck vibrated as first the bow-thrust cut in and then the main diesels answered. Rudder hard over, wash churning white at her stern, *Marlin* came round in a tight, heeling turn. Down below, it meant curses in the engine room and crockery crashing in the galley. One of the bridge lockers flew open and a bundle of signal flags cascaded out.

It was a spectacular, not totally necessary piece of seamanship. As the engines died again, Shannon was grinning. They'd rounded the Russian's stern and were steadying on a new parallel course along her port side.

Then Shannon's grin froze. Where there had been two fishing boats alongside the *Zarakov,* there was only one. The other was moving away from the factory ship, about thirty yards clear, speed little more than a crawl—and she was directly in *Marlin*'s path.

Carrick swallowed. The helmsman swore and grabbed at the wheel for an emergency turn to port.

"Belay that," snarled Shannon. "Hold your helm midships. Full astern, both engines." He glared at the fishing boats as Carrick jumped to slap the telegraph levers. "Move, you damned idiots. Move her!"

Excited figures were shouting and gesticulating on the factory ship and the other fishing boat. The crewmen on *Marlin*'s deck were open-mouthed and helpless.

Already, in the space of seconds, *Marlin*'s engines were answering the sudden new demand. A white froth was beginning to boil at her stern as her twin screws clawed and spun to arrest her progress. But it still had to be a gesture. They would cleave the fishing boat exactly midships. Her name was the *Harmony* and she had dark red paintwork, details that registered in Carrick's mind like a wild irrelevance, in the same way as he noted the cloud of gulls which had risen from the Russian ship, their screams adding to the general chaos.

Suddenly black smoke seemed to erupt from the fishing boat's exhaust stack. Her engine hammered to full life and she seemed to lunge forward.

It had to be too late. The gap was still shrinking and now *Marlin*, engines still thrashing full astern, looked like hitting her aft, near the wheelhouse. Fists clenched, willing the smaller boat on, Carrick tensed for the impact.

The fishery cruiser's bow began to blank out his view. Then, unbelievably, the *Harmony* was clear, they were shaving past her stern with inches to spare, the distance between them increasing with every second.

"Jesus," said the helmsman reverently. "I thought—"

"Watch your helm," rasped Shannon. He drew a breath. "Mister, resume slow ahead both."

Moments later they were murmuring on, continuing their slow crawl down the *Zarakov*'s length. The *Harmony,* well clear, had stopped and was drifting. A fair-haired man who had to be her skipper had erupted from the little wheelhouse and was shouting and shaking his fist.

"Not exactly pleased," said Shannon with an unusual mildness.

"No, sir." Carrick drew a deep breath and glanced up at the *Zarakov*'s crowded rail. "We gave that lot a fright."

"Or a disappointment," muttered Shannon. He fell silent and stayed that way until *Marlin* had cleared the factory ship's bow, passing close to her rusting anchor chain. The mouth of the loch and the open sea lay ahead. He glanced round. "Where's our friend?"

Carrick followed his gaze. The fishing boat was under way again, on a similar course, moving at a modest but steady pace.

"Take over, mister," ordered Shannon. "Bring her up to full ahead both. Finish the rest of the usual patrol pattern along the coast, then set course for Port Ard." He began moving towards the companionway which led below, then stopped. "The *Harmony* is a Port Ard boat. We'll see her again."

He went below, in the direction of his day cabin. Drawing a deep breath, Carrick let it out slowly, then reached again for the engine-room telegraph. Gradually the bridge deck's vibration began to increase as *Marlin*'s diesels commenced their buildup.

"Sir." The helmsman chuckled. "Fishing boat signalling." He paused and grinned. "Angry, isn't he?"

The smaller craft was well astern, but the light which had begun winking from her wheelhouse was spitting out a ragged stream of Morse as fast as the operator could trigger his lamp key. The words were blistering.

Carrick considered the fishing boat, then the long black hull of the Russian factory ship further astern. He shook his head. The *Harmony*'s skipper was wrong, Shannon had been right.

Holding *Marlin*, refusing to attempt to steer her out of trouble, had been their only chance. Anything else, with so small a gap, would have ended in disaster. Turn to port and they'd have rammed the *Harmony* as she tried to get clear. Try to avoid her stern and *Marlin* would have ended up embedded in the factory ship.

Knowing there was no way they could have stopped in time, Shannon had made his decision and had made it instantly. Instantly—that was what mattered.

Deliberately, Carrick wondered just how fast his own reactions would have been if he had had to make the decision. Could he, would he have been able to cope? It mattered.

The starboard door swung open and Jumbo Wills came in from the bridge wing. Clutching his camera gear, he looked pale. He was closely followed by Clapper Bell, but the bo'sun was grinning.

"Where's the Old Man?" As he asked, Wills dumped the camera equipment on a locker top.

"Gone below," answered Carrick. "How did it go? Did you get those photographs?"

"We tried," said Wills defensively.

"Till the fun began," said the red-haired Bell. He placed the camera he was carrying beside the rest of the gear, considered the light still flashing from the *Harmony*, then frowned. "Not much good with a lamp, is he? And who's he calling a maniac?"

"I can guess," said Wills. "Webb, if you'd been up where we were—"

"Tell the captain," said Carrick.

"He'd like that." Clapper Bell winked at him. He and Carrick worked too much together as *Marlin*'s scuba-diving team to stick to formalities. The kind of partnership demanded by underwater work bred its own style of discipline. "Go on, Mr. Wills—death or glory."

"Get lost," said Wills. He scowled at Carrick. "Webb, I think—"

"Don't," said Carrick wearily. "When you do, we usually land in trouble."

It was near enough the truth to hurt. Wills flushed, but persisted. "Look, I think we were set up."

"By the Russians?" Carrick showed his surprise.

"Why not?" Wills became enthusiastic. "We chop one of our own fishing boats in two. They're taking pictures of us taking pictures of them, and—and—" he came to a halt, uncertain how to finish.

"We make page one in *Pravda?*" suggested Carrick. The deck gave a quivering lurch beneath his feet. They had lost the shelter of the sea-loch, and the lazy, lumping swell from the Atlantic was welcoming them again. "Forget it. They've better things to do." He noticed the helmsman eavesdropping. "So have we. Like staying on course." The helmsman tightened the wheel a token fraction.

Wills and Clapper Bell went below. Then Carrick was relieved by Ferguson, *Marlin*'s third watch-keeping officer. Oldest by several years, middle-aged and grey-haired, Ferguson was taciturn by nature. He rated as Junior Second Mate, a man who had come back to sea after several years ashore. No one knew much about him, and he kept it that way.

Carrick handed over, left the bridge, but stepped out on the main deck before he went below. The sun was past its midday high and they were still about an hour from Port Ard, sailing south and half a mile out from the empty, rocky coastline. The only other ship in sight was a single-funnelled MacBrayne coaster plugging along close to the horizon on some inter-island run.

He heard a clatter and looked round. *Marlin*'s cook was emptying a bucket of galley slops over the side.

"What are we eating?" asked Carrick.

"Stew, sir." The cook, a fat man who sometimes ran an illegal dice game, eyed him cautiously. "Irish stew—the captain likes Irish stew." He paused, then added defensively, "It smells all right."

"Surprise me. Try and keep it that way," suggested Carrick.

He watched the man retreat towards his galley, then went below. Officers' living quarters were 'tween decks and aft of *Marlin*'s modest wardroom. Carrick stopped there to pour himself a mug of coffee from the pot kept heating on a side table. The only other person in the wardroom was the off-watch Second Engineer, a young Cardiff Welshman named Butler. Butler looked up from a book and gave a cheerful nod.

"Have we stopped playing at battleships?" asked Butler.

"Go and oil something," suggested Carrick. "Then maybe you'll win a medal."

Butler chuckled and went back to his book.

Taking the coffee with him, Carrick went to his cabin and closed the door behind him. Then he stood for a moment, sipping the coffee, thinking again.

A stockily built, reasonably handsome man, five foot ten and in his early thirties, he had dark-brown hair. Usually, even when he was thinking, he had an easygoing air. His broad-boned, weather-beaten face had lips that were slightly thin and which often resulted in a mildly cynical expression even when he didn't intend it.

But the easygoing air wasn't totally reliable. Even Captain Shannon had learned that fairly quickly. Webb Carrick could have a stubborn mind of his own.

At that moment, though he didn't know it, Shannon was part of a decision Carrick would have to make by the time the *Marlin*'s current patrol ended.

His uniform jacket was hanging behind the cabin door, the letter was in an inside pocket. It had been delivered aboard just before they sailed from the west coast patrol base at Greenock.

Carrick set down the mug, took the letter, and read it again, though he knew the words by heart.

On Department notepaper, it was more a cautious sounding than an offer and was signed by the Protection Squadron's Marine Superintendent. A new ship would be commissioned in a matter of months. Her captain would be appointed before that time, to be on hand while she was fitted out. The last paragraph was the important one.

"Currently, an appointment to this command is being actively considered. If you wish your name to go forward, advise me by the end of this month."

Her name was *Barracuda*. Smaller than *Marlin* but faster, crammed with electronics, with a new type of hull design and a small helicopter pad aft, she gave direct bridge control of just about everything except the coffee machine.

Reading between the lines, he could have her.

A new ship as his first command. Lips pursed, Carrick folded the letter and tucked it away. Frowning at himself in the mirror above his tiny wash basin, he took another sip of coffee. His dark-brown eyes narrowed as he thought about it for the hundredth time.

Deciding what he should do was more than difficult. Even though to have any doubt might seem crazy.

He looked around the cabin. It was small, with one porthole almost on the waterline. Even in calm sea, spray flecked the glass every few seconds. The furnishings amounted to his bunk, locker space, a folding table, a chair and a few other basics. When *Marlin* was in a pursuit situation it vibrated like a drum.

But it was the nearest thing he'd had to home for the last couple of years.

Until then, he'd been deep-sea Merchant Navy. A newly acquired master's ticket in his pocket but without a ship and nothing on the

horizon, he'd grabbed the appointment as *Marlin*'s First Mate under
Shannon.

Almost immediately he'd learned how little he really knew about
the sea.

The Scottish Fisheries Protection Service was, in practical terms, a
sea-going police and emergency organisation—a unique civilian force
responsible for patrolling some one hundred and thirty thousand
square miles of Scottish offshore waters along one of the most dangerous coastlines in the world.

Marlin's police beat was among the toughest. From the gale-swept
Butt of Lewis in the north to the shifting sandbanks of the Solway in
the south, she covered an average of forty thousand sea miles a year.
With her sister ships, she enforced the law and tried to keep order in
a tough multinational industry which didn't particularly want either.

Zones and limits, conservation and detection—the stakes were
high. The Scottish fishing fleet alone landed a reported £180 million
of fish a year, and even the cynics couldn't guess how much more
came ashore illegally. Other nations had varied rights, varied quotas,
varied prohibitions. Dutch and German, French or Norwegian, the
Eastern Bloc fleets all worked and nibbled round the edges of a web
of rules and regulations intended to protect fish stock for tomorrow.

But fish meant money. The result could be miniature wars between the boats of different nations—with such unexpected con-
tenders as Spaniards from the Mediterranean and the occasional Bul-
garian arrivals all the long way from the Black Sea.

Carrick prowled his little cabin, stopped at the porthole and
looked at the foam-dappled sea sliding past only inches away.

Fisheries Protection played a complex role. Even the average fishing skipper, ready to curse all "fishery snoops," would admit that,
could even maintain something not far short of a love-hate relation-
ship at times.

Caught on an illegal fishing charge, a skipper could face jail, a fine
of up to fifty thousand pounds, and confiscation of his boat, catch
and gear. Balanced against the profit if undetected, that kind of risk
was often acceptable. Not that any fishing boat surrendered easily—
more often that came at the end of a nightmare chase through reefs
and currents and only after a hardfisted Fisheries Protection boarding
party had proved ready to subdue any remaining opposition.

But Fisheries Protection also meant a search-and-rescue service, an
arbitration court, the people who sorted out things like oil pollution

from drilling rigs or tankers, who could turn up in a score of vital one-off security and trouble-shooting roles.

An old Scottish proverb flickered through Carrick's mind and he grinned. *Better the devil you know than the devil you don't.*

When *Barracuda* came along, she'd be in the thick of it. He wanted her command. But, hell, was he ready for that?

"Damn all indecision," he told himself aloud.

And gave in. He needed a cigarette. Two patrols back he'd officially stopped smoking. But he now had a pack, plus a book of matches, taped to the underside of his bunk. Where they were hard to reach, the way a reforming alcoholic might hide an emergency bottle.

Stooping, he got them out, lit one, and drew on it with relief.

There was another aspect to a command in Fisheries Protection—the sheer whitewater seamanship it demanded along a devil's cauldron of a coastline.

He knew he was still learning every day he spent with Shannon. That perverse, often ill-tempered little bear of a man could read all he wanted from the lump of a wave, the sheer texture of a dawn sea, or even how gulls were behaving overhead.

Shannon taught by example, seldom explaining. But it was all there to be learned, and Carrick knew what had just happened was yet one more example.

So, was he really ready?

He took another long draw on his cigarette, then, almost angrily, stuffed what was left of the thing down the wash basin outlet.

There was little room for doubt in Fisheries Protection. The sea was even harsher.

He had the rest of the patrol to decide.

Marlin reached Port Ard at three in the afternoon and eased into a berth on the west side of the little harbour, a berth vacated by a small oil tanker. They saw her leave, a squat utilitarian craft riding high in the water, most of her cargo now in supply tanks ashore.

It was a smooth berthing with only a mild rubbing of fenders against the granite quay, where an exposed edge of green slime emphasised it was low tide. Carrick was aft, Jumbo Wills similarly occupied on the foredeck, and Shannon beside Ferguson on the bridge.

"Cheering crowds in every street," said Clapper Bell sardonically as *Marlin*'s engines stopped, leaving only the hum of her main generator. He grinned at Carrick, then thumbed at the bollard holding the fishery cruiser's stern lines. A large dog was using it as a lamppost. "Think that's the official welcome?"

"Maybe," said Carrick. Two harbour workers had helped them secure and had ambled off again. There were at least thirty fishing boats in harbour, more than he'd expected, but there was little sign of life aboard them. "Wait until the *Harmony* gets in, then we'll really be popular."

Though the fishing fleet would know already. Ferguson had told him of the irate account the *Harmony*'s skipper had pushed out on trawler-band radio, and had been amused. But Ferguson had been asleep in his bunk when the crisis had occurred.

"I met her skipper once," mused the bo'sun. "Jamie Ross—it was a Friday night poker game in Oban."

"And?" Carrick had lost count of the money he'd given to Bell in alleged short-term loans after similar sessions.

"Remember that Swiss watch of mine?" Bell grinned ruefully. "He won it. Last hand—I was chancin' a pair of kings an' he hit me with a full house."

Carrick grunted. The words "Swiss made" had been on the face of Bell's wristwatch, but the rest had come from Hong Kong. The Glasgow-Irishman had won it in another poker session with navy men from a destroyer and had thrown a raging fury when he'd found out. But by then the destroyer was far away.

"How does Ross rate as a skipper?" he asked.

"Younger than most," Bell said. "Wild at the edges but can handle a boat." He paused, eyeing the village beyond the harbour. "If there's a chance ashore tonight—"

He didn't get to finish. Captain Shannon was coming along the deck towards them. He nodded to Bell, then turned to Carrick.

"I've business ashore, mister," he announced. "You'd better come too. Be ready in half an hour." He looked Carrick up and down and gave a critical sniff. "That gives you time to eat and to smarten up— I'd prefer people to know you're my First Officer, not here to rent rowboats from the beach."

"Sir." Carrick couldn't totally fight down a grin. He saw Bell mouthing at him behind Shannon's back. "Harbour routine, sir?"

"Meaning shore leave?" Shannon nodded. "But the usual gangway watch. We're here till morning, maybe longer—I'll have a better idea when we get back." He faced Clapper Bell. "Stay aboard till then, bo'sun. I may need you."

He had gone, stumping off along the deck, before Bell could answer.

"Now, what might that mean?" asked Bell wryly. "What has the wee man got on his mind this time?"

Carrick could only shake his head.

At exactly 2 P.M. Captain James Shannon came down *Marlin*'s gangway to join Carrick on the quayside. Shannon's beard was neatly combed, he wore his second-best shore-going uniform, the one with a row of World War II service ribbons, and he carried a briefcase under one arm.

"Right, mister." He gave a slight nod of approval at Carrick, who was also in uniform with a clean shirt and tie, then flickered a self-conscious attempt at a smile. "We're going to see a lady, a reasonably important lady—who also happens to be an aggressive bitch of a woman if you rub her the wrong way. Which, of course, is what we're not going to do." He saw Carrick's bewilderment. "One Mrs. Alexis Jordan, for some reason, known only to God and the Department, now acting Senior Fisheries Officer in this area."

Carrick blinked. Fisheries officers were shore animals. They kept a tally on catches landed, prepared statistics, collated information, and generally acted as listening posts for the fishery cruisers. Women were a new breed in the job, partly because the average fisherman was still only vaguely aware that women had been given the vote. A woman who reached senior rank had to be better than average.

"You know her, sir?"

It was the wrong thing to ask. Shannon made a heavy throat-clearing noise, ending it like a growl.

"Yes. But until now they've kept her in a cage at Headquarters." The reply came curtly and Shannon started walking.

Following him along the granite quay, Carrick looked around with interest. It was his first time in Port Ard. Coming in from the sea, it had seemed a typical West Highland fishing port, though with a not too easy approach. A tall, long finger of grey granite sea-cliff to the north acted like a giant natural breakwater and was topped by the ruined remains of an old clan fortress keep. A twin of the ruin was perched on a small rock-fringed island lying about two miles offshore.

The rest was a rock-strewn curve of bay. The harbour, built of local granite, was shaped like two cupped, slightly overlapping hands. Entering meant a careful lineup of two marker posts, then coping with a brief undertow swell which lurked just where the hands overlapped—and part of the east side of the harbour dried out at low tide. Some fishing boats were lying on exposed muddy shingle, temporarily stranded.

Then the village. It began at shore level with a few two-storey buildings, some of them small warehouses around the harbour's edge, then became a sprawling mixture of low, white-walled cottages and small modern houses which clung to the lower slopes of a steep, grassy hill. The hill was topped by a community TV mast and a radio transmitter aerial. From signs, like the number of new-model cars parked near the quay and the lavish equipment on most of the boats, there was reasonable prosperity.

"They're doing all right," said Shannon suddenly, as if reading his thought. *Marlin*'s commander slowed for a moment, looking up at the hill. "A lot of these houses didn't exist last time I was here. Mackerel money, mister—and don't ask me how much the taxman ever heard about."

A knot of fishermen were gossiping beside a big Volvo tractor-trailer outfit parked at the shore end of the quayside. The fishermen displayed a calculated indifference as Carrick and Shannon passed by, only a couple returning Shannon's nod of greeting. They were several yards on when the silence was broken.

"Anyone want to buy some extra fenders?" suggested a raucous voice. "Seamen? That bunch on *Marlin* are more like learner drivers!"

Shannon flushed, his mouth clamping shut as the group roared with laughter. But, though it took an effort, he didn't look round and kept walking.

The harbour master's office was a two-storey brick building near the main gate. It had an observation window on the upper floor. At quayside level, the second door in the brickwork carried a sign FISHERIES OFFICER and the Department badge.

Reaching it, Shannon paused for a moment to regain his composure.

"Damn them." He drew a deep breath. "Self-control, mister—I practice it when I can. Otherwise I'd—"

"Kick a few heads in?" suggested Carrick.

"No." Shannon sighed and twitched an unexpected grin. "But that would do for a start."

As he spoke, the door opened. Tall, thin and in his forties, the man who came out gave them a friendly nod and thumbed over his shoulder.

"She's all yours," he said in a dry voice which had a slight English accent.

The stranger, who had thinning black hair and wore a Lovat grey sports suit, walked over to a black B.M.W. coupe parked a few yards away. He got in, started it, and drove off towards the village.

Shrugging, Shannon turned towards the door. They went in, down a short passageway, and arrived in a modestly furnished office. The furnishings were the inevitable Civil Service issue, but the walls had been brightened by full-colour poster illustrations of fish and fishing boats issued by one of the oil companies.

"Hello." The girl sitting behind one of the two desks smiled. "Captain Shannon?"

"That's right." Shannon's manner thawed. She was in her twenties, with long, fair hair, a good figure and an attractive face. "To see Mrs. Jordan."

"She's expecting you." The girl, who wore a dark-red shirt-blouse and tartan trews, made an awkward business of rising.

Then they saw why. She picked up a stick and used it, limping heavily, as she crossed to a partition door at the rear. She went in, spoke briefly to whoever was inside, then turned and smiled at them. "Come through, Captain."

They went over and she waved them through into a smaller office which held a desk, a filing cabinet, an old leather couch, and not much more. The tall, well-built woman seated behind the desk rose and came round to meet them.

"Welcome to Port Ard, Captain Shannon," she said, considering Shannon with amusement. "I gather you've been having a busy day."

The girl in the doorway made a noise close to a chuckle, but her face stayed innocently composed.

"We had a small problem," admitted Shannon. "You heard about it?"

"Yes." The older woman exchanged an amused glance with the girl. "Maybe my secretary didn't introduce herself. Her name is Katie Ross. Her brother is skipper of the *Harmony*." She enjoyed Shannon's discomfiture, then nodded. "I think I can handle him, Katie. If you hear fighting, look in."

"I will." Katie Ross turned. She managed a slight wink in Carrick's direction as she limped out and closed the door.

"Now." Alexis Jordan glanced at Carrick. "You brought a body-guard, I see."

Shannon made the introductions. When he'd finished, Alexis Jordan gestured to the leather couch. As they settled in it, she went round to her chair again.

She looked in her late thirties. She had high cheekbones, sharp blue eyes, a pleasant but firm mouth, and her auburn hair was neatly styled. Her only jewellery was a plain gold band on her wedding finger, and she was dressed in a blue two-piece suit and matching sweater. The desktop in front of her was tidy, but the well-filled ash-tray in the middle showed she was a heavy smoker. Carrick was beginning to note that kind of detail.

"It's been a few years since we met," said Shannon heavily. "How are you—ah—Alexis?"

"Fine." The blue eyes turned to Carrick for a moment. "I presume you've already been told, Chief Officer. Your captain and I sometimes have different opinions." She didn't wait for an answer but turned back to Shannon. "But I'm glad you're here of course—James. You've a package to pass on?"

"Yes." Shannon opened the briefcase, took out a bulky envelope and slid it across the desk. "Three rolls of film. You know about them?"

"Our Russian." She tapped the envelope with a fingernail. "I keep them until a navy messenger gets here." She paused and sighed. "How much do they matter?"

Shannon scowled. "You've seen the *Zarakov?*"

"I've been aboard her." She paused. "By invitation. But the same thing happened last month. Another captain, another Fisheries Protection ship—it was *Stonefish*—and the same business of photographs."

Shannon glanced at Carrick. "Explain it, mister."

"The *Zarakov—*" began Carrick.

"Is probably a part-time spyship," she said wearily, taking a cigarette from a box beside her. She lit it. "I know that bit."

He nodded. That was the other role filled by some of the Russian factory ships and any number of their deep-sea trawlers. They had sophisticated hydroacoustic gear, which explained why they often cruised through submarine exercise areas. It was incidental that ships of the *Zarakov* class could be adapted to carry Styx surface-to-surface missiles.

What mattered was that the *Zarakov* would have several communications experts aboard who would only know a fish if it came cooked on a plate.

"Aerials and radar gear," he said slowly. "That's what it's all about, Mrs. Jordan. You've seen the *Zarakov*. You know she looks like an electronic Christmas tree up top."

"Yes. But—"

"A ship like the *Zarakov* can monitor defence traffic over half of Scotland," emphasised Carrick. He grinned. "Except that our mob, the Americans and most of NATO monitor them monitoring us—and learn a hell of a lot in the process. Part of that is knowing anytime they change their aerial rig or radar gear. So we take pictures."

"They know why?"

Shannon nodded. "They know."

Alexis Jordan's mouth tightened. "Which makes it like some stupid schoolboy game." She sighed. "That's an end to it for you?"

"We're back to normal patrol status, if that's what you mean." Shannon paused, then let his curiosity take over. "Any reason why there are so many boats in harbour?"

"A death in the village—the funeral was this morning." She stubbed her cigarette in the ashtray, one more for the collection. "He was a fisherman. Most of the older skippers are staying in port for the day."

"A mark of respect?" Shannon exchanged a glance with Carrick and nodded. Old customs died hard, particularly along the West Highland coast. Television and dishwashers might have arrived, some fishermen played the Stock Exchange. But when it came to such things as births, a marriage or death, the older generation were still staunch in their ways.

"This is yours, Captain Shannon." Alexis Jordan took a folder from the pile in front of her and passed it over. "My local situation report—the usual summaries."

"Thank you." Shannon put the folder in his briefcase and was cautiously polite. "How long have you been in Port Ard?"

"Four—nearly five months." She was suspicious. "Why?"

Shannon shrugged. "It's quite a change for you. From working behind a desk in Edinburgh to this—your own territory, senior shore officer."

"Senior in name," she said with a slight grimace. "I had one assistant. He left last month to drive a truck. There's no replacement in sight. Apart from Katie, I'm on my own."

"Difficult," said Shannon innocently. "This assistant. The—ah—job got too much for him?"

"No." Her manner chilled. "Truck driving paid more. What else did you have in mind?"

"Nothing." Shannon grinned at her. "So—Port Ard. What's the general picture?"

"Record fish catches, landings up to maximum quota. Plenty of money being made—seasonal money, mackerel money."

"But not so good the rest of the year?" suggested Carrick.

She nodded, still eyeing Shannon with suspicion. "The rest of the year the average skipper is lucky if he can cover his costs and pay the grocery bills. Though Port Ard does have one advantage—a good road link, easier transport to the real markets."

"Hence the need for truck drivers," murmured Shannon. He became serious. "What about problems, the kind I should know about?"

"Illegal fishing?" Alexis Jordan shrugged. "I'm not fool enough to imagine it isn't going on. If you want rumour, three French trawlers raided a sea-loch south of here just before the storm. Cleaned it out in a night. But there's no proof." She paused and glanced towards her office door. "Katie told me about it. She's usually reliable—but I don't ask her about local boats."

"Would she tell you if you did?" asked Carrick.

"No. Katie has her own brand of loyalty—both ways. The Ross family have been a fishing family for generations—her father was drowned at sea when the last *Harmony* sank in a storm, and the same thing happened to his father."

"What about your tame Russians?" persisted Shannon.

"The *Zarakov?*" She made it plain she was trying to be patient. "There's no trouble from that direction. Her people know the regulations and don't break them. The Port Ard skippers are glad they're here. If you read my last report to Department you'd know I calculate they'll have bought close on five thousand tons of mackerel by the end of the season."

Carrick couldn't suppress a whistle.

"A lot of fish," she agreed.

"And a lot of money," said Shannon. "Who handles payments and paerwork? The usual system—a shore agent?"

"Yes. He's John Maxwell, one of the Port Ard buyers." Her voice softened. "Maybe you saw him leave—a dark-haired man."

"If he drives a B.M.W.," agreed Carrick.

"He does." Her smile made Carrick certain Maxwell had been a welcome visitor. "He also runs a refrigerated haulage business. His trucks take a lot of fish out of here by road, long-distance."

"A man worth meeting," said Shannon, fastening his briefcase and preparing to leave. "We'll be in harbour overnight. I'll probably base *Marlin* at Port Ard for a day or two." He hesitated. "You'd be welcome aboard, of course. This evening, or—"

"Tomorrow would be better." Her cheekbones reddened a little. "I'm busy this evening, Captain."

"Tomorrow, then." Shannon glanced at Carrick and they got to their feet.

"And your own plans, Captain?" she asked.

"Nothing in particular," said Shannon. "There's a man I want to look up while I'm here. I haven't seen him for a spell, so we'll probably have a drink or two." He chuckled. "You may know him, Gibby MacNeil."

Alexis Jordan stared at him.

"Something wrong?" asked Shannon, puzzled.

"I'm sorry." She moistened her lips. "I—well, there's no way you could have known."

Shannon frowned at her. "Known what?"

"He's dead," she said simply. "That funeral this morning—"

"His?" Shannon froze.

She nodded.

"I see." Shannon's face might have been carved from stone, but there was an odd glint in his eyes. He said nothing for a moment, and Carrick could hear the sound of a typewriter coming from the outer office. At last, Shannon spoke again. "What happened?"

"An accident." Alexis Jordan moved uneasily in her chair. "I'm sorry, Captain. But your friend MacNeil had a regular habit of getting drunk. Then he'd sleep it off, anywhere handy." She drew a deep breath. "This last time he ended up in a boat's fishhold, in the ice bin —it was empty then. Nobody noticed when they took on ice." She stopped there and looked at Carrick, as if for support.

"When did they find him?" asked Carrick.

"A long time later. Frozen and dead." She turned to Shannon, her manner sympathetic. "Was he a close friend, Captain Shannon?"

"No." Shannon had recovered, whatever his feelings. "We were shipmates once, years ago—in wartime. I saw him now and again." He cleared his throat heavily. "Which boat?"

"The *Cailinn*. The skipper is a man named Campbell."

Shannon nodded. "Was there a postmortem?"

"Yes. At the Cottage Hospital. Dr. Blair carried it out. She—"

"A woman?" Shannon frowned. "There was a Dr. Harding."

"Who was about ninety, with wandering hands," countered Alexis Jordan. The sympathy evaporated. "He retired. The Blair girl is new and she's good. Don't disappoint me, Captain. Distrust of a woman doctor is one of the last strongholds of the inadequate male."

"I reckon myself still reasonably adequate," said Shannon with a deliberate politeness. "Depending on the woman, of course. Depending on the woman."

He nodded good-bye, walked to the door, opened it, and went out. Following him, Carrick heard a strange, snorting gasp. He glanced back. Alexis Jordan had slumped back in her chair and was grinning from ear to ear.

Katie Ross was still pecking at her typewriter in the outer office. She stopped and looked up at them. The partition wall was thin. Carrick had a feeling she would hear most things that happened.

"You'll be back, Captain?" she asked brightly.

"Probably." Shannon's face softened as he looked at her. "So—your brother is skipper of the *Harmony?*"

She nodded. "Skipper and part owner. It's a family boat."

"Well, don't believe too much of what he tells you tonight," said Shannon dryly. "Nobody was terribly clever."

Shannon walked on. Katie Ross eyed Carrick quizzically. He grimaced, shrugged, then followed Shannon.

Outside the building, two heavy container trucks were heading out of the harbour. One had Belgian registration plates, and a long journey ahead of it. As the vehicles cleared the entrance gates, Shannon glanced along the quayside towards *Marlin,* then seemed to make up his mind.

"Mister, I've a grave to find, my respects to pay," he said grimly.

"Like me to come?" asked Carrick.

"No. I'll do it alone—but thank you." Shannon paused. "Webb, afterwards I want to know more about this place, a lot more. I'm going to put you and the bo'sun to work on that."

"Sir?" Carrick watched him carefully. When Shannon used his first name, which wasn't often, it meant *Marlin's* commander had something important on his mind.

"Big Gibby MacNeil. I want to find out how it happened—and, more important, *why* it happened." Shannon stuffed his hands in his jacket pockets and scowled. "MacNeil always liked drink too much for his own good. But when he was sober, he was nobody's fool."

"How well did you really know him?" asked Carrick.

"Better than I admitted to her. It seemed better that way." He drew a deep breath. "Some mail came aboard before we sailed."

Carrick nodded.

"There was a personal letter for me from MacNeil," said Shannon. "All it said was he had to see me. He'd come across something he didn't like. He had to talk to someone he could trust."

"Any hint what he had in mind?"

"None. But he'd never written me before, and he'd known I would be here."

Carrick nodded again. There was no particular secrecy about Fisheries Protection patrol schedules. MacNeil would know *Marlin* was due to take over the Port Ard sector. But he could guess what was gnawing at Shannon. The storm which had ravaged the Minch had delayed their scheduled arrival by three full days.

Time enough for MacNeil to die.

A Klaxon rasped from the harbour. A fishing boat was coming in, edging round to tie up beside the other boats at the east quay. Fenders out, she eased past a dark-red hull, one Carrick recognised. The *Harmony* was already in.

"Damn." Shannon had seen her too. "Mister, first thing you'd better do is go round and soothe that lot down. Then maybe you can find out if any of them will talk about MacNeil. But don't push it."

"There's the medical side," suggested Carrick. "If we saw the autopsy report—"

"By some wet-behind-the-ears female, newly licensed to cure?" Shannon asked. "Later, maybe. But I won't necessarily believe it."

"Why not?" He met Shannon's glare and knew he had to force the older man to come out into the open. "Do you want to treat it as murder?"

"Maybe yes, maybe no," said Shannon. "Mister, a man wrote me a letter. Next thing, he ends up dead under a load of crushed ice." He smacked a clenched fist against an open palm. "I owed Gibby MacNeil. He more or less saved my life once, before you were born. So it's personal, maybe. But we're going to find out anyway. Understood?"

Shoulders squared, he strode away.

Carrick watched him go. Then he rubbed a hand along his chin, sighed, and started for the fishing boats.

CHAPTER 2

The tide was on the turn, lapping its way back into the harbour. It signalled a gradual start to activity aboard several of the boats along the east quay. Nets put ashore to dry or be repaired were being gathered in. A few boats were taking on ice and fuel while gear was being stowed or a deck hosed down. Even the gulls seemed to sense things were happening and had begun circling overhead again, calling impatiently.

Webb Carrick walked along the edge of the quay, checking the names of the boats, looking for the *Cailinn*. He found her about half-way along the little armada, lying in the middle of one group of three. The boat on which Gibby MacNeil had died was older than most, with a broad band of blue paint around her hull.

But she seemed deserted. A box of provisions had been dumped outside her wheelhouse, waiting her crew's return. Some washing, including a pair of long johns, had been hung out to dry over her aerial rigging.

One down. Carrick moved until he came to the *Harmony*. She was the outside boat in another row of three and there was certainly life aboard. A pair of trouser-clad legs protruded from the open door of her wheelhouse. Whoever was working inside seemed to have problems. Above the steady tapping of metal came the sound of his voice, shouting to a deckhand loafing on the middle boat's forepeak.

Clambering down to the nearest deck, Carrick picked his way over ropes and gear and crossed to the middle boat.

"Hey." The deckhand scowled at him. "Lookin' for someone, mister?"

"On the *Harmony*," answered Carrick. He thumbed towards the wheelhouse. "Any chance that's her skipper?"

"Why?"

Carrick eyed him casually. "Mind your own damned business."

The man raised his voice. "Jamie. There's a Fisheries snoop come to see you."

The legs in the wheelhouse jerked in surprise. Then a voice bellowed back.

"Send him over. If he's lucky, I'll just drown him in a bucket."

Grinning, Carrick stepped onto the *Harmony*'s deck as the figure in the wheelhouse squirmed out from somewhere behind the control gear and scrambled to his feet.

"So what the hell do you want?" asked Jamie Ross. He was tall and lean with fine-boned features and a nose that had been broken at some time. He was shirtless, skin tanned to a near bronze, and sun and sea had bleached his long fair hair to a shade close to white. He had streaks of oil and dirt on his arms and face, and blood was oozing from a gashed knuckle. He glared at Carrick. "Come round to grovel, have you?"

"Not particularly," said Carrick mildly. "What are you complaining about? Your boat's still in one piece."

"Uh?" Ross swallowed hard, his eyes widening. "What am I supposed to do—thank you?"

"No." Carrick leaned against the wheelhouse doorway and gave a sympathetic grimace. "We probably scared the hell out of you, and I've a captain who came close to a cardiac attack. It was pretty close."

"Close?" Ross scowled at him. "It was damned near homicidal."

"Of course, we didn't expect you'd come wandering out from the Russian," said Carrick.

"Meaning it was *my* fault?" Ross stared at him in near amazement. "I'm the one who nearly got rammed, remember?"

"It didn't happen," soothed Carrick. "How about calling it a general foul-up?"

"I'll go along with that." Ross considered Carrick's uniform. "Yes, I saw you on *Marlin*'s bridge. What's your name anyway?"

"Webb Carrick—I'm Chief Officer." Carrick thumbed towards the wheelhouse controls. "What's the problem?"

"The linkage on one of the rods has fractured. I told the crew we'd pack in for the day, that I'd stay and fix it." Jamie Ross stuck his thumbs into the broad leather belt at his waist, then added sarcastically, "Want to ask how it happened?"

"I don't think so," said Carrick.

"Then, how about a reason why I don't throw you over the side?" Carrick shook his head. "Your sister wouldn't like it."

"You've met Katie?" Ross frowned. "Hiding behind a woman isn't heroic."

"It's practical," murmured Carrick.

"And she'd have my guts," admitted Ross. "Having a sister working for you people is a liability at times." He sighed. "All right, it
was just one of those things. A foul-up. And I'm going to have a beer
—I need it."

He led the way aft and into a tiny deckhouse. Gesturing Carrick
towards one of the bench seats, he produced two cans of beer from a
small refrigerator and tossed one over.

"Thanks." Carrick caught the can and opened it. "You'll call it
square?"

"But I don't want a next time." Ross took a long drink from his
can. "The Russians actually waved me clear. Maybe they guessed
what might happen, maybe they didn't. They're an unpredictable
bunch."

"But good customers?"

"They keep buying as much mackerel as comes their way," said
Ross. He settled on the seat across from Carrick. "Once you've
unloaded, they give you a chit for the agreed weight of fish. Then a
couple of days later you get the money from John Maxwell, their
local agent."

"I heard about him," said Carrick.

"Probably from Katie's boss, Mrs. Jordan." Ross sipped his beer.
"Maxwell is divorced, she's a widow—the rest is their business."

Carrick looked around the little deckhouse. It was shabby but
clean, showing the scars of hard use. A set of oilskins hung behind
the door, and two lobster pots had been dumped in a corner beside a
well-oiled shotgun. But his real interest was roused when he saw a
single-cylinder aqualung unit lying under Ross's bench.

"Yours?" he asked.

"Yes." Ross bent and touched the cylinder affectionately. "It's an
old model, but sweet to use. You do scuba work?"

"Sometimes." Carrick left it at that.

But he was curious. Not many fishermen used scuba gear. Most
said they earned their living on the water and to hell with going
under it. It was like an offshoot of the same stubborn philosophy
which meant many fishermen deliberately avoided learning how to
swim. If they were going to drown, they argued, they'd rather it happened quickly.

"There's some reasonable diving territory around here," volunteered Ross. "Interested in wrecks? Or are you one of the underwater cave clan?"

"Whatever comes," said Carrick.

"Then maybe I'll show you something I've found." Ross brushed a strand of that long, almost white hair back from his forehead, his manner suddenly enthusiastic. "It happened last summer. I made a dive close in to Targe Island—you know, that little island out beyond the bay. Wham—straight off, I found this cave. It's a narrow enough entrance, but once you're through it's the nearest thing I've ever seen to an underwater grotto." He stopped short, his eyes narrowing. "Scuba diving. Hold on—do you know a character named Clapper Bell? Plays poker like it's his life's work? Hell, yes, I think he was on *Marlin*—"

"He still is," said Carrick.

Jamie Ross smiled. "I bought a watch from him once."

"Bought?" Carrick raised an eyebrow.

"All right, won it," said Ross. "He conned me—it was rubbish." He shook his head at the memory. "Tell him he's a damned pirate."

"I do, regularly." Carrick finished his beer and tossed the can into a wastebucket. "About that cave—I'd like to see it."

"Right." Ross looked pleased. "I'm just a poor innocent fisherman who could use some help exploring out there. The damned thing goes on and on."

"Poor innocent fishermen are in short supply," said Carrick. "Everyone should help them when they can." He got to his feet. "Where can I find the *Cailinn*'s skipper? He's my next stop."

"Hugh Campbell?" Jamie Ross frowned. "Is he in trouble?"

Carrick shook his head. "I want to talk to him about Gibby MacNeil's death."

"Hugh was staying in harbour for the funeral." Ross rubbed his chin. "I thought about it. But I decided I couldn't afford to lose a day's fishing—not right now. This month's payment on the boat won't wait—in fact, it's overdue. I've had some pretty hefty overheads lately."

He rose as he spoke and they left the deckhouse, then stopped again in the open, beside the fishing boat's winch gear.

"How well did you know MacNeil?" asked Carrick.

"He used to work for me." Jamie Ross pursed his lips. "Not regularly, but now and again—he filled in that way aboard a few boats, when a skipper was shorthanded." He shrugged. "Big Gibby's problem was drinking—like he was trying to support the whisky trade on his own. Sober and needing money, he was all right."

"I've met them." Carrick looked across the harbour to where *Mar-*

lin was berthed. He thought of Captain Shannon, on his way to visit
a grave, then turned to Ross again. "How about the night MacNeil
died? How many people saw him?"

"Hardly anyone. The storm was still blowing and most folk were
at home, hoping the roof wouldn't blow away." Ross considered the
deck planking at his feet. "Anyway, it seems he splashed in out of
the rain at the Clan Bar, had a couple of drinks, bought a half-bottle
of whisky to take away, then left. No one saw him after that—until
they found his body." He looked up. "If you want Hugh Campbell,
try the Memorial Hall. Go through the harbour gates and you're in
Shore Street. Turn left, keep walking, and you can't miss it. He's usually there when he's ashore, keeping clear of his wife—anytime she
sees him she sticks a paint brush in his hand."

Carrick made his way back across the fishing boats to the quay
again, walking from there to the harbour gates, then turned left as
he'd been directed.

Port Ard's Shore Street was well named. It directly faced the sea, a
single line of shops, offices, two banks and a church as its centre. The
rock and shingle of the shoreline began on the other side of the narrow roadway. A scatter of parked cars left little manoeuvring room
for through traffic.

He crossed over to the shopping side of the street as a jam between a mail bus and a farm tractor pulling a trailer stopped everything. Some of *Marlin*'s shore-leave men were already over there,
window-shopping, ready to try a grin at any passing female under
pension age.

The Clan Bar was located just beyond the second bank. Gibby
MacNeil's last-known port of call was a long, flat-roofed building
with fancy ironwork guarding its windows. A painted sign above the
door showed a group of Highland warriors with claymores poised,
about to do something unpleasant to a suitably alarmed English red-
coat. The door was firmly closed. But come opening time, Carrick
knew that *Marlin*'s men would be among its customers.

He kept walking. Further out, towards the end of the village, he
reached a row of small fishing cottages. Brightly painted, with glinting brasswork on the doors and white lace curtains at the windows,
they had an old-fashioned charm only partly spoiled by their TV
aerials.

The last cottage had a showpiece garden. It also had a police sign
almost obscured by rosebushes, and as he passed Carrick caught a

glimpse of a police car parked at the rear. He smiled to himself. Being the local law in a place like Port Ard couldn't be the most arduous of jobs.

There was a stretch of waste ground beyond the police cottage, then, at last, he reached the Memorial Hall. It was an ugly red brick structure with a corrugated-iron roof, and it stood where the road began to curve inland towards the hills. When he reached the front porch, he saw a brass plate. It detailed a long-ago fishing tragedy when a Port Ard boat had been lost at sea and the hall had been built.

The front door was open. He went in, passed a notice board in a corridor, then heard voices and a familiar clicking come from behind a door to his right. He pushed it open, and found himself in a large room which held four snooker tables. Three were in use, and a few spectators were watching the players and gossiping.

He was spotted immediately. An elderly man in caretaker's overalls came over and blocked his path.

"No visitors allowed," said the caretaker. "Sorry—only fishermen and locals."

"I'm not visiting," said Carrick. "Is Hugh Campbell here?"

"He might be," said the caretaker. "Why?"

"Mind your own damned business, Archie," said a voice from the tables. Leaning on his cue, one of the players nodded to Carrick. "I'm Campbell."

The caretaker retired and Carrick went over. Hugh Campbell was a tall, thin man with greying hair. He was wearing his obviously Sunday-best dark suit, with a white shirt and a black tie.

"Well?" He glanced at Carrick's uniform. "What brings Fisheries Protection looking for me, eh? Think you've caught me on some of your damned regulations?"

"Nothing like that, skipper," said Carrick. He glanced across at Campbell's opponent, a thick-set man in overalls. He had a broad, unshaven face and didn't look pleased at the interruption. "But I need your help."

"Help?" Campbell frowned, then nodded. "Wait."

He went back to the table, considered the game, then used his cue in a smooth, deliberate stroke. The white cue ball gently nudged a red, trickled past it, and stopped jammed against the blue, close to a corner pocket.

"Sort that out," Campbell told the other player. Then he led Carrick away from the table towards a window. Leaning against the sill, he brought out a pack of cigarettes, lit one, and eyed Carrick quizzically. "So, what's this about?"

"Gibby MacNeil," said Carrick quietly.

"Aye, we buried him this morning." Campbell drew on his cigarette. Behind him, the view was out towards the sea-cliff to the north of the village. "What's your interest?"

"Accident statistics," lied Carrick smoothly. "It's a Department survey, linked to safety procedures."

"Do I order my copy now?" Campbell was unimpressed. "Man, I gave a statement to the police. Read it."

"I will." The cigarette smoke made Carrick's nostrils twitch. Campbell smoked a pungent blend. "Look, this is different. Sometimes, after a spell, people may remember a detail they couldn't recall earlier."

"It can happen." Campbell's attention strayed to the snooker table. The unshaven man was still scowling at the problem he'd been left. "What's on your mind?"

"Any reason why he chose *your* boat?"

Campbell shrugged. "She had an inside berth, against the quay. And Big Gibby had sailed with me a few times, so he knew the *Cailinn*."

"But why the fishhold?"

Campbell sighed. "Maybe he wanted a dark corner. How would I know?"

"How about the fo'c'sle and wheelhouse? Were they locked?"

"Locked?" Campbell blinked at the notion. "No. Folk up here trust their neighbours." He grinned a little. "Most of the time, anyway."

It was the answer Carrick had expected. The fishing coast had to be one of the last areas where it could still be regarded as an insult to others if a man locked his door at night.

He tried again. "Did he have many friends—close friends?"

"Everybody knew him. But"—Campbell drew on his cigarette again—"no, there's not a man or woman who was really close to him."

"How about you?" persisted Carrick. "When did you see him last?"

"I was in the Clan Bar that last night," said Campbell with a deliberate patience which meant he didn't feel that way. "But the mood Big Gibby was in, he didn't want company. A few folk said hello to him, but he just ignored them." His attention switched to the snooker table again and his face registered concern. "Now, what's that about?"

Carrick turned. The other player had company, the dark-haired man he'd seen leaving Alexis Jordan's office. They were talking and neither seemed happy. The dark-haired man came towards Campbell.

"Sorry, skipper," he said briskly. "I need Ferdie for a job. I'm going to have to break up your game."

"Now?" Campbell winced. "I've money on this, Mr. Maxwell. A couple of minutes—eh?"

His plea brought a resigned nod. Quickly, he faced Carrick.

"We're finished anyway. If I do remember anything, I'll let you know."

"Right," said Carrick. He watched Campbell hurry back to the fray, then turned to the other man. "You're John Maxwell?"

"Yes." Maxwell gave him a slight smile. "You're from *Marlin?*"

"Yes. Carrick, her Chief Officer." He shook hands with Maxwell. "We heard about you from Mrs. Jordan."

"Alexis' version?" Maxwell chuckled. He had strong white teeth and a sallow complexion. Carrick had an idea that beneath the man's tweed suit was a thin body built like whipcord. "I wish I'd been there. How did I make out?"

"As fairly prosperous," said Carrick as play began again at the snooker table. "She said you're shore agent for the *Zarakov.*"

"It's a sideline. Good money, but the Russian's only here a few weeks of the year," Maxwell said easily. "I earn my real living at the harbour, buying fish and trucking it out—refrigerated container traffic, mostly long-distance style."

"For the London market?"

"No, that's sewn up by the big traders." Maxwell shook his head. "I go further, into Europe—generally France or Belgium. I've two trucks leaving for Brussels tonight, and that's my problem. One of them has just been hauled in with a dead engine."

"Bad luck."

"The kind I can't afford—that's why I'm here." Maxwell grimaced at the snooker players. "The unshaven gorilla playing your skipper friend is Ferdie Renfrew, my foreman mechanic—hell, my *only* mechanic. I need that truck back on the road. He can have the rest of his time off later."

A groan came from the handful of spectators who'd drifted round the table. Campbell had failed to sink the last red. Grinning, his opponent despatched it into a pocket with a stroke which left him perfectly placed.

"Get on with it," muttered Maxwell. He faced Carrick again. "What brought you here, Carrick?"

"Campbell. I needed his help."

Maxwell eyed him shrewdly. "Meaning you're interested in the late Gibby MacNeil?"

"MacNeil's an accident statistic," said Carrick. "An unusual one."

"Anything about MacNeil was unusual," said Maxwell. He pursed his lips. "Didn't your ship have—ah—an incident with the *Harmony* when you were playing tag with my Russians this morning?"

"You could say we met," agreed Carrick.

Maxwell nodded. "Well, if you want to know about MacNeil, talk to the *Harmony*'s skipper."

"Jamie Ross?" Carrick wondered what was coming. "I did, but—"

"Did he tell you how MacNeil set fire to the *Harmony?* It was two, nearly three months ago. MacNeil got drunk one night and tried the same damned-fool trick—except that time he crawled into the *Harmony*'s wheelhouse, then tried to light a cigarette. He dropped the match into a locker full of signal flares."

"Good-bye wheelhouse?" Carrick raised a startled eyebrow.

"And very nearly good-bye MacNeil," said Maxwell acidly. "Except he'd sense enough left to go over the side. Young Jamie Ross was ready to kill him on the spot. That was one boat he didn't work on again."

A shout of triumph came from the snooker table. Ferdie Renfrew had just cleared the last ball, and Hugh Campbell was gloomily counting money into the man's outstretched hand.

"Thank God for that," said Maxwell. He glanced at his wristwatch. "About your trip round the *Zarakov*. Some of her people are coming ashore this evening—they run a sort of liberty boat twice a week." He chuckled. "I'm meeting a couple of their officers who speak English. I'll let you know their version later."

He walked over to his mechanic, clapped a hand on the man's shoulder, and led him off.

Hugh Campbell had gone off to sulk somewhere after his defeat. The fishermen who remained studiously ignored Carrick and made it very clear he'd outstayed any suggestion of a welcome at the Memorial Hall.

He watched play at one of the other tables for a couple of minutes, then left. But when he reached the outside porch two men lounging in the doorway moved in to block his path. One was tall and thin, wearing a red wool shirt with jeans and cut-down seaboots. The other was smaller, stocky, hands still in the pockets of his dark-blue duffel jacket.

"Hello, snoop," said the taller man softly. "You know something? I've been promising mysel' one of your kind for a long time."

His companion grinned, showing a mouthful of bad teeth. Carrick knew their kind, the dregs from some fishing crew with an old score to settle. He eyed them bleakly, knowing that talk was useless.

"Try it," he said.

They came in together. The stocky man dragged a short leather-covered cosh from one pocket and swung it experimentally. But the tall man was first. Carrick took a half step clear as he lunged, blocked a swinging fist, and slammed an elbow into his attacker's mouth.

A moment later, though he tried to avoid it, the cosh took him on the left shoulder. It was a glancing blow, but hard enough to leave the arm almost paralysed. Gasping, he managed to ram a knee into the stocky man's stomach, saw him reel back, and followed up fast. A judo *atemi* slash with the edge of his hand, deliberately only hard enough to stun but not kill, took his opponent on the vital point just under the nose. The man gave a strange gobbling noise and slumped.

The tall man had been shuffling in again, blood streaming from his damaged lips. But he hesitated as his companion collapsed face-down on the floor. Then he turned to run. Carefully, happily, Carrick booted him hard in the rear and heard him howl with pain before he started running.

At last some of the snooker players made a cautious appearance from the Memorial Hall. They stood gaping while the other man, still dazed and groaning, made a feeble, pawing effort to sit up.

"Better look after him," Carrick told them. "It must have been something he ate."

He walked away, rubbing the numbness from his left arm.

The road took him back again past the police cottage. A police-man in shirtsleeves was sunning himself by the garden gate. He was middle-aged, with greying hair, a comfortable paunch, and a ser-geant's chrome-plated insignia on his shoulder straps.

"Grand day." He gave a slightly weary grin as he considered Carrick's uniform. "From *Marlin,* eh? Would you have been up at the Memorial Hall?"

"That's right," said Carrick. "Why?"

"There was this man in a red shirt. He went down the road in one hell of a hurry." The sergeant chuckled. "Maybe *I* should have asked why."

"You knew him?"

"No. But we've plenty of outside boats in harbour, here for the mackerel." He eyed Carrick shrewdly. "Any problem?"

"Not particularly," said Carrick.

"Good." The sergeant sighed. "Now, if you're here for that wee captain of yours, he's been and, thank the Lord, he's gone."

"How long since?" Carrick leaned on the gate. There were two men at work further down the garden, digging in a vegetable patch with minimal enthusiasm.

"Minutes, no more. You'll be Carrick—he mentioned you." The sergeant eased his paunch off the gate. "I'm Ballantyne—Donald Ballantyne. These"—he thumbed over his shoulder—"these are two fishing gentlemen from the Islands doing penance for an unfortunate misunderstanding they had the other night." He winked. "Nothing like gardening for calming a man, eh?"

"It looks that way." Carrick considered the reluctant gardeners. One gave him a wan smile. "What do you call it, Sergeant? Fringe benefit?"

"Just practical," said Ballantyne. "It saves all that tiresome business of charges and cautions—let alone getting involved with some damned fool of a magistrate. Of course, if any prisoner really wants it that way—" He shrugged.

"You've a neat garden," said Carrick dryly.

"Aye." Ballantyne gave a satisfied nod. "The best. Your Captain Shannon was more interested in a death. But you'll know about that?"

"Gibby MacNeil." Carrick nodded.

"My wife was fond of Big Gibby. Aye, he did a grand job when he painted her kitchen last winter." Pausing, still amiable, but his eyes hardening, Ballantyne asked, "And what makes your wee captain so interested in my report, eh?"

"They were shipmates once, a long time ago." Carrick sought a diversion and looked past him. "Captain Shannon doesn't like leaving stones unturned, Sergeant. Which is more than I'd say about these two—have you seen what they're doing to your vegetable plot?"

"Eh?" Ballantyne swung round, growled, and headed at a trot towards his two penitents. "You pair, what's going on?"

Carrick escaped and kept walking until he reached Shore Street. Then, deciding he'd like to know the place better, he explored his way around the rest of the village for a spell. A chandler's store located in a lane had a sideline in sports equipment which interested him, from hunting crossbows to deer-stalking rifles. Going in, he bought a cork-handled diving knife to replace one he'd lost, but resisted the temptation to linger over the rest.

Further up the lane, he discovered another street and found himself at the rear of the Maxwell Transport yard. A high chain-link fence surrounded a weed-grown parking lot with an office and workshop area to one side. Maxwell's black B.M.W. was parked outside the office hut, but the only other vehicle in sight was an old Dodge breakdown truck, a four-wheel-drive unit with spotlights and a crane.

Curious, he made a deliberate circuit of the fence until he reached the big workshop shed, a ramshackle corrugated-iron structure. The main door was open. Inside, a young mechanic wearing goggles was using welding gear at a bench. But that was all. Maxwell's truck that had "died" must be somewhere else.

Without realising it, he'd climbed a reasonable slope in his wanderings. He stopped for a moment, looking down across the lower level of shops and houses towards the harbour and the sea beyond. Two fishing boats were heading out, keeping to the south of Targe Island. *Marlin* had a new neighbour on the west quay, a big white catamaran yacht. Somebody with money on a cruising trip, probably heading for the Outer Isles. If the weather held, and it should, then the crew would only have to worry about their suntans.

Knowing that was plain jealousy, he started back. As he reached the harbour gates, a foursome who had to be from the catamaran were coming out. The men were middle-aged, with sunglasses and yachting caps. The two girls, a blonde and a redhead, wore tight white shorts and sailor shirts. As they passed, the men were talking loudly about sailing, but the girls looked bored. The redhead caught his glance and gave a slow, deliberate wink.

Carrick whistled under his breath and kept walking. Stir that foursome into what was already ashore in Port Ard, and it could be an explosive mixture.

A petty officer, bored in the sunlight, gave a token salute as Carrick returned aboard *Marlin*. But, almost inevitable when they were in harbour, the thin, stoop-shouldered figure of Ferguson was lurking on deck. He came padding over with a complaining air.

"What's wrong?" asked Carrick.

"Andy Shaw." Ferguson managed to make their Chief Engineer's name sound like a disease. The grey-haired Junior Second Mate took a suspicious sideways glance to make sure the petty officer was out of earshot. "He's gone too far this time, Carrick. He's stealing ship's stores—I can prove it."

"How?" Carrick waited. Shaw and Ferguson fought regularly, the Chief Engineer often deliberately stirring it up.

"I saw him," said Ferguson primly. "He went ashore with a bag full of new electrical cable. Drink money."

"Did you ask him about it?"

"No." Ferguson looked surprised.

"I'll check." Then, knowing Ferguson wouldn't, he asked, "Want a spell ashore? I'll take the watch for an hour or so."

"Ashore, here?" Ferguson visibly shrank from the idea. "What for?"

"Forget it," shrugged Carrick. "Anything else happening?"

"Captain Shannon came back aboard, then left again. He talked to Bell, not me," said Ferguson peevishly. "Then—yes, someone came looking for you. A girl. Pleasant, but she had a bad leg. She seemed to know Bell too—she talked to him." He scowled. "Damn it, sometimes I wonder who runs this ship, captain or bo'sun."

"Depends who you're asking," said Carrick.

Leaving Ferguson, he went aft along the main deck. Clapper Bell's private domain was the scuba-gear storeroom, located near the stern. As usual, the door was hooked open and Bell was inside, sprawled back in the comfort of an old armchair which had mysteriously appeared there one day. Looking up, the Glasgow-Irishman grinned a welcome, heaved himself out of the armchair, and removed the cigarette smouldering between his lips.

"I wondered when you'd show, sir," he said amiably, and nodded towards the stern. "Seen her?"

"Yes. And what was aboard." The white catamaran's hull was too low in the water for more than her masthead to be visible. But as he'd come aboard, Carrick had seen her name was *Carthusa* and that she flew the Danish flag and a Royal Copenhagen Yacht Club burgee. If that meant she'd crossed the North Sea and had come round by Cape Wrath, then the foursome ashore were no mere gin-and-tonic sailors. "Nice neighbours."

"You should have seen the rush to help them tie up." Bell's rugged face split in a grin. "Can I put in for a transfer?"

"If we get the girls." Carrick sat on an equipment box. "Any coffee?"

Bell had a flask. He poured hot black coffee into a tin mug and handed the mug over.

"Thanks." He took a sip while Bell settled back in his armchair. The coffee came ready-laced with rum. Carrick didn't know where Bell kept the rum bottle, and he wasn't going to ask. "I expected you to be ashore by now. If you're really tight for cash—"

"No." Two five-pound notes appeared like magic between Bell's stubby fingers, then vanished again. "I've got a float—courtesy of our beloved captain."

Carrick sat upright. "To do what?"

"Sort of socialise," said Bell. "Chat up the natives."

"About MacNeil?" Carrick pursed his lips a little. "Then go easy. I met up with a couple who wanted to play rough. They could have friends."

"I'll cope." The Glasgow-Irishman's humour faded. "The Old Man seems pretty sensitive about this MacNeil business."

Carrick nodded. "Did he tell you why?"

"Enough," said Bell. He took the stub of lighted cigarette from his lips and used a calloused thumb to flick it expertly across the storeroom. It landed inside another tin mug lying on the floor and sizzled and died there among the coffee dregs at the bottom. "How much sense does it make to you, sir?"

"Not a lot—yet." A thin, white contrail was moving in an arrow-straight line across the blue sky outside the scuba room. Carrick watched it absently. The high-flying jet up there might be a scheduled passenger flight on the Polar route to North America or an air defence patrol. Both flew the northwest route, probably without any notion of a place called Port Ard. He sighed. "Any idea what he's doing now, Clapper?"

"The Old Man?" Bell shook his head. "He just told me he'd be ashore till late and to let you know." He brightened. "Did our happy Mr. Ferguson tell you Jamie Ross's sister was aboard?"

"He muttered about it."

"He's good at that," said Bell sardonically. "She brought an invite from Ross. Something about he's goin' out to Targe Island this evening and that you're welcome to come along." He scratched his chin, puzzled. "What's going on? I was to tell you to wear a wet suit but that you wouldn't need scuba gear."

"There's a cave out there. He found it, he's proud of it," explained

Carrick. The invitation was a surprise, but useful. "I'll go. Ross knows more about MacNeil than he admitted—more than I asked him about, anyway."

"She said they'll pick you up at seven." Bell's face took on a surprisingly gentle cast for a moment. "That's a nice kid, his sister. Rough on her, having a bad leg. How'd it happen?"

Carrick shook his head.

"Rough," said Bell again. He shrugged, then grinned. "If they ask you for a repeat visit, say I'll come too. But it's time I got to work, eh?"

He heaved himself out of the armchair, winked at Carrick, and ambled off towards the gangway.

Carrick changed out of uniform into a shirt and slacks, packed his black neoprene rubber wet suit into a canvas bag, then went along to the wardroom. *Marlin*'s cook and the steward had gone ashore together, which he knew could be compared with Attila the Hun having a night out with Genghis Khan. It also left the galley assistant in charge, and his idea of catering was thick-cut cheese sandwiches and boiled tea.

But Carrick still felt hungry enough to eat. His only company was Ferguson, whose main topic of conversation was still Andy Shaw and his claim he'd seen the Chief Engineer smuggling ship's stores ashore.

He escaped and went up to the chartroom. It was quiet and peaceful, the only sound an occasional muted crackle of sound from the bridge radio, tuned to the fishing wavelength. Plenty of boats seemed to be out, and their skippers seemed to be heavily into mackerel.

The Admiralty large-scale chart for the Port Ard and Loch Armach stretch of coastline was already out on the chart table. Shannon had obviously been studying it, and Carrick did the same for a spell. Loch Armach was about four miles north of Port Ard in a straight line, but ships didn't operate that way. He reckoned the sea distance to the *Zarakov* was nearer seven miles, but if the Russian wanted a sheltered offshore anchorage without direct contact with land, then her captain had chosen well. The rest—he frowned over the chart's details for a spell, from coastal contours to sounding lines and the small-print warnings scattered among the tiny islands.

It was good fishing territory. It also had tidal rip currents, shoal rock, dangerous wrecks, and a dry warning that certain data might be incomplete.

In other words, things were about normal.

He left *Marlin* at 7 P.M., dumped his canvas bag on the quay, and went over to look at the catamaran moored astern. He was staring down at the deserted yacht, admiring her lines, when he heard a vehicle approaching.

A small white Ford van came along the quayside. Decorated with extra spotlights, a front spoiler and a long whip aerial topped with a foxtail pennant, it swung in a tight turn and braked to a halt beside him. Grinning from behind the wheel, Katie Ross beckoned.

"Get in," she invited.

He went over, opened the passenger door, threw his bag into the rear of the van, and got aboard.

"Before you ask, the decor is Jamie's," warned Katie. "His taste is mostly in his mouth."

Carrick blinked. The interior had been enthusiastically customised. Seats and dashboard had sheepskin trim, a line of extra instruments occupied an overhead console, and an elaborate radio panel with a built-in cassette deck was set under the fascia, just forward of the automatic gear change. Behind the seats were further mysterious bumps and humps of fitments.

"It's different," he said dryly. "Can it go?"

"Usually." Katie Ross flicked the transmission stick and hit the accelerator. The little vehicle took off in a scream of tyre rubber which jerked him back in his seat. He had a fractional glimpse of the open-mouthed seaman on *Marlin*'s gangway watch, a blur of quayside, then Katie was braking because they were almost at the harbour gates.

"Sorry," she said demurely.

"Blame Jamie, not you?" suggested Carrick, pulling himself upright again.

She nodded. "He did a few things to the engine."

"I'll take your word for it."

They began to purr quietly along Shore Street, but in the opposite direction to the way he'd gone earlier. "Where are we heading?"

"Our place—it's not far." She drove confidently. The automatic transmission meant the crippled leg didn't matter, and she seemed to guess what he was thinking. "You're safe enough."

"I had that feeling." The overhead instruments included a compass and a digital cruise control. "Why no radar?"

"He thought about that," she said seriously. She was wearing tan slacks and a white shirt, her hair tied back by a narrow red ribbon.

"You know, you must be fairly persuasive, Mr. Carrick. Jamie hasn't taken anyone else out to our cave before."

"Call me Webb," he suggested. "And I didn't persuade. It was his idea."

"Then take care." She smiled to herself. "There's bound to be a reason."

They passed the last of the village, the road narrowing and pot-holed. Another half mile on, a small cottage was located on its own between the road and the shore. Katie Ross swung the van onto a pebbled track, drove round the side of the cottage and stopped. Behind the cottage a small dinghy bobbed against a wooden jetty at the water's edge. Jamie Ross was there, wearing a grey rubber wet suit, pouring fuel from a can into the dinghy's outboard engine. Looking up, he waved a greeting but finished the job before he came to meet them as they left the van.

"Brought your gear?" He gave a satisfied nod as Carrick produced the canvas grip from the van. "Your stuff's aboard, Katie."

"Then I'm ready." She came round from the driver's door, leaning on her stick. "Where's Mother?"

"Coming." Ross pointed towards the cottage. A grey-haired woman, small and plump, had emerged from the back door and was coming briskly towards them.

"Hello." She smiled at Carrick, then switched her attention to her children. "Now, don't do anything foolish out there."

"We won't," promised Jamie Ross.

"Meaning, Shut up, you old fool?" Amused, his mother stuck her hands in the pockets of the tweed jacket she was wearing over a hand-knitted wool dress and appealed to Carrick. "You look reasonably sensible. Watch them for me, will you?"

"I'll try," said Carrick mildly.

"Diving. I tell myself, 'Morag Ross, if the Good Lord had meant folk to go under the sea, he'd have given us fins and a tail.'" Then she smiled, in a way that took years from her age. "Enjoy yourselves. I'll be down in the village."

They left her, crossed the shingle to the jetty, and got aboard the dinghy. Katie sat near the bow, with Carrick between her and her brother, who took his place on the stern thwart and pull-started the outboard engine.

The dinghy contained several small oilskin-wrapped bundles, and Katie began opening a canvas bag similar to Carrick's.

"We can change on the way," she told him. "It saves time." As she spoke, she brought out a yellow scuba suit. Unfolding it, she glanced up again. "You look your way, I'll look mine."

"That's for my benefit," said Jamie Ross dryly. "If I wasn't here—" He chuckled and avoided a chunk of waste rag she threw in his direction.

Turning to face Ross, Carrick got out his own suit and began to change while the little craft rode through the slight, chopping swell, heading on a course which would take them slightly north of the rocky bulk of Targe Island.

"This way we pick up a current, gain a couple of knots speed," explained Ross, lounging back with one arm over the rudder bar. "Coming back, we try to dodge it." He swore good-humouredly as a wave slapping against the dinghy's side drenched a fine curtain of spray across its length, and watched for a moment as Carrick pulled on his suit. "I'm not planning anything clever. All I want to do is have a look at the first cave and maybe leave some of this gear we're bringing out."

"That's why you brought him along," accused Katie, and Carrick guessed she was busy with her suit. "He wants another damned porter."

"Why not?" agreed Ross cheerfully. He eased down into a more comfortable position, one foot jammed against the centre thwart. "Still interested in Russians, Carrick?"

"Right now?" Carrick shrugged.

"Take a look—starboard bow. Don't worry about Katie, she's more or less decent."

Carrick turned. Katie Ross was pulling on the top of her wet suit and he had a brief glimpse of firm, suntanned breasts. Her eyes mocked him in a surprising way, then she gestured seaward.

"Over there."

A large grey launch was coming into the bay. She had a small cockpit area for'ard but otherwise was open-decked. Still about a mile away, she was heading for the harbour at Port Ard.

"She's from the *Zarakov*," explained Jamie Ross. "Usually there's around forty of them aboard. They get a couple of hours or so ashore, then they get marched back aboard again and off they go."

"Ever any trouble with them?" asked Carrick, watching the launch. Making about eight knots, she was a drab workhorse of a boat, despite the way the evening sun highlighted the white wash at her stern.

"Ashore?" Ross shook his head. "The word is, they only let some of their people come in—the ones they can trust. They drink a little, walk around a little, one or two of the shops stay open for them— that's all."

"And the others?"

"Never set foot on land, Webb." Katie answered him, with surprising bitterness. "It was the same when another of their ships was here last year." She pursed her lips. "All those people—"

"It's probably not too bad for them." Her brother shifted with a degree of unease. "We don't know, Carrick. They don't encourage visitors on the *Zarakov*. But they're supposed to have a cinema, amusements—"

"It's like a damned prison ship," snapped Katie.

"Quoting your boss?" countered Carrick.

She flushed. "No."

"No chance," said Ross. "Alexis Jordan wouldn't say anything that might upset them. Not when the man in her life wouldn't like it."

"Maxwell?" asked Carrick.

Ross nodded, ignored his sister's glare, and, humming to himself, eased the outboard's throttle open an extra notch.

Fifteen minutes later they were drifting in close under a raw cliff of rock on the west side of Targe Island. The outboard had been cut back to a murmur and Ross eyed the rock above, using its features as markers. In the bow, Katie had a grapnel anchor ready.

The west side was the seaward side of the island. Port Ard and most of its bay lost from view, the mainland bulk of Claymore Point was the sole reminder they existed. As the dinghy pitched in a heavier swell, Carrick looked up at the ruins which crowned Targe Island and then across at the remains of the old fortress on the Point. Katie had explained about them, two old clan strongholds built in the days when Viking longships still raided the Scottish coast.

Between them, Targe and Claymore had defended the bay. Centuries after the Vikings had gone, they'd served the same purpose when Scot fought Scot in bitter clan feuds. Till that ended too.

No one lived on Targe Island now. For generations it had been left to the seabirds. Seabirds and seals. He saw one swimming a few yards out from the dinghy, the small, grey, old man's face considering them with a puzzled curiosity.

Ross signalled, and Katie let the anchor run out. As it splashed and sank, the seal dived.

"Right." Ross cut the engine as the dinghy's motion changed to a steady bobbing on the end of the anchor rope. He clipped a waterproof torch to the belt of his scuba suit, then pointed down. "You can see it from here."

The sea was clean and clear. Peering down, Carrick could make out a black shimmering outline in the rock face. He guessed it was about twenty feet below them.

"I'll take a look on my own first. We haven't been out since before the storm." He glanced at his sister. "I'll check through, then be straight back."

As she nodded, Ross slipped over the side. Then, taking a deep breath, he duck-dived down. For a few seconds, Carrick followed his shape as he swam down. Then Ross reached the black hole and vanished inside.

"Exactly what's down there?" he asked Katie.

"A clear entrance, broad as a tunnel, maybe twenty feet of it, then we surface." She spoke confidently. "There's no problem, no snags. Even at high tide there's air space—in the first cave, anyway." She wrinkled her nose. "Beyond that, the other caves aren't so easy—the ones we know about, anyway."

While she spoke, she moved awkwardly down from the bow. Then, taking Carrick by surprise, she made a strange sideways flip with her body and splashed into the water. She surfaced beside the boat, tossing back her wet hair, grinning at him, then began swimming with a lazy style and effortless ease. She circled the dinghy, then rested a hand on its combing and floated happily.

"You know something, Webb Carrick?" she said softly. "You haven't asked a damned thing about my leg. Why? Too polite?"

"Maybe." He leaned close towards her. "What happened?"

"Two fishing boats. One was my father's, the old *Harmony*. I was on board, helping him berth her as we came into harbour." She twisted a quick, bitter smile. "I slipped, fell between them—and grunch."

Carrick fought down a shudder. He'd once seen a man die that way, would never forget it.

"When?"

"I was still at school." The dinghy bobbed on another wave, which broke lightly over the shoulders of the yellow scuba suit. She spat water, then laughed at his expression. "Don't look so worried about it. Everything else is in good working order—I guarantee it."

"I've noticed," agreed Carrick.

"Good." She let go of the boat, swam a few strokes, then floated back. "Now you tell me something. Why is everyone suddenly so interested again in what happened to Gibby MacNeil?"

"Everybody?" He leaned his elbows on the side of the dinghy, her face inches from his own.

"You, your captain—and Sergeant Ballantyne was on the phone to Mrs. Jordan this afternoon about it." She frowned at him, waiting for an answer.

"Captain Shannon sometimes stirs things up," he said.

"That's all?" She didn't believe him.

Before she could speak again, there was a splash in the water a few feet away as Jamie Ross suddenly surfaced again. He floated where he was for a moment, breathing deeply.

"Everything all right?" asked Katie.

"No." His voice was hoarse. He swam over to the boat, dragged himself aboard, and sat silent for a moment on the stern thwart, water dripping from his scuba suit. "No, it's not."

"Why?" Katie reached the side of the boat again in a couple of strokes and grabbed for support. "What's wrong, Jamie?"

"Don't ask me how, but there's a dead man down there," said her brother. He looked up at Carrick. "Dead—and I think he's a bloody Russian."

CHAPTER 3

When Jamie Ross dived down again, Carrick went with him. Once the water closed over their heads and they began swimming, he let Ross take the lead into the dark maw of the undersea cavern.

The familiar initial chill of the Hebridean sea penetrated the scuba rubbers as he followed. Within a moment, the water had changed from bright and clear to darkness deeper than night, then Ross switched on the torch clipped to his waistband. Carrick used it like a marker beacon and stayed close. He could see that the natural tunnel through the rock stayed broad, sides worn smooth by tide and time and scoured clean of all but an occasional wavering strand of marine weed.

A few strokes more, and he had still plenty of lung capacity left when they rose and surfaced together in a new black darkness, the inner cave. The air smelled salt-damp but clean; the only sound was the lapping of water.

"This isn't how I planned it, but here we are." Jamie Ross's voice echoed eerily. Floating for a moment, he unclipped his torch and used it in a slow, deliberate arc around the cave.

It was roughly bowl-shaped, perhaps sixty feet across, with the rippling black water covering about half its surface. The rest was a broad shelf of rock which sloped from water level upward. The torch moved and gave Carrick a glimpse of a jagged roof high overhead. Then the beam came down again, to settle on the shelf. Much of it was covered in a thick carpet of debris, splintered driftwood and tangled weed mixed with everything from small boulders to dead fish and the smashed remains of a lobster pot. But two shapes bulkier than the rest lay close together on the left.

"Over there?" asked Carrick.

Ross nodded.

A few more strokes, and Carrick's feet touched the start of the shelf. He waded in the rest of the way, took his own torch from his waistband, and switched it on as Ross joined him.

Crunching over the debris, Carrick reached the first of the shapes. It was the limp carcase of a dead sheep. But beyond it, lying face-down, was the body of a man in the torn remains of a black rubber scuba suit.

Facedown—Carrick found himself remembering yet again the dispassionate, long-ago lecture he'd been given on why a drowned man was usually found that way and why a woman came in faceup. The reason was basic anatomy, and so far the lecturer concerned had always been right. Which was a pity. Carrick had disliked every minute with him.

He stopped beside the dead frogman, used the torch beam in a slow head-to-toe inspection, and winced. Whatever had happened, it was as if he'd been ripped and torn by giant claws. The tough neoprene rubber suit had been reduced to rags, one entire leg completely torn away. The pale exposed flesh below showed a crisscross of deep gashes. One began at the back of the frogman's neck and ran high up into his dark, close-cropped hair. There was no air-tank harness, no scuba mask, and his feet were bare.

"Well?" Still dripping water, Jamie Ross came up beside him. "What do you think?"

"He's a mess," said Carrick.

"And the suit?"

Carrick nodded. The scuba suit, what was left of it, was oddly different in style and cut from any make he'd come across.

"Take a look at his left wrist," invited Ross.

Stooping, Carrick lifted the limp, cold arm. A broken compass was still strapped to the dead man's wrist, but something else glinted above it—a chrome metal identity bracelet. He found the nameplate. It was engraved in a bold Cyrillic script, the first name Andrei, the second name impossible to decipher.

"Russian, right?" said Ross.

"It looks that way." Easing back on his heels, Carrick turned the dead man over, faceup.

He heard Ross give a quick, retching gasp and felt pretty much the same. The frogman's badly damaged face had also been partly eaten away. Several small, almost transparent crabs scuttled away from their feast, fleeing from the light.

"God Almighty," said Ross shakily, stepping back a couple of paces. "I could have done without that."

"So could he." Forcing himself to ignore the horror of the man's empty eye sockets and the other areas where the crabs had been busy, Carrick began a closer inspection. "Look round," he suggested without turning. "See if you can find anything else."

Ross obeyed without protest.

One of the suit pockets was still, by a miracle, intact. He opened it. Inside, wrapped in waterproof plastic, he found a packet of British cigarettes and a cheap gunmetal cigarette lighter which had a hammer-and-sickle badge on the casing. There was nothing else.

But the dead man had been wearing breathing apparatus. The marks were there, on the suit and on his body, to show how some terrible force had ripped the air-tank harness away. A deep, oddly shaped cut on his right cheek could only have been caused by a face-mask being smashed.

There wasn't much more he could do. Carefully, he turned the body over facedown again, exactly as he'd found it. He rose as Ross came back along the shelf.

"Nothing." Ross shook his head.

"All right." Carrick shifted his feet and heard a piece of unseen driftwood snap with the move. He suddenly found himself hating this black piece of underworld which had become a tomb. "But how the hell did he get in here?"

"I could take a guess," said Ross slowly.

He stopped there, startled, as a loud splash came from the darkness beyond the ledge. They swung their torches and the beams settled on Katie Ross, who had just surfaced. She swam in and let her brother help her out onto the rock shelf.

"You were to stay out there," he said harshly.

"That's right." Eyeing him stubbornly, she pushed back her dripping wet hair. "I changed my mind."

She limped past him, reached Carrick, and looked down at the dead man. Her face paled in the torchlight, then she went over to the remains of a large wooden box and sat down.

"Is he a Russian?" she asked quietly.

Carrick nodded. "Had they reported anyone missing?"

"From the *Zarakov*?" She shook her head. "I'd have heard at the office—"

"Everyone, anywhere, would have heard," said her brother. "Port Ard's a good place for gossip."

"Meaning what?" She glared at him.

"Sort it out later," Carrick told them. He heard his voice echo back from the roof of the cave as he paused and nodded towards the dead frogman. "Jamie, what about him?"

"How he got here?" Jamie Ross shrugged. "The same way everything else did. It's all new—almost all of it, anyway." He had a question of his own. "How long would you say he'd been dead?"

Carrick thought of the crabs. "A few days—not much more than that, but not less."

Ross glanced at his sister. She gave a slow nod of agreement to his unspoken question, any flare-up forgotten.

"Which means either during the storm or just before it," said Ross. He spoke slowly but with an underlying confidence. "Remember, I told you this cave system goes right back, most of it underwater?"

"Yes." Carrick waited.

"So at peak tidal times you can have one hell of a lot of water pouring in or being sucked out." Ross grimaced at the thought. "No way would I go diving down here when that's happening. And in a storm, a real storm—"

It would be an underwater hell, an irresistible syphoning back and forward. Carrick knew exactly what he meant, had once been caught in something similar, and had felt lucky to get out alive.

But the young fisherman wasn't finished.

"If he did get sucked in, then I'll bet on where he was diving," he said almost casually. "Ever heard of the Sump?"

Carrick shook his head.

"Jamie, we could show him it on the way back," suggested Katie. She was still pale and shivered a little. "It would be easier, and I'd rather be out of here."

Her brother nodded. "You and me both, girl." He glanced at Carrick. "What about—?"

"Moving him? No." Carrick had already decided on that. "I'll come back with one of *Marlin*'s boats—tomorrow morning will be soon enough."

"He'll still be here," said Ross without humour. He swung the beam of his torch in a last, slow inspection of the cave and sighed. "No, I don't think I'll feel the same about this place again. All right, we're ready."

"Lead on," said Carrick.

He stood watching as Ross and Katie went together into the water. Then they went under and for a few seconds the submerged glow of Ross's torch marked their progress. It vanished as they entered the tunnel.

Stooping, Carrick unclipped the metal identity bracelet from the dead man's wrist. He tucked it into a pocket of his scuba suit, then rose again.

"I'll be back," he promised the silent figure.

Then, the torch clipped to his belt again, he waded out into the rippling black water. He stopped and heard tiny scuttling noises from the shelf. The crabs were returning. Suppressing a slight shudder, he took a deep breath and went under.

Dusk was beginning to creep in when he reached the world outside. The wind had risen a little, there were some clouds overhead, and the sea had a new restlessness. A change in the weather might be on the way.

Aboard the dinghy, Jamie Ross took command again. He insisted they change out of their diving suits. When that was done and they were dried down and dressed again, he was in no hurry to haul up the anchor.

"You want to see the Sump, right?" he said to Carrick. "Then we wait—the tide's about right, but we'll give it another ten minutes."

Carrick made no objection and they stayed where they were, the dinghy bobbing as the sea slapped and swirled around its varnished wood. Finally, Ross was ready. The anchor and its dripping line in a neat heap near the bow, the little outboard engine throbbing, they began moving again and headed out from Targe Island, steering on a southwest course, which still kept the island's rocky bulk and ruined castle like a barrier screen between them and the approach to Port Ard.

"About here," said Ross after a very short time. Throttling back, he used the outboard and rudder to hold their position. "Katie?"

She still had a towel round her neck and had been quietly combing her hair into some semblance of order. Now she nodded, touched Carrick's arm, and gestured at the stretch of sea now between them and the island.

"It's starting," she said.

A broad patch of water was gradually beginning to fleck and whiten. Then, as Carrick watched, the sea beneath that surface foam began to change in colour to an angry green.

The outboard's beat increased a little. The boat eased out still further from the island while the same patch of sea increased its strange turmoil. Sharp, lumping waves began to appear. Suddenly there were birds circling overhead, sea-fishing fulmars and black, sharp-billed skuas. They were watching, waiting expectantly, but none ventured down to the surface.

Another minute, and Carrick found himself watching an isolated turmoil of broken water surrounded by relatively peaceful sea—and understood.

The tide was on the turn and they were on the edge of an overfall, that occasional combination of an isolated reef of rock not far beneath the surface in a surround of deep water. With, in this case, all the signs of a narrow undersea valley running through the middle.

"The Sump," said Ross grimly. He had to raise his voice as he went on. Where before there had been the throb of the outboard and the steady clamour of the waves, there was now something else—a strange, muted rumbling as the overfall's currents sent unseen boulders clashing one against another. "It's a good place to stay away from."

Carrick nodded, the rumbling growing louder, the broken water still increasing in fury.

"What you've got is a five-fathom depth at low tide suddenly rising to less than two fathoms—but with a twenty-fathom ribbon running down the middle." Ross looked at him and shrugged. "That's why we call it the Sump. Anything caught by the tide—"

"Hasn't a chance," said Katie. She frowned up at the hovering seabirds. "Even they know that. But sometimes, afterwards, there are fish."

There were other overfalls along the coast and sometimes surprisingly far out at sea. All were dangerous. But Carrick guessed the one off Targe Island was as near as nature came to a murder machine. On an outgoing tide, the water retreating through that underwater chasm splitting the rise of rock would suck with an awesome strength, suck and devour anything into its depths, living or dead.

With no escape. If the dead frogman had been working anywhere between Targe Island and the Sump, he would have been sucked in too. Hauled along, smashed against bottom rock, battered, broken, taken down into the currents of the chasm. Then spewed out again as the next tide came scouring in.

"The main current feeds towards the caves?"

Ross nodded.

Then the storm had come. Carrick drew a deep breath. Already the surface turmoil above the Sump was dying. But down below it would still be raging.

He ran a hand along the dinghy's varnished wood. There was nothing more to say. Not for the moment, at any rate.

It was true dusk, a grey half-light, when the dinghy murmured back in towards Port Ard. The approach lights for the harbour entrance were already burning, but Jamie Ross steered away from them, heading home again. Carrick had hoped for the harbour, but Ross apparently still disliked the idea of sailing in with a Fisheries Protection man aboard.

"I'll give you a lift in the van," offered Katie as they bumped the little jetty beside their cottage. She watched her brother tie the dinghy's painter to a mooring ring, then added bluntly, "That's the least we can do."

Ross grunted, stepped across to the jetty, and helped her ashore. As Carrick followed, Ross faced him with a slightly shamefaced frown.

"How much do we need to get involved?"

"You'll have to give some kind of a statement—both of you," Carrick told him. "But it can wait."

"Good." Ross looked relieved. "The less I'm caught up in this, the better. I'll have the *Harmony* out fishing by first light tomorrow—and the *Zarakov* is still my best market."

He turned away, striding towards the cottage. Katie sighed, then, leaning on her stick, limped over to the parked Ford. Carrick followed her and they got aboard. Setting the engine running, the girl engaged the automatic transmission with a jerk that sent gravel spinning from the rear wheels as they began moving.

"Sometimes I could kick Jamie," she said tightly as the white van bumped back onto the road. Then she gave a wry grimace. "Except if I tried, I suppose I'd fall flat on my backside—damn him."

The van gathered speed, Katie leaned forward and flicked on their lights as a car came towards them, travelling with dipped headlamps.

"Those people on the *Zarakov*," she exploded suddenly. "If they lost a man, why didn't they say anything, tell people?"

"Sometimes that's the Russian way," said Carrick. It could also have depended on what the frogman had been doing. He had no theories, just a knowledge that Russian ships' captains usually adopted a stubborn stance towards the rest of the world. "What about John Maxwell? Would he know anything?"

"Him?" She crinkled her nose at the fish buyer's name. "I doubt it. Or if he did, he'd tell Mrs. Jordan."

"And you'd know." Carrick smiled in the grey light. "Still, he's their front man."

"They use him, that's all," she said with a positive authority. She grinned, keeping her eyes on the road. "But he must be reasonable in bed. Mrs. Jordan certainly likes having him around."

"I don't think I asked about that," said Carrick. "What your boss does in her spare time is her business."

"True." Katie Ross was unperturbed. "How do you think she would be—that way?"

Carrick swallowed.

"I wouldn't know," he said weakly.

Katie Ross laughed and left it at that.

Shore Street was busy. Small groups of men, some from *Marlin,* others obviously from the *Zarakov*'s shore party, seemed everywhere along its length but particularly around the brightly lit Clan Bar. The locals were out too, bunched in shop doorways or at street corners, watching, taking note when a girl went by on a stranger's arm.

Port Ard showed all the ingredients for possible trouble. Carrick let the scene register as the van purred along, hoped things would stay peaceful, but knew he had more important things to worry about.

The van swung in through the harbour gates, bounced over a couple of potholes, had to weave through some parked trucks and unloaded cargo, then came to a halt exactly level with *Marlin*'s gangway. The fishery cruiser's deck lights were on and a small spotlamp had been rigged to throw an extra pool of light at the quayside end of the gangway.

"Now, then, you can't park there." Ferguson's thin figure pushed past the petty officer on watch and strode officiously down the gangway. Then the grey-haired Junior Second Mate saw Carrick in the passenger seat and grunted a reluctant apology. "I didn't expect you back this early."

"That makes two of us." Carrick gestured towards the fishery cruiser. "Is the Old Man aboard?"

Ferguson shook his head. "Been and gone again. He got hold of a car—the local Fisheries Officer's transport, borrowed for tonight."

Carrick swore under his breath. "Where was he heading?"

"That fisherman MacNeil's cottage." Ferguson scowled. "Whether he got there is something else, the way he drives."

Carrick grinned. Shannon might be a master mariner, but he handled anything on wheels with an awesome clumsiness that terrified any innocent trapped into being a passenger.

"I'll find him." He glanced round at Katie. "Any chance of another lift?"

She nodded. "It isn't far."

Ferguson frowned. "He said he didn't want company."

"Well, he's going to have it," said Carrick. "How are things at this end? Any troubles in the village?"

"No, it's early yet," said Ferguson gloomily. "But there will be. And I'm still reporting Shaw for stealing ship's stores—remember that."

He left them, stalking back up the gangway, and Katie laughed softly as she set the van moving again.

"What's so funny?" asked Carrick.

"Nothing." She shook her head. "Just men."

Back in the village, they turned off Shore Street and the van took a narrow road which was little more than a track. It snaked up the hill behind the village, winding past a thin scatter of small cottages. Katie eased back on the accelerator as they reached one which had a grey Volvo station wagon parked outside the door.

"That's Gibby MacNeil's place—and Mrs. Jordan's station wagon." She pursed her lips appreciatively. "Webb, your captain must be pretty persuasive. She doesn't usually let anyone touch that Volvo."

"He has hidden charms," said Carrick. Light showed at one of the cottage windows, a narrow strip from behind closed curtains. He reached for the passenger-door handle as the van stopped, then turned towards her. "Thanks for the lift. I'm sorry about the way things happened."

"It wasn't your fault." For a moment, in the dim light from the instrument panel, he saw her face tighten at the stark memory of what they'd seen in the cave. Then, unexpectedly, she leaned over and her lips brushed his cheek. "I like you, Webb Carrick. Now move—Jamie's expecting me back, probably timing me with a stopwatch."

He climbed out, closed the van door, and watched for a moment as the little vehicle turned on the narrow track. Then, as it began to travel downhill again and the taillights vanished, he walked past the empty Volvo and headed for the cottage. Small and old, built of rough stone which had been whitewashed, it had a corrugated-iron roof which was held down, islands style, by a net of ropes weighted at each corner by heavy stones. A TV aerial was attached to the single chimney at one end, a narrow strip of garden round the cottage probably hadn't been tended in years, and what had once been a wooden garage shed near the rear was a dilapidated wreck.

Carrick reached the front door, used the old-fashioned horseshoe knocker, and waited. No one answered. Frowning, he tried the handle and the door swung open.

"Captain?" He went in as he called. "Where are you?"

"Damn," said a disappointed voice. The door was kicked shut and a light came on.

A metal poker still clutched in one hand, Captain Shannon stepped out from where he'd been hiding behind the door. He looked at Carrick, then at the poker, and lowered it almost reluctantly.

"Expecting someone, sir?" asked Carrick politely.

"Not you." Shannon's round, bearded face reflected a momentary embarrassment. "But I heard someone prowling outside earlier—caught a glimpse of him trying to look in through a window." He made a sheepish throat-clearing noise. "At my age, you don't take chances, mister. Anyway, what the hell are you doing here?"

"Something came up," said Carrick.

"Did it?" Shannon scowled. "I didn't want company here. I still don't."

Carrick shrugged. "I found a dead Russian."

"You found—" Shannon's eyebrows shot upward and his mouth fell open. He purpled for a moment, then drew a deep breath. "My God, that's all we needed."

"I didn't exactly go looking for him," said Carrick.

"That helps, I suppose," said Shannon bitterly. He sighed. "All right, mister. Come through and I'll listen. Don't worry about this place—I bullied the keys out of the local sergeant."

They went through the small lobby. The cottage had three modestly furnished rooms, a tiny kitchen and a small bathroom which looked as though it had been tacked on as a halfhearted late-Victorian afterthought. Shannon led the way into the living room, at the rear. Two battered armchairs flanked a stone hearth which held the cold ashes of a peat fire.

"I'm damned if Gibby would grudge us a drink." Opening a cupboard, Shannon took out a half-empty bottle and gave a grunt of satisfaction as he examined the label. "He always kept a special bottle of the best, for visitors. Wouldn't touch it on his own, just drank the ordinary stuff. So—we're visitors."

Finding two chipped, dusty tumblers, Shannon poured a hefty

measure of whisky into each. He gave one to Carrick, then settled in a chair.

"Well?" he asked, as Carrick did the same. "Your alleged Russian, mister—how did it happen?"

Even keeping to essentials, the story took a few minutes to tell and Shannon asked several questions along the way. At the finish, both tumblers were almost empty. Rising, *Marlin*'s captain padded over, collected the whisky bottle, poured himself another measure, then looked pointedly at Carrick's tumbler and shook his head.

"You've had enough. You're driving when we leave." He pondered for a moment. "Where's the identity bracelet?"

Carrick handed it over.

"Nothing else on him?"

"No, sir."

"Can you find this cave again, or do we need Ross?"

"I can find it."

"Good." Shannon studied the identity bracelet for another moment, then stuffed it into an inside pocket of his uniform jacket. "The next thing is, do we tell them—or do we wait until we've collected him?"

"The *Zarakov*'s people?"

"Who else?" Shannon looked around the room and sighed. "You know why I came here, mister. To—well, to try and find something. Anything. Suppose there's a connection between MacNeil's death and this one?"

"There doesn't have to be," said Carrick.

"Then what the hell was a Russian frogman doing, working out there?" demanded Shannon in a harsh voice. "You don't know, I don't know—and if they haven't even reported him missing, do you imagine they're going to tell us?"

"I wouldn't bet on it," said Carrick.

He knew from experience that when Shannon was in that kind of mood it helped to go along with him at least part of the way. They had two strange deaths—that much was hard fact. They might be accidental, they might not. Go beyond that, and the way was open for a nightmare labyrinth of possibilities.

"How about the people you've seen so far?" he asked. "Were they any help?"

"No." Shannon took a sip from his drink, frowning, but letting his temporary wrath subside. "I've seen statements, reports, talked to Sergeant Ballantyne, to that female doctor, other people. None of them have any doubts—MacNeil got drunk, then froze to death." He shrugged. "And I don't believe it. Anyway, you may as well help me to finish off here, mister. Look around for anything unusual, anything that doesn't seem right."

Shannon had already explored most of the cottage. They went through it again, including a small bedroom at the front. The bedroom curtains were closed, but a large pair of binoculars, mounted on a tripod, faced the window.

"Like to know what the view is, mister?" asked Shannon. "Straight out across the harbour to your Targe Island. With glasses like that pair, MacNeil could look out to that chunk of rock and count the fleas on a resident rabbit's backbone. Does that interest you?"

The binoculars were certainly powerful, though it was too dark outside to put them to any test. The only other thing that mattered in the bedroom was a large envelope lying in a drawer beneath a tangle of washed but unironed shirts and neatly darned underwear. It held several faded photographs of ships and seamen. His face impassive, Shannon leafed through the photographs one by one, then returned them to the drawer.

"I knew a few of them," he said softly. "The ships and the men. All right, we're finished."

He led the way back into the living room. A piece of elaborately embroidered canvas, still in its wooden hoop, lay on top of the scarred wooden sideboard. Shannon picked it up. The embroidered picture, picked out in fine detail in a delicate selection of coloured wools, showed an old-fashioned sailing ship. An embroidery needle was still attached to a strand of black wool, used to create a stylised pattern round the outer edge of the canvas.

"Like it?" asked Shannon.

Carrick nodded. "His?"

"Yes." Shannon eased the embroidered canvas from the hoop. "He always promised me one."

Carrick watched him fold the canvas and put it inside his jacket. He didn't feel any surprise that Big Gibby MacNeil, whatever his reputation, should have been an expert at embroidery. Seamen—particularly seamen of MacNeil's generation, when voyages were longer and shore leave scanty—often took up hobbies afloat that would startle a landsman.

One of *Marlin*'s stokers was a grandfather who knitted baby clothes—he'd learned how to use the needles in jail. On Carrick's last ship, they'd had a cook who created ivory-like jewellery from old soup bones, and a deckhand had had a passion for making soft toys.

"That's it." Shannon took a last look around and nodded. "I'll give Sergeant Ballantyne the keys, you can tell him about your Russian."

They were heading for the cottage door when the noise came from outside, a sudden clatter, then the sound of running feet.

"He's back!" Shannon made a rush for the door. In the process, he blocked Carrick's way out. But they still reached the open in time to see a figure disappear round the side of the cottage, trying to escape towards the rear.

Carrick began sprinting, hearing Shannon pounding along behind him. Night had closed in, but there was enough moonlight to see the prowler, now running hard for the tumbledown wooden garage. As Carrick began to close the gap, the man ahead glanced back. He wore a black hood over his head and what looked like overalls, and after the glance, which made him slow for a moment, he swerved off in a new direction, to go round the side of the garage.

Shannon was baying somewhere behind, but Carrick knew that, effectively, he was on his own. His quarry seemed to stumble and, as the man recovered, Carrick threw himself forward in a tackle which took him just below the knees. They went down together, smashing against the fragile wooden planking of the old garage, then rolling away from it, locked together.

The hooded man had a strength and ferocity which took Carrick by surprise. A knee took Carrick low and hard in the stomach, a fist hammered a blow against his head, which jarred his senses. Then the man had torn free, was scrambling up, and was grabbing at a thick length of rotted timber.

Struggling to rise, Carrick saw Shannon come charging in like a squat, enraged bear. The length of timber in the hooded man's hands swung like a club and smashed against the little captain's chest and shoulder. Shannon staggered. The wooden club swung again in another two-handed blow, this time at Shannon's head.

The rotted timber cracked and splintered under the impact, and Shannon pitched forward. Hurling the remaining stump of wood at Carrick, the hooded man ran again and vanished into the shadows.

Shannon lay still. Carrick reached him, knelt quickly, heard a faint groan, then looked up again as the bark of a motorcycle starting up cut through the night.

Throttle jammed wide open, engine racing to a screaming note, the machine burst into view from behind a patch of bush. Riding high off the saddle, clinging to the handlebars, the hooded man took it bouncing and bucking across the rough ground beyond the cottage straight towards the road. Then, making a skidding turn, the machine went snarling down the road towards Port Ard and disappeared.

Shannon groaned again, louder this time. He started to move, the groan became a curse, then very slowly, Carrick helping him, he sat up.

"Damn him," he managed. "What the hell did he hit me with, mister?"

"That." Carrick pointed at the splintered wood.

"Just that?" Shannon moved his head experimentally, winced, then stared in disbelief. "It felt more like a telegraph pole." He sat where he was for a minute longer, breathing heavily, then his mouth tightened. "All right, what are we hanging about here for?"

Carrick helped him up, then assisted him back. When they reached the cottage, Shannon insisted on going past it and got into the passenger seat of his borrowed station wagon. He sat there while Carrick took the cottage keys and locked up. When Carrick returned, Shannon had the Volvo's interior light on and was ruefully examining a long, shallow cut across the top of his scantily thatched scalp.

"That's all," he said with something close to awe. "I was ready for a lot worse, mister."

"You need a doctor," said Carrick.

"Me?" Shannon snorted with disgust. "No, thanks, I've met her. I'd rather trust a vet."

Carrick shrugged. "That could be arranged—sir."

"Thank you." Shannon had a padded handkerchief clutched in one hand and used it again to dab away some of the blood oozing from his scalp wound. Then he settled back with a sigh. "Sergeant Ballantyne, mister—that's an order."

Reluctantly, Carrick obeyed. The Volvo handled smoothly, the heavy Scandinavian suspension making light of the potholed way back to Port Ard, and in a few minutes he brought the station wagon coasting to a halt outside the police sergeant's house.

"Company," said Shannon, breaking his silence for the first time since they'd started. He leaned forward and scowled. "Isn't that Maxwell's car?"

Carrick nodded. The black B.M.W. was parked outside the house, behind Ballantyne's police car, and the house itself was a blaze of light.

"Damn." Shannon used the rearview mirror to inspect his scalp again, mopped away another trickle of blood, then scowled round. "My hat."

Carrick reached over, picked up Shannon's hat from the rear seat, and Shannon rammed it firmly on his head.

"Ready," he said curtly.

They walked together up the path to the house, Shannon moving with an awkward stiffness and his lips tightly closed. They'd been seen. Sergeant Ballantyne's wife, a large, capable-looking woman wearing a knitted sweater and slacks, opened the front door to them with a resigned air.

"He's in there." She nodded to a door to her right. A low murmur of voices was coming from beyond it. "Don't keep him too long, please—his supper's ready."

"I'll remember," said Shannon.

She left them and they pushed open the door.

On the other side, they were in the office area of the house—and the little room which was Sergeant Ballantyne's official domain was already crowded. The conversation stopped short and Shannon stared at the people in the room, startled.

"What the hell?"

Carrick shared his surprise. Clapper Bell was leaning against a wall and greeted him with a slight grin and an almost apologetic shrug. Seated behind his desk, Sergeant Ballantyne looked almost as startled as Shannon.

The others were Alexis Jordan, John Maxwell, and a calm-eyed stranger, a man with short, jet-black hair who was about Carrick's age and build. They sat together on a bench, and Alexis Jordan didn't seem dressed for a police station visit. She was in a white silk shirt and a black velvet skirt. A fur jacket was draped over her shoulders, and a heavy gold chain hugged her throat.

"Good evening, James," she said. "I wondered when you'd show up."

"I think the captain probably doesn't know—yet," said Sergeant Ballantyne, frowning. He cleared his throat and looked deliberately at the calm-eyed stranger. "But we've had a wee spot of trouble in the village, Captain Shannon."

The stranger gave a slight nod. He was dressed in a grey suit, neatly tailored, but with a vaguely foreign cut. Maxwell had also smartened his appearance, and was wearing a dark-blue blazer with plaid slacks.

"Were any of my crew involved in this?" Shannon shot a suspicious glance in Clapper Bell's direction.

"Only in stopping it, Captain," soothed Maxwell. He got to his feet. "You haven't met the *Zarakov*'s executive officer, Commander Vasilek—"

"Fedor Vasilek, Captain." The man rose as he spoke, greeting Shannon with interest. What might have been amusement showed briefly in his eyes as he glanced at Carrick. "I know your ship, of course."

"You could say we met," said Carrick politely.

Maxwell completed the introductions, the Russian formally shaking hands with each of them in turn. He had a firm grip. His face, sharply chiselled, badly pockmarked, seemed built to show as little emotion as possible, and his English was almost flawless, with only a faint trace of accent.

"What's your problem, Commander?" asked Shannon.

Vasilek shrugged. "An unfortunate incident involving one of our shore-leave party, Captain. Hopefully, however—"

"It's been sorted out," said Maxwell quickly. "I think the sergeant agrees on that."

"Does he?" Auburn hair glinting as she moved, Alexis Jordan opened her handbag and took a cigarette from its pack. Immediately Vasilek produced a silver lighter. She smiled, bent briefly over the tiny flame, drew deeply on her cigarette, then looked up. "Well, Sergeant? It all depends on you."

"Aye." Ballantyne rubbed his chin, obviously tempted but not totally decided. He glanced at Shannon. "It's simple enough, Captain. One of the *Zarakov*'s crew made a grab at a girl—she's not local, but newly off some damned yacht."

"The blonde or the redhead?" Carrick raised an interested eyebrow. "I've seen them."

"The blonde," said Ballantyne. "The seaman had been drinking. The girl's companions told him to shove off and he went wild. Drew a knife and tried to drag the girl away. There were plenty of people around and it got fairly nasty."

"That's when our peacemaker arrived," murmured Alexis Jordan. She considered Clapper Bell with an interested respect. "It seems you were pretty effective, Mr. Bell."

"As a peacemaker?" Shannon swallowed hard. "Him?"

Bell gave an embarrassed shrug. "All I did was thump him, sir.

For his own good, like. I mean, if he'd stuck someone with that knife—"

"He'd have been lynched," said Ballantyne. He saw Vasilek's disbelief and flushed a little. "That's how it could have been, Commander. Either that or a small war—I saw the crowd who were there."

"Where is he now?" asked Carrick.

Ballantyne gestured over his shoulder at another door. "Back there. My wife isn't very pleased—I keep telling her it's a cell, but she will keep storing her damned homemade jam in it."

"In Russia wives are much the same," said Vasilek sympathetically. "But in this case the problem seems easy to resolve."

"Release him to you." Ballantyne frowned, the fingers of one hand drumming on his desk. "What'll happen to him?"

The black-haired Russian shrugged. "The man will be suitably punished."

"Poor sod," muttered Clapper Bell.

No one challenged him. Slowly Ballantyne got to his feet. Without a word, he went through the door.

"And that's that," said Maxwell with relief. "The best solution all round, eh?"

Shannon ignored him. His eyes were on Alexis Jordan.

"How did you know about this?" he demanded.

"Sheer chance." She took a last draw at her cigarette and stubbed it carefully in an ashtray. "John and I were having dinner with Commander Vasilek and—"

"That's right," agreed Maxwell, cutting in. "At Clachan Lodge, Captain. Maybe you know the place—it's a hotel about a mile out of Port Ard."

Shannon grunted. "I've heard of it. And?"

"One of my crew telephoned," said Vasilek. He sighed. "A pity. It was a good meal. But I'm grateful to your Mrs. Jordan for offering to help."

"It's Department policy—we try to avoid friction, don't we, Captain?" Her eyes challenged Shannon to argue.

The rear door swung open again and Ballantyne returned, pushing a tall, thick-set but distinctly frightened seaman ahead of him. The man had a swollen jaw and a badly split lip and he stiffened, paling, as he saw Vasilek.

"He's yours," said Ballantyne.

"Thank you, Sergeant." Vasilek looked the seaman up and down in silence, then turned to Maxwell. "Could you drive us to the harbour?"

"No problem. We'll see you off." Maxwell grinned at Alexis Jordan as she rose to join them, then nodded to Ballantyne. "Thanks, Sergeant. I owe you one."

The freed seaman with them, they were heading for the exit door when Shannon spoke, his voice grating across the room.

"Commander, I'd like a word with you. Alone."

The Russian frowned, hesitated, and glanced at his seaman while Maxwell and Alexis Jordan looked puzzled.

"Only for a moment." Shannon signalled Clapper Bell. "My bo'sun can keep an eye on your—ah—comrade."

"Very well." Vasilek waited while Clapper Bell and the others left, Alexis Jordan looking both annoyed and suspicious. Then, as the door closed, he asked, "Is there some mystery?"

"*You* tell *me*." Suddenly, Shannon tossed the chromed identity bracelet on Ballantyne's desk. "Recognise it?"

Slowly, almost reluctantly, Vasilek crossed over and picked up the bracelet. His mouth tightened as he looked at it.

"Where did you find this, Captain?" he asked quietly.

"My Chief Officer took it from a drowned man wearing what was left of a frogman's outfit," said Shannon. He ignored Sergeant Ballantyne's exclamation of surprise. "Was he yours, Commander?"

"Yes." Vasilek laid down the disc again and sighed. "His name was Andrei Krymov, one of our—our technical officers. Diving was his hobby. He went missing several days ago."

Shannon walked across to a chair and sat down heavily. Suddenly Carrick realised how grey and strained he looked. Vasilek also seemed to realise something was wrong.

"Are you unwell, Captain?" he asked.

"Well enough." Shannon nodded to Carrick. "Take over, mister."

"Did you search for Krymov?" asked Carrick.

Vasilek flushed. "Of course."

"But you didn't report he was missing?"

"To the British authorities?" Vasilek shook his head.

Carrick touched the identity bracelet with a finger, enough to make the chain links jingle. "Where did you search, Commander?"

"Andrei Krymov disappeared while diving from a small boat in Loch Armach, close to where the *Zarakov* is anchored. He was spearfishing." Vasilek moistened his lips. "We searched that area. May I ask where you found him?"

"A long way from there." Carrick had caught Shannon's warning glance. He gave thanks that Sergeant Ballantyne was still managing to stay quiet. "Strange, isn't it?"

"So are tides and currents, my friend." The dark-haired Russian turned firmly to Shannon. "Captain, I would appreciate your cooperation in having Comrade Andrei Krymov's remains brought aboard the *Zarakov*."

"Sorry." Just as firmly, Shannon shook his head. "He may have been a Russian national, but his body was found in British waters. We have to keep him for now." He glanced at Ballantyne, a slight, partly forced smile twisting his bearded face. "Correct, Sergeant?"

"Correct." Ballantyne couldn't keep the indignation from his voice. "That's the law. We hold his remains until enquiries are complete—including why you didn't report this. Then you can have him, Commander."

"I see." Vasilek pursed his lips but didn't argue. "Very well, I'll advise my captain when I return to the *Zarakov*." He paused, looking at the identity bracelet, then at Shannon. "May I take this?"

Shannon nodded. "But give the sergeant a receipt."

Angrily, Vasilek took a pencil and paper lying on the desk, scribbled, then tossed the result towards Ballantyne. Picking up the identity bracelet, he headed for the door and opened it.

"Good night, Commander Vasilek," said Carrick softly.

The Russian turned. For a moment his eyes met Carrick's. They were no longer calm. Then, without a word, he was gone and the door had slammed shut again.

They heard Maxwell's car start up and pull away, then Clapper Bell came back in. It was a signal for Sergeant Ballantyne to start asking questions.

Still slumped in his chair, Shannon parried most of them. At last, Ballantyne gave up.

"I'll make the arrangements," he said gloomily.

"A dead Russian in a frogman suit," mused Shannon. He rubbed a thumb along his beard, watching Ballantyne. "That's trouble, Sergeant. Do you really want him?"

"No." Then Ballantyne grinned. "Damn you, Captain. You're welcome to him."

"Not me—other people." Shannon heaved up off the chair. The short rest seemed to have done him good. Reaching into a pocket, he brought out the keys to Gibby MacNeil's cottage and handed them over. "I'm finished with these for now."

"Find anything?" Ballantyne scooped the keys into a drawer with minimal interest.

"A prowler," said Shannon.

"Eh?" Ballantyne blinked. "You're sure?"

With care Shannon removed his hat, leaving some congealed blood and hair sticking to the leather headband.

"I'm sure," he said with dignity. "What I want to know is why."

He motioned Carrick and Clapper Bell towards the door, then led the way out. Carrick hung back.

"Sergeant—there's something else."

"What?" asked Ballantyne weakly.

"Your supper's ready."

Ballantyne swore at him.

CHAPTER 4

It was 8 A.M. next morning, the sky dull and cloudy, the sea a sullen, lacklustre grey, when Her Majesty's Fisheries Protection Service cruiser *Marlin* idled her way out of the tight confines of Port Ard harbour.

She had been ready to sail since dawn, when Shannon had first appeared on the bridge. But Fleet Support in Edinburgh said Shannon had to wait for orders. What had to be done might be simple, but it had to have the official stamp of approval.

So *Marlin* had waited, while a steady trickle of fishing boats headed out to sea. Others had left for the fishing grounds before first light. Even the big catamaran yacht had gone, motoring out across the greasy water of the harbour, only hoisting sail once clear of the breakwater. There had been no sign of the two girls, probably still snug in their bunks below. Which had caused a few imaginative comments from some of *Marlin*'s disappointed deckhands.

Then, at last, the teleprinter link in the radio room chattered out the signal which meant go ahead. A minute later, Shannon in the command chair, the fishery cruiser was under way.

Carrick was beside him. He eyed Shannon again as they manoeuvred out, noting the way he hunched lower than usual in the command chair. The older man's face looked haggard and strained in the morning light; his hat covered the wound on his head. When Carrick had asked him much earlier how he felt, Shannon's answer had been an ill-humoured snarl.

"Port ten," Shannon ordered as they cleared the overlapping stone fingers. He watched *Marlin*'s bow come round. "Midships. Give me half ahead both, mister."

"Half ahead." Carrick flicked the telegraph levers, felt the diesels respond, and saw a seaman on the foredeck return a wave from a small boy who stood watching them from the breakwater's point. He glanced at Shannon. "I'll get ready."

Shannon nodded. *Marlin*'s bow was pointed squarely towards

Targe Island. They were to take the dead Russian aboard, then head south to a rendezvous with a Royal Navy rescue helicopter. Andrei Krymov's body would be flown from there for a full postmortem examination. Several people wanted to know how he'd died. That way, they might find a pointer to the other question. Why?

The initial telex to Fleet Support had been sent from *Marlin* as soon as they'd got back aboard the previous night. A priority signal had come hammering back, wanting more details. Then, after a few more exchanges, the one-word signal: "Wait."

Which they knew meant till morning. Shannon had announced in an oddly quiet voice that he was going to his bunk. Before he did the same, Carrick had asked if Alexis Jordan should be told what was going on.

"She'll know," Shannon had said. "From Vasilek or Maxwell—or both. If by some miracle she doesn't, I'll tell her tomorrow. I said she'd have her car back by noon."

Carrick hadn't argued. But he had a feeling that a certain local Fisheries Officer was going to be in a fury at being deliberately ignored.

Ferguson was lurking in ambush when Carrick reached the main deck. Usually, when off watch, the grey-haired Junior Second Mate stayed below. But he stopped Carrick, his thin shoulders squared determinedly.

"Have you told him yet?" demanded Ferguson, jerking his head towards the bridge.

"Told him what?" asked Carrick wearily.

"About Shaw—about his Chief Engineer being on the fiddle with ship's stores," snapped Ferguson. "Look, Carrick, if you won't tell him—"

"You will, I know," agreed Carrick, "but I wouldn't do it right now. He's not in the mood."

Lips pursed, Ferguson turned on his heel and clattered down a companionway stair, heading for his cabin. Carrick walked aft, towards the scuba compartment. On the way, Jumbo Wills hailed him from the boat deck and he looked up. Wills and a couple of seamen were preparing one of the inflatables for launching. The little rubber boats made an ideal diving platform at water level.

"This what you want, Webb?" Wills held up a long tube of canvas, sewn closed at one end, a cord running through eyelets at the other. "It's about the best we can do."

"I don't think he'll complain," said Carrick.

Getting the dead frogman out of the grotto cave wouldn't be the easiest of tasks. But the canvas would make it less gruesome and more practical than having to cope with the alternative.

Satisfied, Wills bent to check the inflatable's outboard engine. Targe Island was now slightly on *Marlin*'s port bow, growing nearer, Shannon steering a course which would take them round the north side before they crept in towards the rocks which marked the underwater cave. Carrick glanced up at the shimmering exhaust quietly pulsing from the fishery cruiser's squat funnel. There wasn't much wind, there wasn't much of a sea. In fact, there wasn't much of anything, including enthusiasm, for what lay ahead.

In the scuba compartment, Clapper Bell was already dressed in his diving rubbers and was making a final check of their scuba breathing gear. He grinned as Carrick entered.

"You reckon we'll really need these?" he asked.

Carrick nodded. "While we're there, I want to take a look around, check further back on those caves." He saw Bell's expression. "No, I don't mean a full exploring trip. But I'd like to know more about them."

He changed into his own neoprene suit while Bell continued the meticulous checking. The bo'sun's thick fingers moved quickly and delicately over hose clips and demand valves, webbing harness and gauges. Both men had too much underwater experience to take anything for granted.

Ready, Carrick deliberately double-checked the readings on the twin steel air cylinders of his aqualung. They were fully charged, giving an underwater endurance far longer than anything he was likely to need.

"Okay?" asked Bell, lighting a cigarette. He blew the smoke deliberately in Carrick's direction, chuckled, and tucked the pack away. "About last night—before the rumpus, I mean. Did you find out anything that mattered about Gibby MacNeil?"

"No." Carrick eased his new diving knife in its sheath, which fitted snugly against his thigh. "You?"

"Not much. A few said they'd miss him as a fiddle player. But he'd run out of skippers who'd take him aboard." Bell drew on his cigarette. "Mostly, the only work left for him was loading fish into trucks."

"Which firm?" Carrick asked it almost automatically.

"Any of them," shrugged Bell. "Casual."

"Maxwell Transport?"

Bell nodded, then was interrupted as a lanky, bald-headed figure in overalls stepped into the compartment. Andy Shaw, *Marlin*'s Chief Engineer, had a warlike expression on his horse-shaped face.

"How the other half live," he muttered half to himself, looking around. He pointed an accusing finger at Clapper Bell. "You. Who the hell told you to help yourself from my personal tool kit?"

"It's called borrowing." Bell reached into a box and heaved a large ring-spanner across. As Shaw caught it, Bell winked at Carrick. "Give some folk an oily rag, and they think they rule the world."

Carrick grinned. Their Chief Engineer certainly made no bones about his belief that few things happening outside his hot, oily underworld had any lasting importance.

"Andy." He saw his chance and probed gently. "I might have bought you a drink yesterday if I'd seen you ashore. Where did you get to?"

"Me?" Shaw shook his head. "I was trapped, Webb. I—"

He stopped there and blinked as *Marlin*'s siren boomed unexpectedly. One short, one long, two short—the three men stared at each other in surprise. The Morse letter *L* was the international "Stop Immediately" warning to any craft.

At the same moment, *Marlin*'s engines began to quicken. The deck shuddered and vibrated as in a buildup towards full speed.

Shaw was first out of the scuba compartment, hurrying back towards his engine room. Carrick and Clapper Bell were close behind him and stopped on the main deck, staring ahead.

Marlin had rounded the north end of Targe Island. On ahead, Carrick saw the rock formation which marked the location of the underwater entrance to the caves. Close in under the rocks, making no attempt to run, a fishing boat bobbed gently in the light, chopping sea. She had a dark-red hull.

He swore aloud. What the hell was Jamie Ross's *Harmony* doing back there?

Minutes later, they found out. The *Harmony* stayed where she was, keeping position by engine and rudder, as the fishery cruiser stormed down towards her. Shannon had Jumbo Wills beside him on the bridge, and even Ferguson had turned out on deck.

With an awesome precision, Shannon left it until almost the last minute before he juggled *Marlin*'s diesels and steering to bring her round in a lurching, foaming turn which ended with the fishery cruiser lying tight alongside the smaller craft, fenders out and almost touching.

On the *Harmony*'s deck, her crew looked up at the grey steel hull of the fishery cruiser with expressions of bland innocence. But two figures emerged from her wheelhouse, and Carrick, seeing them, fought down a groan. One was Jamie Ross, who gave a slightly apprehensive grin as he recognized Carrick. The other was Commander Fedor Vasilek. The Russian was in uniform, his face as usual wiped totally clean of emotion.

"Commander Vasilek." Shannon's voice rasped metallically from the bridge loudhailer. "I suggest you come aboard."

Vasilek raised one hand in a signal he understood, as a rope ladder tumbled down from *Marlin*'s main deck. Waiting until the two vessels' fenders rubbed, he stepped across, hauled himself up, and gave Carrick a nod of thanks as he was helped aboard.

"Good morning." He gave Carrick a faint, polite smile, then glanced deliberately at his wristwatch. "I've been waiting for you, Chief Officer."

"That's nice," said Carrick. He glanced round. Jumbo Wills was out on the bridge wing and hand-signalled towards Shannon's day cabin. Carrick nodded and turned to Vasilek again. "This way, Commander. And the best of luck—you're going to need it."

"More than likely," murmured the Russian, unperturbed.

Captain James Shannon's day cabin was big when compared with any other aboard. Chintz curtains at the portholes had been supplied by his wife on *Marlin*'s last refit. She'd also insisted on the rubber plant which occupied one corner, and it clung stubbornly to life on a diet of coffee slops and cigarette ash.

Shannon was seated at his desk when Carrick brought Vasilek into the cabin.

"Good morning, Captain." Vasilek stiffened and his heels clicked as he snapped a salute which shouted his navy background. "It's good to see you again."

"Is it?" Shannon only scowled. He looked deliberately over Vasilek's head at the roll pendulum and repeater compass on the opposite bulkhead.

"He says he's been waiting on us, sir," said Carrick.

"Does he?" Shannon's bearded mouth tightened into a hard, angry line. "All right, Vasilek. Tell me why."

"Sir." Vasilek gave a fractional shrug. "I have to tell you that, acting on the orders of Captain Rudichev of the Soviet factory ship *Zarakov,* two Russian divers this morning recovered the body of our Technical Officer, Andrei Krymov." He paused and gave a slight, apologetic gesture. "I think I should add, Captain, that one of the *Zarakov*'s launches was used in this operation. It left some time ago. By now, Andrei Krymov's body will be back aboard the *Zarakov.*"

"I see." Shannon's face might have been carved from rough granite. But his hands were visible, and were clenched knuckle-white. "You stayed. Why?"

"Captain Rudichev agreed that it might be—well, diplomatic, Captain." A small, nervous tic twitched a corner of Vasilek's mouth. He moistened his lips. "I'm sorry, Captain. But Captain Rudichev's instructions came from—"

"A lot higher up?" Shannon growled the words. Then suddenly he relaxed and grimaced. "So did mine, Commander. So did mine."

Vasilek nodded. From his manner, Carrick could guess that there had been a busy night's radio traffic between the factory ship and her base.

"Mister." Shannon got to his feet as he spoke, moving slowly, strangely, carefully. "I'm inviting the commander to join me in a drink before he leaves. You don't need to stay."

"Sir." Carrick knew what he meant. Nodding to a surprised Vasilek, he left them. As he closed the cabin door, he could hear the clink of glasses.

Clapper Bell was lurking in the companionway outside. He followed Carrick out on deck, where several of *Marlin*'s crew were lined along the rail exchanging reasonably good-humoured insults with the fishermen below.

"Going over?" asked Bell.

"Yes." Carrick sighed. "All right, you too. But it's a visit, not an invasion."

Fishery cruiser and fishing boat had drifted slightly apart, but when he signalled the *Harmony* someone threw a line. It was secured, the fishing boat's engine muttered briefly, and she came in again. As the two sets of fenders kissed, Carrick and Bell jumped down onto the *Harmony*'s deck.

"Hello, Webb." Jamie Ross was leaning against the wheelhouse door. He scratched his chin as Carrick came over. "I suppose I'm not too popular."

"It's possible," said Carrick frostily.

"Yes." The young skipper considered Carrick's diving rubbers. "All dressed up and nowhere to go?"

"Why?" asked Carrick.

"Why not?" Ross was unrepentant. "I sell them a hell of a lot of fish. All I did was show them where to dive—I didn't go down. Is that breaking any law?"

"No." Carrick shoved him back into the wheelhouse, kicked the door shut behind them. They were alone. "All right, Jamie, I want the story. What happened?"

"Simple." Ross eyed him warily. "John Maxwell brought Vasilek round to our place last night, late on. He knew you'd been out with me—"

"How?"

"Someone must have seen us," shrugged Ross. "Anyway, Vasilek said the frogman was their property and they wanted him. So—well, I agreed to show them where to look."

"How much did they pay?" demanded Carrick.

"Not a lot." Ross was defensive. "Look, it's straight business. I'm losing fishing time. I've a crew to pay, a boat to run—"

"I'll weep for you later," said Carrick.

The sound of a short scuffle and a yelp of pain came from outside. He turned. Clapper Bell had his back planted firmly against the other side of the wheelhouse door, and one of Ross's crew had fallen on his back against a pile of fishnets. Sucking the knuckles of his right fist, Bell gave a cheerful wink at him through the glass. The rest of the *Harmony*'s crew were hovering aggressively but seemed uncertain what to do, probably because of the men watching from *Marlin*'s rail.

"Damned fools," muttered Ross. He slid open one of the wheelhouse windows and called to them. "Back off, you idiots. There's no problem."

The hurt fisherman retired sullenly to join his companions. Slamming the window shut, Jamie Ross used both hands to comb his long, fair hair back from his forehead.

"Anything more?" he asked.

Carrick nodded. "Did Katie know about this?"

"Yes." Ross grimaced at the reminder. "She didn't like the idea. The only way to shut her up was to tell her I wouldn't do it."

"But?"

"So now I tell her I changed my mind. I'm skipper of this boat, right?"

Carrick nodded. Between them, Maxwell and the Russian had worked fast, almost impossibly fast, and if Vasilek had gone back to the *Zarakov* with the leave party, then he must have come back in again by boat very quickly.

But who had told them? Who else had known about his trip out to Targe Island? First the prowler at the cottage, now this—if there was any kind of a link, what the hell was really going on in Port Ard?

He talked to Jamie Ross for another couple of minutes, learned nothing more, and left the wheelhouse as Commander Vasilek came over the side from *Marlin* and reached the *Harmony*'s deck.

"Finished?" asked Vasilek.

"For now," he agreed.

"Good." Vasilek stuffed his hands in his pockets and sighed. "Your captain and my captain—they have a lot in common. Maybe we have too, eh?"

"I wouldn't know," said Carrick. "I wouldn't bank on it."

He motioned Clapper Bell towards the rope ladder, then followed him up. As soon as they had returned aboard *Marlin* the fishing boat's line was cast off. She eased clear, then headed away on a course which would take her towards Loch Armach to deliver her passenger to the factory ship.

Captain Shannon was still in his day cabin. There was an empty glass on the table beside him, but his own drink had hardly been touched. He heard Carrick out in silence, then gave a resigned grunt.

"Not much, is it?" he said.

"How about Vasilek?" asked Carrick.

"Nothing," admitted Shannon. Then he gave a sudden wince and sat for a moment with his eyes closed.

"How do you feel?" asked Carrick.

"Mind your own damned business." Shannon opened his eyes quickly and scowled up at him. "All right, mister. We're here. We'll still check that cave. Get on with it."

They did. Using the rubber inflatable as a tender, *Marlin* lying close at hand, Carrick and Bell took to the water a few minutes later. Diving down, they swam through the short tunnel that led to the hidden cave.

Lit by their battery lanterns, the scene on the rock shelf was unchanged except where the frogman's body had been. One of the *Zarakov*'s divers with a warped sense of humour had left them a small Soviet flag attached to a piece of wire.

The delay with the *Harmony* had cut the time they could stay down. Swimming in, Carrick had felt the first, deceptively gentle movement of water, which meant the tide would soon be on the turn. Before that happened, he wanted to be clear. But they still weren't finished and they had discussed what they had to do.

Quitting the shelf, they waded out into the lapping darkness again, and went under. Staying close together, bubbles of exhaled air rising from their breathing masks like twin plumes, they soon located another underwater split in the island rock.

It led into another cave, one in which the water lapped against sheer sides of rock. Clapper Bell played the beam of his lantern up towards the dark roof, let it glint for a moment on a vein of exposed quartz, then swam closer to Carrick and pointed questioningly back the way they'd come. Carrick shook his head and pointed down again, though he knew time was running out.

Finding the entrance to the third cave was more difficult. It was little more than a jagged crack in the rock. A man might have squeezed through, but only with difficulty—and the water was now tugging fiercely. Tapping Bell's shoulder, Carrick signalled and they headed back.

The water in the second cave was acquiring a strange, swirling motion. They didn't linger, dived again—then suddenly Clapper Bell grabbed Carrick's arm and pointed down to something just visible in the beam of their lanterns. Twisting round, the bo'sun sank beside it on the bottom rock. Then he held up his find, a compact aqualung. The cylinder seemed intact but the back-straps were broken, and all that was left of the face-mask was a wavering fragment of tubing.

They brought it out with them. Getting through the final stretch of natural tunnel beyond the first cave was a minor battle against clawing, unseen currents, and Carrick surfaced beside the waiting inflatable with a feeling of relief.

Helped aboard, he spat out his mouthpiece, shoved back his face-mask, and grinned as Clapper Bell heaved in beside him, still clutching their find.

"Finished," he told the two seamen who were crewing the inflatable. "Head for home."

"Looks like we'd better, sir," said the nearest man. "*Marlin*'s been signalling. You're wanted aboard, in a hurry."

Outboard motor rasping, the inflatable bounced and slammed her way at top speed towards the fishery cruiser. Carrick was first up the accommodation ladder as they came alongside, and when he reached the deck he came face to face with a strangely agitated Jumbo Wills.

"What's happened?" demanded Carrick.

"It's Captain Shannon." Wills's freckled face was pale and serious. "Ferguson found him in the day cabin about ten minutes ago. He'd collapsed, Webb—hell, at first Ferguson thought he was dead."

"Damn." A memory of Shannon being clubbed down the previous night came flooding into Carrick's mind, along with the way *Marlin*'s commander had looked ever since—and the way he'd stubbornly refused to admit anything was wrong. "Right. Heave that boat aboard, Jumbo. Then head back to Port Ard. And don't waste any time."

He headed along the deck at a run, his scuba rubbers still dribbling water. When he got there, the door of the day cabin stood open. Inside, James Shannon was slumped back in an armchair, with Ferguson and Shannon's steward fussing around him.

"How is he?" asked Carrick.

Ferguson shrugged, his lined face worried. "Talking—better than he was, but there's something badly wrong."

Thumbing the steward out of the way, Carrick bent over the armchair. Shannon's face was pale, saliva had dribbled from his mouth and down his beard, but he managed a twist of a smile.

"You—you're back." His voice was hoarse and slurred. "Right, mister. I—I'd be obliged if you—if you'd take over."

"How do you feel?" asked Carrick.

"Hellish." Shannon sighed. "Unstuck, Webb—totally unstuck."

Carrick stood back. They were already under way and he could hear *Marlin*'s diesels building up speed.

"He took a bash on the head last night, didn't he?" murmured Ferguson.

Carrick nodded.

"A pity." Ferguson's lips pursed with a mixture of concern and disappointment. "I was going to talk to him about Shaw. You know, about yesterday afternoon—"

"I know." Carrick cut him short. "Now get out."

Ferguson shrugged but obeyed.

Jumbo Wills temporarily in the command chair, *Marlin* took the direct way back to Port Ard. That meant cutting in close to the edge of the white, boiling fury of the Sump, where the overfall was in full spate, then steering a course which brought the fishery cruiser almost under the shadow of the south end of Targe Island. Whole colonies of nesting seabirds erupted from the stark cliffs as *Marlin* thundered on, her wash breaking on the rocks.

Port Ard was in sight when Carrick reached the bridge. He took one glance at Wills, at the determined concentration on his face, and stayed back. Clapper Bell, already there, met Carrick's eyes, gave a fractional nod of agreement, then thumbed towards the trawler-band radio.

"I called up one o' the boats in harbour," he said softly. "Told them to ask the local doctor to stand by."

"Good."

"*His* idea." Bell indicated Jumbo Wills. "When it matters, he's reasonably bright."

Carrick nodded; the same thought had only occurred to him as he reached the bridge.

Marlin entered harbour smoothly and berthed without fuss. There were several fishermen on the quayside, silent men, any feud forgotten, who helped as the mooring lines snaked ashore. One of them pushed forward as soon as the fishery cruiser's gangway touched the quayside. Coming aboard, he made straight for Carrick.

"Doctor Blair's heading straight for the medical clinic," he said without preliminaries. "You're to take him straight there. How is the old devil?"

"Not too good," admitted Carrick.

"But he's the kind that survive," said the fisherman. "Have you got transport?"

"Yes." Carrick nodded. The grey Volvo station wagon borrowed from Alexis Jordan was still parked on the quayside. He'd found the keys on Shannon's desk. "Just tell me how to get there."

When they were ready, Clapper Bell brought Shannon out on deck, wrapped in a blanket and cradled effortlessly in the bo'sun's muscular arms. Shannon cursed weakly and indignantly as he was unceremoniously placed in the Volvo's rear seat. Carrick at the wheel, Bell beside him, they set off.

The clinic was a new flat-roofed building located not far from the Maxwell Transport yard. As the Volvo drew up beside it, the door opened and a tall, fair-haired girl wearing a white medical coat came out to meet them.

"Bring him straight in," she instructed without preliminaries. "Handle him carefully."

They did. This time between them, they carried Shannon from the car into the clinic and followed the fair-haired girl into a room which held a hospital cot and an examination couch. The sheets on the cot had already been turned down.

"On the couch, please." She gave a brief, reassuring smile as they eased Shannon down. "Fine. I'm Dr. Blair—Jan Blair. Now, what happened?"

"He took a blow on the head last night," said Carrick. "Afterwards, he said he was fine—"

"Though he didn't look it," said Clapper Bell caustically.

She frowned. "When did he collapse?"

"Less than an hour ago." Carrick rubbed his chin. "I suggested he should have a medical check last night, but he wouldn't listen."

"That doesn't surprise me. Not after meeting him yesterday," she said. "All right, both of you outside. Please."

The door of the room closed firmly as they left. Clapper Bell took out a cigarette, grimaced at a NO SMOKING sign on the corridor wall, and tucked the cigarette behind his ear.

"Well, she looks all right," he said softly. "I was ready for an old goat with whiskers."

"That, at least, she's not," said Carrick.

Port Ard's resident physician was attractive as well as tall. Her fair hair was shoulder-length and she was slim with, as far as he could judge, beautifully proportioned legs. He guessed she was in her late twenties. The rest included a slightly snub nose, grey eyes and a quiet style of confidence. Jan Blair's voice had a distinct Borders lilt, and he wondered briefly what could have brought her north of the Highland line to an outpost like Port Ard.

Clapper Bell sighed and shuffled his feet.

"What's wrong?" asked Carrick.

"I'm not much good at this kind o' hanging about." Bell gave him a shamefaced grin. "Sorry."

"Then I'll give you something to do." Carrick had been thinking of several potential problems ahead. One, at least, had to be dealt with. "Get back to *Marlin* and tell Jumbo Wills to stay ready to sail. If any signal comes in from Headquarters, he gets word to me fast."

"Like about our frogman being hijacked?" Bell raised an eyebrow.

Carrick nodded. He knew Shannon had sent a long signal to Fleet Support telling what had happened. So far, all that had come back was a brief acknowledgement. That meant someone somewhere was still trying to make up his mind what should be done.

"What about him?" Bell gestured towards the closed door. He

considered Carrick soberly. "If the Old Man is out of the game for a spell, it becomes your show."

"Maybe." Carrick had had the same thought. At that precise moment it wasn't attractive. His more immediate concern was what was wrong with Shannon.

"If it happens, the best of luck," said Bell in a tone of sympathy. "You'll need it." Then he brightened. "Still, he's the old-fashioned kind—barbed wire and concrete. Give him a rest and a couple of aspirins—"

He left it at that, gave Carrick a grin that was meant to be encouraging, and went away.

Carrick found a chair and sat down. There were several health-education posters on the corridor walls and he had time enough to read assorted advice on everything from prenatal clinics to dental care. A telephone rang somewhere and kept ringing until the caller gave up. Then, at last, the room door opened. He got to his feet as Jan Blair came out.

"How is he?" asked Carrick.

She beckoned him over and let him look past her. Shannon was in the hospital cot, the sheets tucked round him, and seemed asleep. His uniform lay in a neatly folded bundle on the couch.

"You moved him on your own?" Carrick showed his surprise.

"He wasn't particularly able to argue," she said. "Now—"

Closing the door, she led Carrick across the corridor and into a small consulting room. Perching on the edge of the desk, she considered him seriously.

"You're one of his officers?"

"Yes. Carrick, his Chief Officer."

"Right. First, I'm fairly certain your captain is simply suffering from delayed concussion. There's no apparent skull fracture. But to confirm that, we'll need X-ray examination and tests."

Carrick nodded. "Where?"

"Here. We have the facilities." A glint of amusement showed in her grey eyes as she noted his surprise. "Including radiology. I can have any outside help I need by this afternoon. Then—well, we'll see."

"And afterwards?"

She frowned. "That depends."

"On what?"

"Several things." She came down from the desk and went over to a coffee pot which was simmering near the window. "Like some?"

"Please." He waited while she took two mugs from a cupboard, filled both, and brought one over. "You said 'several things.'"

"Yes." She waved him towards a chair; then, as he sat down, she perched on the desk again and nursed the second mug between her hands. "Look, I'll spell it out in plain language. When anyone gets a real clout on the head, the brain reacts like a football being bounced off a wall. There doesn't have to be any sign of external injury—that's the danger."

"Haemorrhage?"

"Yes—bruising, laceration or haemorrhage." She grimaced. "That's why every medical student learns that you never show a head-injury case the door. You hold them for observation if you can."

"And Captain Shannon?" pressed Carrick. "I've got to know."

"Let's say that he's probably going to be in drydock for a few days, for rest and observation. Plus, in his case, mild sedation." She smiled apologetically at him over her coffee mug. "I'm fairly certain that's all. But I still can't say for sure—until the tests are done."

"That's fair," said Carrick. "Did he talk to you?"

"No. At least, just a few words." She frowned at him. "I found wood splinters in that head wound. What happened?"

"Someone hit him with a chunk of wood—we don't know who it was. But it happened at Gibby MacNeil's cottage."

"Up there?" Jan Blair lost a little of her professional air of composure. "But—"

"Why?" Carrick shrugged. "We don't know that either."

She frowned down at the floor, tracing a pattern on it with one of her shoes. Then, setting down the coffee mug, she looked up.

"Yesterday, when he came here, Captain Shannon stopped just short of calling me incompetent."

"And *are* you?" Carrick grinned at her.

"No. I don't think so." She got up again, went behind her desk, opened a drawer and took out a folder. "This is what caused the trouble."

"The postmortem report on MacNeil?" He nodded and leaned forward. "I'd like to hear about it—your version."

"I only assisted—the real work was done by a pathologist from the Regional Pathology team. That's standard procedure in any accidental death."

"But you agreed with his findings?"

"Yes. That's usual. The cause of death was a combination of cold and asphyxia. Evidence of freezing still present, internal organs congested, and enough alcohol in the stomach to be a contributory factor."

Carrick frowned. "Meaning?"

"Gibby MacNeil had downed the best part of a half-bottle of whisky. That amount of alcohol, apart from leaving him drunk, would also reduce body temperature."

"And time of death?"

"Impossible to say. The pathologist wouldn't even try."

He sighed. "No doubts, no reservations?"

"None." She glanced away as they heard someone knock on the door. "Give me a moment."

She went over, opened the door, and Carrick caught a glimpse of a middle-aged woman standing outside. She wore an outdoor coat over her nurse's uniform. Jan Blair spoke to her briefly and the woman nodded. She left, and Jan Blair closed the door again.

"I've a midmorning clinic, patients waiting, and calls to make, Mr. Carrick." She checked her wristwatch. "I'm throwing you out. But don't worry, we'll take care of your captain—whether he likes it or not."

Carrick got to his feet. "And the results from those tests?"

"We should know by this evening. Come back then, but no other visitors allowed—not until we're sure."

He nodded his thanks and left, almost brushing against her as he went out. She used a light, oddly tantalising perfume, one that momentarily caught at his senses.

Then he was out in the corridor and back with reality, walking past a seated row of waiting patients. A woman with a child on her knee looked up. The child's face was covered with spots, and the woman directed a disapproving sniff in Carrick's direction, obviously blaming him for the clinic's delay.

"Mr. Carrick." It was the middle-aged nurse. She cleared her throat. "Captain Shannon—we're supposed to know next of kin. Is he married?"

"Yes." Carrick hesitated. "But she doesn't know about this."

"We need a name," frowned the woman.

"You've got mine," he told her.

He walked on before she could argue.

Outside, the heavy clouds which had been overhead since dawn had begun to break up a little. There were a few patches of blue sky, but the wind was still cold and the threat of rain remained in the air. Carrick stuck his hands in his jacket pockets and paused, glancing along the little street towards the opened gates of the Maxwell Transport yard. John Maxwell had some questions to answer, and now might be as good a time as any.

A car horn gave a short peep just beside him. The grey Volvo was still parked outside the clinic, and Alexis Jordan was in the driver's seat. As she beckoned, he went round to the passenger side and got in beside her.

"Well? How is he?"

"Dr. Blair says it's delayed concussion." Carrick saw the lighted cigarette between her fingers and two more stubbed out in the Volvo's ashtray. Her usually neat auburn hair was tousled and her whole manner was tense. "She wants to run some X-ray shots and tests, but he should be all right."

"Thank God for that." She gave a long, relieved sigh, then took an equally long draw on her cigarette. "I heard a garbled story that he'd been hurt and went along to *Marlin*. One of your officers, the young freckle-faced one—"

"Wills. He's Second Mate."

"Yes." Alexis Jordan wasn't interested. "He told me some of it. Your bo'sun got back as I left, and he was helpful." She relaxed against the seat and gave a short, humourless laugh. "I should have known, I suppose. Shannon has the world's thickest skull, in more ways than one. Can I see him?"

"No visitors yet."

"All right." She seemed disappointed. "But if it happened before we met last night, why didn't he tell me?"

"He told hardly anyone, Mrs. Jordan," said Carrick.

"I'm supposed to be a colleague," countered Alexis Jordan indignantly. She took a last draw at her cigarette, then mashed it into the ashtray. "I'm Senior Fisheries Officer for this area. Damn him, he didn't tell me about it, he didn't tell me about the Russian frogman, he just ignored me—the way he always has. He's a chauvinistic old—" She stopped with an effort. "I'm sorry. But he *is*."

"I've called him worse," said Carrick. He gave her a sideways glance. "When did you hear about the Russian?"

"Katie told me this morning." She flushed at his quizzical expression. "Before you ask, Commander Vasilek didn't mention it last night. Not while I was with him."

"He told John Maxwell," said Carrick.

"They dropped me at my house first, before they went on to the harbour. He must have told John after that." A frown crossed her face. "I haven't spoken to John about it yet. But I will."

"I'm going to try and do that now." Carrick rubbed a hand lightly along the car's dashboard, watching a farm tractor and trailer rumbling towards them. "Commander Vasilek got in ahead of us this morning, and did a piece of fast body-snatching—with a little help from his friends. Or at least from Jamie Ross. And your friend Maxwell was the go-between."

"But"—she sat wide-mouthed—"but Katie told me—"

"Jamie changed his mind," said Carrick. "Want to come with me, Mrs. Jordan?"

"No." She shook her head quickly.

"That's a surprise," said Carrick with sarcasm. "I thought you wanted to know what was going on?"

"I do, but—" She broke off, hands resting on the steering wheel, fingertips tapping in uneasy irritation. The tractor passed them, its trailer crammed with sheep, and had gone before she spoke again. "Look, I have my job and you have yours. The Department employs me to—to compile reports, supply statistics, run an office. People like you—"

"Do the dirty work." Carrick grinned at her reflection in the windscreen. "Maybe. You've no other reason?"

"You know there is." She swore under her breath, angrily.

"Like the way things are between you and Maxwell?"

"Yes." She nodded reluctantly. "But I know John. Whatever happened, there had to be a misunderstanding of some kind. If you ask him, he'll be able to explain it—but you don't need my help for that, do you?"

"No. Not if it would be awkward," soothed Carrick.

"Thank you." She forced a tight, relieved smile. "Do you still need my car? I had the spare keys in my pocket, but—"

"No, we're finished with it for now." Carrick brought out the other set and handed them over. "But if we need it again—"

"Just ask. It was a fair trade." Alexis Jordan saw he didn't understand. "James Shannon got the use of my car, I got two new power sockets wired up in my office. Your Chief Engineer did the job for me."

"I'll tell him you're pleased." It also solved a small mystery. Carrick opened the car door and got out. "And I'll let you know if—well, anything changes."

Alexis Jordan nodded, then started the car as Carrick closed the door. He stood back, watching it turn and head down towards the harbour. Maybe he should have gone with her, checked if anything had happened aboard *Marlin*. But he still wanted to talk to John Maxwell.

He started walking.

Four big travel-stained diesel trucks were parked in a neat line inside the Maxwell Transport yard. Their refrigerated containers lay open and empty and a driver was standing at one of the tailboards, hosing down the interior. A small man, as travel-stained as his vehicle, he turned off his hose as Carrick came over.

"Is John Maxwell around?" asked Carrick.

"The boss?" The man nodded and used the hose to point towards the workshop shed. "In there. Or he was."

Thanking him, Carrick walked on across the weed-covered yard. The workshop's main doors were open and another truck blocked most of the entrance. An inspection panel had been removed, the engine was running, and the burly, unshaven figure of the foreman mechanic, Ferdie Renfrew, stood scowling at the throbbing diesel.

He didn't hear Carrick approach. But the diesel switched off, the truck's cab door opened, and John Maxwell climbed down.

"Saw you coming in," said Maxwell. "I'd a notion I was going to have a visit like this. Hold on, then we'll go to the office."

Maxwell turned to Renfrew. His foreman, grimy in his overalls, looked at Carrick with disinterest, then both men bent over the silent engine for a moment in a brief murmured conversation.

"Try it, Ferdie," said Maxwell, standing back. He brushed his hands together and shrugged as he joined Carrick. "Temperamental brute, that one."

Carrick presumed he meant the truck. From the expression on Renfrew's broad face, the foreman mechanic could also qualify.

Maxwell led the way from the workshop to the small brick-built office building. Plain and shabby on the outside, the interior was very different. Two girls were in the outer office, both young, reasonably pretty, one typing and the other working on a ledger. The furniture and equipment were modern, the walls were panelled with a wood veneer, and the floor was covered in a bright cord carpeting.

"Happy offices make happy staff—that's the theory," said Maxwell as they went through. He opened a door at the rear. "I reckon the boss should have his share too."

His private office was compact but comfortable. The panelling was pine, the carpeting a thick-pile wool, and the desk, though untidy with paperwork, looked expensive to match. Dumping some papers from a leather armchair, Maxwell invited Carrick to sit down, then settled in a matching leather swivel chair behind the desk.

"Now." His thin face stayed cheerful, but his voice took on a slightly wary edge. "All right, I've been a bad boy—but can this stay civilised?"

Carrick shrugged. "Why not? It's up to you."

"Good." The man leaned forward. "Before you start, Carrick, how's Captain Shannon? I heard he'd been—well, hurt. Something about him being taken ashore—or that's the word I got from the harbour."

"He should be all right in a day or two." Carrick pursed his lips. "You seem to hear about most things—things that matter, anyway."

"That's on target." Maxwell sighed. "You're here about the *Zarakov*'s frogman, right?"

Carrick nodded.

"And why you lost him," said Maxwell softly. "Don't look surprised, Carrick. I've got a radio link to the *Zarakov*. Commander Vasilek called me about an hour ago." He spread his hands in an apologetic gesture. "Does it help that I didn't know our little Soviet friends would try to pull a stunt like that?"

"What did you think they had in mind?" asked Carrick.

"That they'd get there first, see for themselves. Or be there when you arrived. Hell, they're Russians. Who knows?"

"*We* didn't," said Carrick in a flat voice. "What about last night? It didn't take you long to find out about Jamie Ross. How did that happen? How did you know about Targe Island?"

"That?" For a moment, a guarded look crossed Maxwell's face, then had gone. "I know my way around the harbour—that's part of how I earn a living. I spoke to a few people, found a couple of fishermen who'd been out in the bay tending a line of lobster pots. They saw Jamie and the girl taking you across. They said you had wet suits —it was pretty obvious after that."

"So then you and Vasilek got to work on Ross."

Maxwell frowned. "I told you, I didn't think they'd pull a crazy stunt like snatching that body. I thought—"

Carrick cut him short. "You thought you'd keep the customer happy?"

Maxwell shrugged but didn't answer.

Getting up, Carrick walked over to the only window and looked out. The view was towards the parked trucks and Renfrew was there, talking to the little driver.

"Two trucks arrived last night, the other two this morning." Maxwell had come over beside him and nodded towards the vehicles. "One with a half-load, the other three empty—that's the killer in the transport game, dead-mileage return trips, hauling air."

Carrick nodded. Out in the yard, Renfrew had finished talking to the driver. Turning away, the foreman mechanic headed back towards his workshop. He was limping.

"Notice that?" said Maxwell with a note of irritation. "The damned fool nearly killed himself this morning. He's changing over a radiator assembly on that truck in the shop, and the whole damned unit slips, lands on him. If he breaks a leg, what am I supposed to do?"

"Get a vet." Carrick turned as Renfrew vanished into the workshop again. "Where's your radio link?"

"Over here." Maxwell led him over to a metal cabinet. He opened the door. The radio telephone set inside was compact, obviously powerful.

"Not bad, is it?" Maxwell stood back. "It's legal and licensed."

"And the aerial?"

"On the outside wall. We're high enough here for it to be no big deal." Maxwell closed the cabinet again. "Look, about last night and this morning—I made a mistake, fair enough?"

"Jamie Ross said the same thing." Carrick made his way towards the door, stopped, and eyed Maxwell unemotionally. "Your Russian friends owe you a bonus for last night—you earned it."

He left before Maxwell could reply, and got a childish pleasure from slamming the door. Startled, the two girls in the outer office stared at him. Giving them a slightly shamefaced smile, he went out into the yard.

There was no sign of Ferdie Renfrew, but the truck in the workshop had its engine running again.

The foreman mechanic and the way he was limping had Carrick thinking as he began walking back towards the harbour. Shannon wasn't the only one who'd been hurt in that brief struggle outside Gibby MacNeil's cottage. The hooded prowler had taken punishment.

Could Renfrew have been the man they'd chased?

There was no way of proving it, no reason why Renfrew should have been there. Except that another thought crossed his mind—the powerful binoculars at Gibby MacNeil's window, a window with a view across to Targe Island.

If the prowler could have been in the cottage, could have been in and left again before Shannon arrived, that might be another way in which John Maxwell had known to go to Jamie Ross.

But it was like building a house with a pack of cards. Everything collapsed if he asked why.

A thin drizzle of rain began falling from the grey, broken sky. It didn't look as though it would last, but he quickened his step.

Marlin waited at the quayside with the air of a hound straining to be let off the leash. Exhaust gently fluttering from her funnel, several of her hands lounging on deck not far from their stations for leaving harbour, even the gentle, steady creaking from her mooring lines conveyed the message that she was a ship ready and willing to go.

The seaman on gangway watch snapped an unexpected salute as Carrick came aboard. Then he met Clapper Bell further along the deck, beside the companionway stair that led to the bridge.

"Nice timing," said Bell, then gave a fractional wink. "Nice timing —sir. How's the Old Man?"

"Concussion, probably nothing else. Pass the word for me." Carrick stopped and frowned. "What's the 'sir' bit?"

"Ask Jumbo Wills." Bell grinned at him. "It'll make him happy."

Wills was on the bridge. So was the duty helmsman, and Ferguson was lurking in the background, at the chartroom door. Suddenly Carrick had a feeling he knew what it was about.

"Webb." Wills came forward eagerly. "How is he?"

Carrick told it again. Wills nodded with genuine relief, and without a word handed him a telex message. Carrick read the first line.

"CHIEF OFFICER CARRICK TO ACTING COMMAND, MARLIN . . ."

It was from Fleet Support, Headquarters.

He looked up.

"Congratulations," said Wills, beaming. Then, awkwardly, he added, "All right, you didn't want it this way, but—"

"I'm caretaking," said Carrick. "Temporary, acting—right?"

"Sir." Wills nodded cheerfully. Behind him, the helmsman was grinning. Even Ferguson's face looked as though it might crease into a smile.

"What's been going on?" Carrick asked.

"Headquarters came through, direct, on RT." Wills grimaced at the memory. "It was Captain Dobie at their end. He wanted to talk to Shannon about the frogman. So—well, I had to tell him."

"Yes." Captain Dobie, a man who had won his medal ribbons on destroyers, was senior officer in command of the entire Fisheries Protection flotilla. It was his signature, as Marine Superintendent, on the letter tucked away in Carrick's cabin. "All right, then, what?"

"That came in." Wills gestured at the telex form. The rest of his grin faded. "Better read the rest of it, Webb."

Carrick did, then again, to make sure it really meant what it said.

"MARLIN TO CARRY OUT NORMAL PATROL SWEEP IN SOUTHEAST BOX ONLY OF ALLOCATED SEA SECTOR. WILL NOT REPEAT NOT APPROACH FACTORY SHIP ZARAKOV OR COMMUNICATE WITH SAID ZARAKOV UNTIL FURTHER ORDERS. ACTING COMMANDER TO PERSONALLY ACKNOWLEDGE THIS ORDER BEFORE LEAVING HARBOUR."

"What the heck's going on?" demanded Wills in a puzzled voice.

"Somebody thinks we're an embarrassment," said Carrick grimly. He looked at the faces around him. "All right, Mr. Wills. Let's get the show on the road. Hands to stations. Stand by moorings and fenders."

Carrick heard the order, repeated, squawk out over *Marlin*'s Tannoy as he eased into the command chair. It felt the same as ever, yet oddly different. Only the familiar routine going on around him seemed the same as ever.

He drew a deep breath and got down to the business of taking *Marlin* on patrol.

CHAPTER 5

The southeast box patrol was a dull, frustrating monotony for every man of *Marlin*'s crew. They were being kept away from the *Zarakov*, but why? Lower-deck theorists argued fiercely, divided between whether they'd been hauled out to allow the Navy to whistle up a frigate and move in, or the more cynical declaration that, as usual, the politicians had their knickers in a twist.

But they had the southeast box. Staying about a mile out from shore, *Marlin* completed the first leg of her patrol without coming across anything bigger than a small fishing boat, dredging for clams. Then she turned west, sticking to the perimeter of the patrol area, lurching and juddering through a patch of rough water whipped up by a brief, fierce squall from the north, the sea breaking white along her starboard quarter and spray drenching along her length.

The squall passed, funnelling on down the Minch. A rusting cattle boat plodded by, heading for the mainland from some of the Outer Isles, black smoke lazing from her funnels. A large dog barked at them from her foredeck, and the solitary figure on her open bridge raised a hand in a brief greeting.

A scatter of contacts began to show on the radar ten-mile scan. They came up with the first a little later, a shark-catching boat, the harpoon gun at her bow manned and ready as she closed on the big, black, sail-like fins of a family of basking sharks.

On the bridge, Carrick sipped a mug of coffee and watched with interest. Hunting the basking shark, the largest fish in the North Atlantic, bigger than any elephant, was no easy way to make a living.

A puff of smoke and a muffled bang came from the shark-catcher's harpoon gun. Where the sail fins had been, the sea exploded in a vast white flurry of spray as the alarmed giants dived for deep water.

But the boat had still probably made a kill and, with the coastline of Lewis a thin smear on the horizon, it was time for *Marlin* to change course again.

Heeling round on the north leg, they passed more of the contacts,

a group of purse-netters too busy fishing and too sure of their rights
to give a damn who came their way. They exchanged courtesies with
an American nuclear submarine, heading south on the surface, and
rolled briefly in the wake created by her sheer size and bulk.

Handing over to Ferguson, who had the watch, Carrick left the
bridge. He gained a slight satisfaction from Ferguson's stiff formality
at the handover—the grey-haired Junior Second Mate was still smart-
ing at the way Carrick had first summarily rejected his complaint
against Andy Shaw and then had curtly told him why.

Marlin throbbed on. Briefly, Carrick visited Captain Shannon's
day cabin. It was his to use, if he wanted. But he still felt the little,
bearded figure would march in at any moment. It was more than the
rubber plant, the chintz curtains at the portholes, the old pipe on the
cabin table. Much more.

He made a brief entry in the logbook on the desk, his small, neat
writing in total contrast to the last entry, in Shannon's untidy scrawl,
and checked through the thin folder of signals and papers beside it.
None seemed to have any particular urgency, all could wait.

Leaving, he noticed something on one of the chairs. It was the
embroidered canvas Shannon had brought from Gibby MacNeil's
cottage. He picked it up, fingered the brightly coloured threads, then
cursed as the needle still attached to the stylised black pattern round
the edge jabbed into his flesh. Putting the canvas down, sucking at
the blood oozing from where the needle had stabbed, he turned to
go.

"Sir." The steward was standing in the open doorway, one hand
still raised ready to knock. The man eyed him awkwardly. "Lunch.
Will you want it served here?"

"No. I'll eat in the wardroom—for now." He saw the man's uncertainty, and added, "We'll keep things that way till we know what the
hell's happening."

The steward nodded and went away.

Leaving the cabin, Carrick headed aft along the open deck. It was
deserted, still taking an occasional drenching, but he almost welcomed the cold stinging of spray against his face and the taste of salt
on his lips.

The scuba-compartment door was closed but he heard voices.
Hauling the door open, he stepped in. Clapper Bell was sprawled
back in his armchair, and the other man there was Andy Shaw. The
Chief Engineer, leaning against a bulkhead, nodded. Bell grinned and

rose deliberately as Carrick closed the door on the noise of wind and sea outside.

"Something I can do for you, sir?" Bell stayed on his feet, an unusual note of formality in his voice and manner, friendly, but offering a cautious barrier, the inference plain.

"Knock it off, Clapper," said Carrick wearily. "I'm acting temporary caretaker—and I'm not in the mood."

Bell gave a wary nod and relaxed a little. "Off duty, if that's how you want it—sir."

"But you're running the store," said Andy Shaw. "Better get used to it, Webb. Any word yet from Headquarters?"

"No. We don't exist." He sat on one of the overstuffed arms of Bell's prized chair and grimaced at both men. "So we stay in our box, with the lid on." He remembered the reason which had brought him along. "Clapper, how about that breathing gear you salvaged at the island?"

"The Russian's? There's no way I'd use it to go spearfishing," said Bell. "It's a closed-circuit unit, oxygen rebreathing."

"Soviet Navy issue," said Shaw with certainty. "One of their latest-model units—though it's taken a hell of a knocking around."

Carrick frowned. It was the first chance he'd had to think again about the dead frogman and his mission. In the aftermath of their dive, faced with the emergency of Shannon collapsing, he'd almost forgotten about the breathing gear. But it had looked like a closed-circuit unit, and that told its own story. Oxygen rebreathing apparatus had one major benefit in underwater sabotage or spying missions —it didn't release any telltale trail of bubbles to the surface. It also used a comparatively small oxygen cylinder, and the diver's exhaled breath was cleaned of CO_2 by a soda-lime filter.

There was one major drawback to its use in other, ordinary diving work. Oxygen equipment wasn't safe below about thirty feet. Any deeper dives, unless of minimal duration, brought the threat of oxygen poisoning. There were other dangers—a contaminated oxygen apparatus had been known to explode. Which, as one diving instructor had remarked, wasn't too clever underwater. For deep-dive work, the realistic choice lay between compressed air or, in special circumstances, mixed gas units.

"Commander Vasilek called him a technical officer. Well, we can translate that different ways. But what the hell would interest them around Port Ard?"

"Some funny NATO defence installation?" suggested Shaw, his thin, horselike face looking hopeful.

"No." Carrick shook his head. NATO had plenty on the Scottish west coast, from American and British bases for Polaris and Trident onward, both nuclear and non-nuclear. But his security clearance was good enough to enable him to rule that out. "Something else— but don't ask me what." He turned to Bell again. "How much oxygen had he used?"

"Can't tell." Bell shook his head regretfully. "The demand valve had been knocked to hell, the cylinder was empty."

"And like someone took a sledgehammer to it," said Shaw. He paused, not wanting to be misunderstood. "Figure of speech, that's all."

"Keep the unit locked away. There'll be a Defence boffin some-where who'll scream for it." Carrick got to his feet, balancing instinc-tively as some quirk of a wave pattern made *Marlin* give a shudder-ing jerk, like a dog shaking itself. "I'm going to eat."

Andy Shaw came with him to the wardroom, where their meal was yet another variation on the galley's inevitable stew. But the steward fussed around Carrick considerably more than usual, to Shaw's barely concealed amusement, and for once the cheese which came af-terwards didn't look salvaged from an abandoned mousetrap.

It was two in the afternoon when Carrick returned to the bridge. Jumbo Wills had taken over, there was a different helmsman.

But little else had changed.

They kept the box patrol going, but in a new pattern. The radio-room telex chattered briefly, an updated weather report, then fell si-lent, and Carrick welcomed the break when a lone Dutch trawler, plugging north off the regular shipping track, put on a sudden burst of speed as *Marlin* began to close with her from astern.

Big and broad-beamed, the Dutchman ignored the fishery cruiser's signals until Carrick made a high-speed pass across her bows. Then, reluctantly, she stopped. Ferguson, summoned from his cabin, was in charge of the boarding party, which bobbed across in *Marlin*'s cutter.

But the Dutchman's nets were dry, the wooden-faced skipper the type who decided he couldn't speak English when asked about the fish crammed into his holds. If he'd been on a poaching raid, it hadn't been that day and there was no proof.

The boarding party returned, the Dutch trawler pulled away with a derisive bray from her siren.

It was another half hour later, with *Marlin* back on the southern edge of her patrol box, when the radio room came to life again. On the bridge, Carrick swung round expectantly as the duty operator hurried in.

"Radio telephone for you, sir. Personal from Fleet Support." The operator grinned hopefully. "It's a direct patch-through on scrambler, from Captain Dobie at Headquarters."

Carrick took the call in the radio room on a handset. The Marine Superintendent's voice rasped in his ear a moment later.

"We hadn't forgotten you, Carrick." There was a pause, and Carrick could imagine Dobie sitting in his Edinburgh office, where the view didn't include even a glimpse of the sea. Then the Marine Superintendent spoke again. "Certain—ah—individuals had to be consulted. You appreciate that? Over."

"Yes, sir." Carrick waited.

"Good." Dobie sounded indifferent. "Anyway, that's finished. Proceed to your Russian. Your orders are to go aboard, advise her captain that Her Majesty's Government take a strongly critical view of what happened, and request the immediate surrender of—ah—the deceased. But you'll do it diplomatically. You understand? Over."

"Sir." Carrick glared at the handset, glad the radio operator had left him alone. "Suppose they tell me to go to hell?"

"Maybe they will, maybe they won't." The Marine Superintendent's voice didn't alter. "Whatever happens, you take no action, but I want a priority signal. I've already stressed the diplomatic approach, and no damned boarding-party nonsense." There was another pause, with only a faint background static; then, when Dobie spoke again, he was slightly more human. "It's an experience which can't do you any harm, Chief Officer. Not if you handle it right—particularly with your possible future in mind, eh? Over."

"I'll bear it in mind, sir," answered Carrick woodenly. He drew a deep breath. "Any update on Captain Shannon?"

"We've had a telephoned report from the doctor at Port Ard—condition satisfactory." What could have been a chuckle was almost lost in a rustle of static. "Don't worry, Chief Officer. I've a soft spot for that old devil. His wife has been advised, told not to worry—and I'll try and move him out to civilisation." The Marine Superintendent's manner hardened again. "Any change, you'll be advised. Meantime, you've got your orders. Just remember, the magic word is 'diplomacy'—for now, anyway. Over and out."

Exactly ninety-eight minutes later, *Marlin* sailed into Loch Armach after a sustained high-speed dash which left a broad white wake boiling from her stern. Slowing, her signal lamp flashing, she approached the black twin-funnelled bulk of the anchored *Zarakov*, then lay idling about a cable's length to starboard.

This time there were no fishing boats in sight. They could hear the sounds of the factory ship's machinery at work, and smoke drifted lazily from her for'ard funnel. But the few figures moving on her decks seemed to be deliberately ignoring the fishery cruiser's presence.

Then, at last, a light began winking back from the *Zarakov*'s bridge. Reading the flashes, Clapper Bell gave a grunt of satisfaction and glanced at Carrick.

"'Permission to come aboard.'" He grinned. "Cheeky with it, aren't they?"

Carrick nodded. The signal that he was coming over hadn't asked anyone's permission. Taking a leaf out of Shannon's book, he was wearing full uniform, including a clean white shirt and tie.

Turning, he looked down to Ferguson, who was waiting on the foredeck beside *Marlin*'s high-speed launch. He waved to Ferguson, who nodded, then rapped an order to the work party who were with him. The main derrick boom came rattling to life, lifting the launch from her cradle, swinging her out for lowering. Using the launch, *Marlin*'s largest boat and capable of high-speed pursuit work or an independent role, was a touch of showmanship. But Carrick felt it was a moment when showmanship could do no harm.

Going into the bridge, Carrick had a final word with Jumbo Wills, then went down to the main deck. When he got there the launch was already bobbing alongside *Marlin*'s grey steel hull. Scrambling down a ladder, he stepped into the cockpit. The launch engines were throbbing, a petty officer and two seamen were at their stations.

"Make it look good," he told them.

A cable's length wasn't far, but the launch crew made the most of it, as if they too had caught the showmanship idea. Bucking and snarling over the sheltered water of the loch, the launch approached the towering Russian factory ship like a mosquito delighted to annoy a giant. Humming under his breath, the sound lost under the engines' roar, the petty officer closed his throttles at the very last moment and brought her alongside, fenders gently brushing the *Zarakov*'s rusting plates as she eased up to an accommodation ladder.

Carrick stepped across. As he clambered up, he heard the launch mutter away to lie off, waiting. Then he reached the *Zarakov*'s deck, a Russian petty officer made a token business of helping him aboard, and a waiting detail of other seamen came to attention.

"Welcome aboard, Chief Officer," said a voice. Commander Fedor Vasilek stepped forward and gave a grave smile as they exchanged salutes. "Or it is now 'Captain'? I know your commanding officer is unwell."

"I've acting command." Carrick stopped as a wafting smell hit his nostrils, a smell which might have come from a decaying manure heap.

Vasilek grimaced slightly. "The wind is playing tricks with us today. I'm sorry. We have a fish-meal plant aft and it is—well, something we live with."

Carrick nodded. The bigger factory ships processed their fish offal, for more than waste-not-want-not reasons. The alternatives were to store the stinking offal in tanks or to risk dumping it, something not calculated to make for good relations ashore.

"You've heard from Maxwell?" he asked.

"He radioed." Vasilek gestured him to follow and began leading the way for'ard. "I will take you to Captain Rudichev—I will be present as interpreter, as he speaks little English." He gave Carrick a sideways glance which held what might almost have been a warning. "Your visit, of course, is not unexpected. But then, we all obey orders."

"That's right," said Carrick. "I've certainly got mine."

"Of course." Vasilek slowed and beckoned him over to a large opened hatch. "This may interest you."

Trying to forget the all-pervading smell from aft, Carrick looked down at a vast, brightly lit lower-deck area. At one end, bucket conveyors were dumping cascades of fish onto slow-moving sorting belts. Along each production line a small army of men and women in overalls, rubber boots and aprons were hard at work. Sorting, gutting, discarding or trimming, in pace with the relentless creeping carpet of fish, their small filleting knives slashed and cut in a steel-walled, noisy environment of blood, discarded offal and cleansing hose-jets.

"Before this, of course, there are cooling tanks with a brine solution," murmured Vasilek. He gestured towards the far end of the production deck, where other workers were moving trolleys on a tracked line. As each trolley filled with fish, it vanished into a narrow tunnel. "From here, processing becomes flash-freezing, block packaging, then storage—until the next refrigerated vessel arrives."

Carrick nodded. He'd seen some of it, most of it, before. But never on such a large scale.

"How many people do you carry?"

"Including crew, about three hundred." The Russian shrugged. "We work seven days a week, Chief Officer—there are production targets to meet. Unfortunately, your fishing skippers do not always realise the importance of delivering a catch on schedule."

"Not their fault—there's poor discipline among the fish," said Carrick. "How often do your people get shore leave?"

"Most are happy to remain aboard. We have our own recreation facilities." Vasilek's manner perceptibly stiffened. "Why?"

"Curiosity." Carrick stood back. It was pretty much the answer he'd expected. Any Russian allowed to sample the limited pleasures of Port Ard would be drawn from a totally trusted group. "What happened to the man who pulled a knife last night?"

"He has been punished—suitably." Vasilek frowned. "Can we move on? Captain Rudichev is not the most patient of individuals."

They started off again along the deck, past the tall funnels with their hammer-and-sickle emblems. The production line below had been impressive, but Carrick saw plenty of evidence that, from a sea-man's viewpoint, the *Zarakov* was a slack ship. On all sides there were signs of a lack of basic maintenance, of real shipkeeping. The only exception seemed to be that forest of radio and radar antennae overhead, all apparently leading to a smartly painted area of super-structure aft of the bridge. But that was also something he'd expected.

They entered a companionway door, went up a flight of stairs and through a curtained doorway, and a young, Slav-featured woman in officer's uniform looked up at them from a desk. Getting to her feet, she went over to a cabin door, knocked, opened it, and went in.

"Our Navigation Officer," murmured Vasilek. He smiled at Carrick's raised eyebrow. "At other times she acts as captain's secretary —neither one is an easy task."

She reappeared at the cabin door, held it open, and nodded to Vasilek. They went in past her, and the door closed again.

They were in a large cabin, furnished like an office, lined with steel filing cabinets, the cork covering on the deck scuffed and worn, the large desk in the middle shabby and stained. The man behind the desk didn't get up. He was in his sixties, white-haired, heavily built, and in his shirtsleeves. Small, disinterested eyes in a fat, pale face looked at Carrick briefly, then he spoke for a moment in Russian, his voice flat.

"Captain Rudichev welcomes you aboard and trusts that—ah—any business will be brief," translated Vasilek. He paused as the Russian captain spoke again, then added, "He also hopes the photographs you took the other day were satisfactory."

"They were. Maybe we could get him copies." Carrick gave a faint, appreciative smile. The fat, pale face didn't alter. "I think your captain knows why I'm here, but does he want me to spell it out?"

Vasilek translated. Rudichev grunted and gave a curt headshake.

"Then before I get to the main matter, could he tell me exactly what your Technical Officer Krymov was doing on his last dive?"

Vasilek stiffened. "I can tell you that. I already did."

"Ask him."

"Very well." Vasilek turned to his captain and spoke rapidly. The man listened, then stared at Carrick. For an unguarded moment, an expression of alarm showed on the fat face, then he hurriedly answered.

"Well?" asked Carrick.

"Captain Rudichev confirms. Andrei Krymov was diving from a small boat near the ship. His hobby was spearfishing."

"With a closed-circuit Soviet Navy system?" asked Carrick. "We've got it, Fedor Vasilek. And in case you don't know it, you've got about two hundred feet of water below this ship—and if you check your charts, Loch Armach stays that way almost till you hit the shore."

"No compressed-air system was available." Vasilek glared at him. "Does any of this matter?"

"Would you let me know if it did?" countered Carrick. He faced the white-haired, fat-faced man deliberately. "Tell Captain Rudichev that I officially request the immediate surrender of the body removed from Targe Island this morning, to allow normal process of British law to be carried out."

Vasilek calmed, nodded, and spoke briefly. A slow, deliberate grin appeared on Rudichev's face as he listened, a grin that became a dry laugh as he sat back.

"I've told him," said Vasilek. "But you see, Chief Officer, it's impossible." He made a quick festure to stop Carrick interrupting. "The body of Soviet citizen Andrei Krymov was placed aboard the refrigerated carrier ship *Golovnin,* which made a scheduled arrival here this morning."

Rudichev was still grinning. Carrick swallowed hard, feeling as if he'd been hit in the stomach.

"When did the *Golovnin* sail?" he asked.

"At noon." Vasilek's voice was almost sympathetic. "By now, of course, she should be almost clear of British waters."

"Congratulations." Carrick drew a deep breath, knowing Vasilek was right, that he was totally beaten. "All right, I'll let our people know. Thank your captain for seeing me."

Captain Rudichev was still grinning as Carrick left, Vasilek at his heels. They were out on the main deck again, the same smell wafting over them, before Vasilek spoke again.

"I could have told you when you came aboard, of course." He paused, hands on the deck rail, and grimaced at the sea. "But as you agree, we all obey orders. The *Golovnin* sailed with less than half her normal cargo. You didn't know about her?"

Carrick shook his head. He could see *Marlin*'s launch coming back to pick him up.

"But other people would," said Vasilek. He smiled to himself. "Any Soviet ship is an object of interest to the British, to the Americans, to your allies—also agreed?"

"Agreed." Carrick swore under his breath. *Marlin* had been summarily dismissed to the southeast box, held there, kept there.

Vasilek nodded. "There are times when those above us, those who make decisions, look for simple solutions. Perhaps this was one."

The Russian had to be right. If the *Zarakov*'s captain had still had his Technical Officer's body aboard, the situation could have escalated to a major incident—unless one side or the other climbed down.

But no one had to do that now, not this way.

Marlin's launch bumped alongside, her crew staring up at him from her cockpit. He signalled he was coming.

"Good-bye, Chief Officer." Vasilek saluted him.

"For now." Grimly Carrick returned the salute. He went over to the accommodation ladder, then looked again at Vasilek. "Next time maybe you'll tell me the name of your last ship—and your real job aboard a tub like this. Or were you just banished for stepping out of line?"

Vasilek frowned. His mouth a tight line, he turned deliberately and walked away.

It was a small victory, but better than none. Going down the ladder, Carrick dropped into the launch cockpit.

"Home to mother," he ordered. "I've things to do."

He had *Marlin* under way, heading back to Port Ard, as soon as the launch had been brought aboard. Then, as the fishery cruiser cleared Loch Morlach, Carrick went through to the radio room.

"Telex to Captain Dobie at Headquarters," he told the operator, waving him back into his seat as he started to rise. "Ready?"

"Wait, sir." The operator flicked a couple of switches, then nodded, fingers poised above the keyboard.

Carrick dictated while the keys tapped, keeping the signal brief and curtly factual. If Dobie or anyone else at Headquarters read anything else between the lines, he didn't give a damn. But he'd done what was ordered, he was reporting back.

He finished. As the operator pencilled a time of origin in the signals logbook, the telex machine came to life again.

The incoming message ended. The operator gave a mild whistle of surprise, tore the printed slip from the machine, and handed it over.

"FOR ADVICE. CAPTAIN SHANNON TRANSFERRED BY HELICOPTER FROM PORT ARD TO HOSPITAL, OBAN. CONDITION SATISFACTORY. MOVE TO FACILITATE FURTHER OBSERVATION. SENDER, DOBIE, MARINE SUPERINTENDENT."

Carrick went through to the bridge. Jumbo Wills was prowling the deck behind the helmsman, impatient to hear what had happened on the *Zarakov*. Wordlessly, Carrick handed him the telex message.

"Well"—Wills read it and a hopeful frown creased his freckled face—"seems all right, doesn't it?"

"We'll find out." Carrick didn't feel ready to share anyone's optimism.

He looked ahead through the bridge windows. The broken sky was clearing, helped along by a wind which had swung to the west and was beginning to scud foam from the wavecrests. He could just make out the distant outline of the tall sea-cliff which guarded Port Ard and a smaller, isolated pimple which was Targe Island.

"Uh—about back there," said Wills, unable to hold his curiosity in check any longer. "What happened?"

The helmsman was eavesdropping. They always did. Carrick glanced at the compass binnacle but said nothing. He couldn't. The fishery cruiser was exactly on course. But suddenly he realised that for the moment Jumbo Wills was second-in-command. It was a startling, sobering thought.

"Chartroom," he said. "Let's get out of the draught."

"Draught?" Wills didn't understand.

"Flapping ears," Carrick told him. He saw the helmsman's blink of indignation and added, "Though there's a cure—pin them back, permanently, with six-inch nails!"

The helmsman grinned, mollified. That was one to tell later, off watch. Not as good as Captain Shannon at his best, but worth a hearing.

The sun was setting and the sky mostly a salmon-pink hue as *Marlin* made her approach to Port Ard. Coming in, the fishery cruiser passed the black, bobbing silhouettes of a number of small boats tending some of the lines of lobster creels laid around the rocky fringes of the bay. A few purse-netters were heading out for a night's work.

It was a peaceful scene. The updated weather forecast for the next day was good, confirming what the sky told any seaman. Even the inevitable gulls which appeared to escort *Marlin* into harbour seemed content to plane down and perch on her superstructure and rigging, too lazy to do anything more energetic.

Carrick summoned Clapper Bell to the bridge once they'd berthed. By the time Bell arrived, they were alone. *Marlin*'s gangway had been run out, a few of her crew were already ashore.

"Going to check on the Old Man?" asked Bell without preliminaries.

"For starters." Carrick looked out across the harbour for a moment, at the fishing boats tied thickly along the opposite quay. "Clapper, get hold of Sergeant Ballantyne—you'll probably find him at home."

Bell grunted. "With his feet up. And?"

"Ask what he's done about the character who thumped Captain Shannon." Carrick pursed his lips briefly, with few illusions about the possible answer. "Then—well, something you could do on your own. I want to know if Maxwell's foreman owns a motorcycle."

"Could he fit?" The Glasgow-Irishman allowed himself a soft, appreciative whistle. "No problem. What else?"

"Pick up any gossip you can about the *Zarakov*, about Maxwell—about any damned thing out of the ordinary happening." He looked at Bell and shrugged. "I don't know what I'm after, Clapper. But it has to be here, somehow."

Bell nodded. Like Wills, he and Ferguson had both been given a quick rundown of the general situation before they'd berthed. He knew Carrick's basic problem. Tomorrow—and it was unlikely the orders would be changed—*Marlin* was scheduled to make an extended patrol sweep in her area of the Minch. The kind that would take a couple of days.

If anything was going to happen, it would have to happen quickly.

"That's it, then," said Carrick. He shoved his hat further back on his head and grimaced. "Except for one thing. If you meet trouble, back off—understand?"

"Sir." Bell grinned at him, but nodded.

A few minutes later, Carrick went ashore. As he left *Marlin,* he could hear muffled clanging and banging coming from somewhere down in the engine-room area. Andy Shaw had decided some maintenance work was needed on the starboard diesel and was holding some of his squad aboard until it was finished, something not guaranteed to increase his popularity as Chief Engineer.

Carrick walked along the quay, first passing an islands cargo steamer which had come in during the day, then a gaggle of smaller craft.

He could smell a scent of peat smoke in the air, coming from the village. A few lights were beginning to show; most families in Port Ard were probably settling down to their evening meal, with a TV set flickering in the background.

The harbour area was deserted. But there were lights in Alexis Jordan's office. Her Volvo station wagon and the white van used by Katie Ross were parked outside. Carrick went in. Katie Ross was typing in the outer office, Alexis Jordan standing nearby beside an opened filing cabinet.

"Good evening," Carrick said. "Working late?"

Alexis Jordan closed the cabinet drawer and came over with a file of papers in one hand.

"Fish landing figures—the monthly return for Department," she said. Her mouth tightened slightly. "My kind of work, Mr. Carrick. You know Captain Shannon was moved?"

"Yes." Carrick rested his hands on Katie's desk. "But I want to know why."

"No medical reason—according to Jan Blair, he's doing well." Alexis Jordan shrugged her disapproval. "But some fool at Headquarters seemed to think he'd get better attention somewhere bigger."

"Some fool called Dobie?" asked Carrick.

She nodded.

"What about—well, the other matter?" asked Katie Ross quietly.

She flushed as they both looked at her. "Webb, I'm sorry. That damned brother of mine—"

"He wasn't the only one," said Carrick, and saw the older woman wince. "But it's finished—or it looks that way. They won." He turned deliberately to Alexis Jordan. "Heard from Maxwell?"

"Yes, he called in." Her mouth tightened a little. "We talked, but we didn't totally agree."

"I'm sorry." Not sure what else to say, he glanced at Katie again. "How's Jamie?"

"Sulking. He got back in with a rotten catch. Then when I'd finished with him, my mother started."

He chuckled, and she gave an answering grin. Even Alexis Jordan saw the humour of it and gave a tenuous smile.

A thought crossed Carrick's mind.

"Could I use your car again?" he asked the older woman. "It might be useful."

"Tonight?" She hesitated. "I'm supposed to be at a lifeboat committee meeting—it's a twenty-mile drive down the coast."

"But you could take our van," volunteered Katie. She nodded briskly. "If Mrs. Jordan gives me a lift home, that's all I need. Then when you're finished, just leave the van here, at the harbour. Jamie can pick it up."

He raised an eyebrow. "How?"

"This is his regular once-a-week poker-playing night—they meet on one of the boats, and the game runs late. I'll get word to Jamie and it'll save him having to scrounge a lift home."

He thanked her and took the keys. When he left, Alexis Jordan went with him along the corridor to the outside door.

"Webb." She laid a hand on his arm. "What happened this afternoon?"

"They shipped the body out on a refrigerated carrier." He shrugged. "We were too late. But it was meant to be that way."

"Fewer problems for some people." She sighed. "Well, I suppose John Maxwell will be relieved. What about you?"

"Nobody asked me," he said flatly.

He left her and went over to the Ford van. Starting the engine, he blipped the accelerator a couple of times, checked his way through the instrument layout, and smiled a little at the heavily customised interior. But it could move. Within a few seconds of setting the wheels moving he had to brake twice to slow its pace.

Then, still treating the accelerator cautiously, he drove out of the harbour and headed for the medical clinic.

The main door was closed and the building seemed deserted when he parked outside. Getting out, he tried a bell push which said NIGHT CALLS, then waited. A few moments later he heard footsteps, then the door opened and Jan Blair looked out.

"You." She opened the door wider and beckoned him in. Her voice had a slightly bitter edge. "I thought I'd seen the last of Fisheries Protection for a spell."

"I heard." He looked at her appreciatively as she closed the door. She was wearing a dark-blue wool dress, belted at the waist, with a narrow white lace trimming at the crossover neckline. The white medical coat hadn't done her figure justice. "Off duty?"

"More or less." She thawed. "I suppose it had nothing to do with you. I just don't like it when my prize patient is more or less hijacked."

"But he's all right?"

"No skull fracture, nothing else to worry about. A few days' total rest and he'll be fine."

"Thank you, Doctor." He smiled, relieved. "Maybe you're well rid of him. He wouldn't have given you an easy time."

"That I can imagine," she said. Her eyes twinkled. "Could you use a drink?"

"If that's an invitation, yes."

"Come on through," she said. "I told you I lived behind the shop."

Carrick followed her through the clinic. At the end of a corridor she opened a door marked PRIVATE and led him into a small, tastefully furnished apartment.

"Help yourself." She waved towards a drinks cupboard. "Pour me a brandy and soda—mostly soda—and I'll be back in a moment. I'm halfway through cooking a meal." She started for a door that led into a tiny kitchen, then looked at him again and sighed. "I suppose you haven't eaten?"

"Not yet," he admitted.

"It'll stretch for two. Bring the drinks through."

Carrick fixed her drink, poured himself a measure from a bottle of Tomatin malt, splashed some water into the whisky with a murmured apology to the distillery, then glanced around the room. It had a pleasant, lived-in air, from magazines littering a coffee table to a pair of slippers not quite tucked out of sight under a chair. A photograph

above the small, Dutch-tiled fireplace caught his eye. It showed Jan
Blair in another, surprising role, in army uniform.

He took the drinks through to the kitchen. She was busy at the
stove but stopped to sip her drink and smile her thanks.

"We've got what was meant to be a Spanish omelette, with coffee
and maybe some cheese," she said. "You can help—everything's in
that cupboard."

Obediently, he set two places at a small table.

"When were you in the Army?" he asked.

"After hospital training." She wiped her hands on a cloth. "A
short service commission, two years in Hong Kong. I became pretty
good at treating what are politely called 'social diseases.'" She
paused, then added deliberately, "There was also plenty of autopsy
work."

"And after that—why here?"

"Simple." She divided the omelette between two plates and
brought them over. "I wanted general-practitioner experience, and
Port Ard was all I could get. Now I'm glad. I like the people, I like
the challenge—because you're on your own most of the time. When I
do move on—"

"You'll miss it?"

She nodded, then pointed to his plate. "That's getting cold."

They ate. The cheese, when she found it, was mouldy. They took
their coffee through to the living room and Jan Blair, kicking her
shoes off, curled up in one of the chairs.

"About Gibby MacNeil," she said suddenly. "There are things I
don't understand."

"That makes two of us," said Carrick.

"I'd like to know the story."

He hesitated, met her grey, quietly serious eyes for a moment, then
nodded.

By the time he'd finished, he'd told most of it and she was frowning. Getting up, she brought the coffee pot through from the kitchen,
refilled their cups, then sat down again.

"We could have been wrong," she said slowly. "It can happen,
Webb. The regional pathologist in the MacNeil postmortem is an expert—but sometimes you only look for what you expect to find." For
a moment she fingered the white lace piping at the neck of her dress,
thinking. "I could talk to him. We could try again."

He showed his surprise. "Exhume the body?"

"That would need a court order, and evidence—maybe more evidence than you've got. But it's standard practice to keep tissue and organ samples, for a time." She leaned forward. "But there's nothing more difficult than looking for the unexpected."

Carrick nodded his understanding. "So if I could give you a pointer—"

He stopped there as the telephone in the corner began ringing. Jan Blair swore softly, rose, answered it, and had a brief, professionally soothing conversation with whoever was at the other end. Then she hung up and gave a rueful grimace.

"I'll need to go out. A child on one of the farms—a three-year-old, with a temperature and stomach pains." She pulled on her shoes as she spoke. "I know her mother. She's not the kind to panic without reasonable cause."

"I could drive you over," volunteered Carrick.

"In that thing you've got outside?" The idea amused her, but she nodded. "All right, why not? I'll get a coat and my bag."

It was a moonlit night, with a moderate wind. They drove through the village, took the hill road out, and followed its snaking, climbing route for a couple of miles. Then Jan Blair guided Carrick along a side road for another mile or so, and they stopped outside a small farmhouse.

"You don't mind waiting?" she asked.

"Take all the time you need." He sat back as, bag in hand, she got out and went over to the farmhouse. The door opened before she could knock, a woman ushered her in, and the door closed again.

Idly, Carrick switched on the van's radio and found a foreign station offering a quiet line in jazz. He relaxed to its mood, then, shifting round in his seat, looked out at the night.

He was high up. In the moonlight the view from the hill was out towards the sea. Port Ard was a bright patch to his right; then, out across the silvered water, the stark outline of Targe Island was clearly defined. He could even see the tiny, crawling, beetlelike shape of a fishing boat going in towards the harbour, navigation lights like bright pinprick eyes far below.

The music murmured on, and he sat almost dozing, until suddenly the jazz stopped and a harsh voice began what seemed to be a news bulletin. Cursing mildly, he fiddled with the radio again, found another music station, and checked his wristwatch. Almost twenty minutes had passed.

Sighing, Carrick leaned against the steering wheel for a moment.

Then he stiffened and stared out at the black bulk of Targe Island.

He could see a light. Small but distinct, it moved, split, became two lights, then one vanished. The other persisted for almost a minute.

He waited, tensely. At last a light showed again, briefly, at the same location. It had to be among the ruins to the south end of the island—and he felt certain that the lights wouldn't have been visible from Port Ard. Only the van's position on the hillside, the different angle of view, had left them unmasked as far as he was concerned.

Who was out there on that dangerous, uninhabited buttress of rock —who, and why?

He switched off the radio, no longer in that kind of mood, and kept watching. The lights didn't show again. But he knew he hadn't imagined them.

Five minutes later, Jan Blair came out of the cottage and returned to the van. She was smiling as she got into the passenger seat and closed the door.

"Panic over?" asked Carrick.

"Yes." She tossed her medical bag behind her seat. "Would you believe that child ate a batch of conditioning powders the vet handed in for their sheepdog?" She chuckled. "I'll spare you the details—but I had to wait when I was finished, to make sure."

Carrick started the van and set it moving. A tight turn in the farmyard entrance, and they were heading back the way they'd come. He drove in silence, frowning at the night.

"Anything wrong?" asked Jan Blair after a few moments. "If it's the way I kept you waiting—"

"No, it's not that," he reassured her. "I was thinking. Jan, how much do you know about John Maxwell?"

"Not a lot, and I'd rather keep it that way," she said. "He's certainly not a patient. I know where he lives—he has a cottage about a mile past the Memorial Hall on the coast road. He keeps his boat there too—most of the time anyway."

"His boat?" Carrick steered round a deep pothole which had suddenly appeared in the van's headlamps. "I didn't know he had one."

"Yes. It's an old launch, the *Goosewing*—fairly big and quite fast. I don't think he uses it much. Does it matter?"

"I'm not sure—yet." He kept his eyes on the narrow, badly rutted road, then sensed her irritation at his continued silence. "He's pretty close with Alexis Jordan, isn't he?"

"Yes." She gave an indignant snort. "And with a few others she doesn't know about." She paused and grimaced. "Sorry. That's patients' gossip. Forget it."

A few minutes later they were in Port Ard again. Carrick let the van coast to a halt outside the clinic door.

"Thanks." Jan Blair looked at him for a moment, then touched his arm. "It's still early, but I think I'd better say good night—this time, anyway. You don't mind?"

"This time." He leaned over, gave her a moment to be sure, then kissed her on the lips. She responded, let the kiss linger, her eyes half-closed, then gently eased away.

"My bag." She collected it, opened the passenger door, then smiled at him and got out. "Good night, Webb. Don't make it too long before you come round again."

The door closed. He waited until she had gone into the clinic building, then set the van moving again.

Round the next corner from the clinic, the Maxwell Transport yard lay in darkness. All but one of the trucks had gone and it sat empty and deserted in the moonlight. The main gate was closed and padlocked from the outside; the barbed wire strung along its perimeter fence formed a discouraging tracery against the night.

Carrick took the van past at a crawl, then drove back down towards the village. At Shore Street, where a few people, some of them from *Marlin*'s crew, were still moving about, he turned in the direction of the Memorial Hall. He reached the big hut, its windows brightly lit, and kept along the shore road.

Jan Blair had said about a mile on. He kept by her directions, though the road curved inland, and suddenly found the sea to his left again. Ignoring a cluster of small modern houses, he rounded a bend, then the van's lights showed an isolated cottage just ahead, on the shore side of the road.

He drove past, saw Maxwell's car parked to one side, noted a light at one of the cottage windows, and turned the van about five hundred yards on. Driving past again, he could see no sign of a boat. But another vehicle was parked in the shadows near the rear of the cottage.

Carrick stopped the van well past the cottage, taking it off the road into the shelter of a thick bank of gorse and scrub. Switching off lights and engine, he got out and walked back the way he'd come.

Headlights showed on the road, coming towards him. He took to the beach, hugged a slab of rock until a bus rattled past, then waited, listening, hearing only the mutter of the wind and the steady, scouring rhythm of sea against shore.

He moved on. Gradually, more details took shape in the shadowed moonlight. The second vehicle was an old battered Land Rover with a canvas top. The cottage, a slim TV aerial attached to one chimney, was built West Highland style with its back to the road. Another chink of light showed behind closed curtains at the front, which faced a small stone jetty, little more than a landing place; near the jetty a collection of large lobster creels lay against the side of a squat brick storage shed.

Keeping low, hugging the shadows, Carrick reached the walls of the cottage. When he checked both vehicles, their engines were cold. Easing round, he peered in at the lighted window. Through the gap between the curtains he could see a man sprawled back in a chair, watching television.

The man half-turned, reaching out for a can of beer, showing his face. It was the tall, thin fisherman with the red shirt, one of the pair he had fought off at the Memorial Hall.

Only one other thing in the room caught Carrick's eye. A small walkie-talkie radio sat on top of the television set. Silently he made his way to the other lighted window. It was the kitchen and it was empty.

That left the storage shed. He crossed the stretch of open ground, tried the wooden door, and it creaked open. Moonlight shone wanly on more stored lobster pots, a workbench, tools, and in the middle of it all, a motorcycle. The motorcycle had chunky motocross tyres, the treads heavily caked with mud.

Carrick closed the door with another creak of its hinges. He'd seen enough, it was time to get out.

He had taken barely a dozen steps across the open ground when a light above the front door of the cottage snapped on. The nearest cover was the start of the stone jetty and Carrick threw himself towards it, crouching in the scanty shelter of the roughly cemented rocks.

The door opened. The fisherman came out. He raised the walkie-talkie to his lips, spoke into it, then stood waiting.

A moment later the low throb of a powerful boat engine reached Carrick's ears. He looked round. A large launch, a dark shape moving without lights, was creeping in towards the shore.

Figures moved on the boat's foredeck. The engine rasped briefly, a boathook glinted and swung, dragging in the float of a mooring rope.

As it was secured, the engine was cut. In another moment the men on the launch began lowering a small rubber boat into the water to come ashore—and the fisherman at the cottage came towards the jetty to meet them, a lighted torch in one hand.

The fisherman came nearer, humming, the torch beam swinging casually as he walked. Feeling around in the shingle, Carrick found a hard, moderately sized, almost perfectly rounded pebble, and tensed.

He let the fisherman take three steps nearer. Then, jumping up, he hurled the stone at the man's head.

There was a distinct thud, an anguished cry of pain, and the torch dropped. The man staggered, hands going up to his face, then Carrick took him with a shoulder charge which sent him reeling, and followed it up with a double-handed smash to the side of the neck.

The fisherman collapsed to his knees. Carrick turned and ran, hearing alarmed shouts coming across the water as he pounded over shingle and grass towards the road.

He glanced back once. The rubber boat had reached the jetty. Two men were scrambling ashore. But there was still someone on the launch, using a spotlamp from the cockpit, sweeping its narrow beam around in a fruitless, uncertain arc.

Reaching the van, he tumbled in, started it, and the little vehicle took off.

A few minutes later he was back in Port Ard. He parked the white van outside the Fisheries Office, sat limp behind the wheel for a moment or two, then grinned at himself in the driving mirror.

Carrick was willing to take any bet there had been no chance of his being recognised. And he now had two more counts against John Maxwell—the motorcycle hidden in the store shed, and the way his launch had sneaked in without navigation lights. Back from a trip which somehow had to be connected with Targe Island.

He took the keys from the ignition, tucked them in under the front seat, left the van, and walked through the harbour to where *Marlin*'s reassuring, familiar silhouette lay waiting.

It was after 1 A.M. when Clapper Bell returned aboard. Carrick was waiting for him in the scuba compartment, lounging in the bo'sun's prized armchair, the remains of a pot of coffee from the wardroom at his feet.

"Made yourself comfortable, eh?" Bell grinned at him, then stiffened and gave what was meant to be a smart salute. "Reportin' aboard, sir."

Then he spoiled the effect with a beery belch, sighed, and squatted happily on an equipment box.

"How'd you make out?" asked Carrick.

"Great." Bell beamed at him. "There was this game—"

"On one of the boats?"

"That's right." Bell blinked at him, surprised. "Anyway, half o' them were fishing skippers, wavin' money around like it was too much for their pockets. But the way they played"—he shook his head —"hell, halfway through I took the best pot of the night. Bluffed them with a rotten bobtail straight!"

"So how much did you win?" Carrick had a brief vision of the long list of debts Bell owed him, then saw Bell's expression. "Or *did* you?"

Bell shrugged resignedly. "It didn't go so good after that. I got out maybe evens." He brightened. "The talk was good."

"Was Jamie Ross there?" Carrick leaned forward.

"Part of the time." Bell fumbled for his cigarettes and lit one. "I stayed quiet when he was around." He drew in a lungful of smoke. "I checked with Sergeant Ballantyne first. He made some noises about out-of-town fishermen, not much else. But I got some of what you wanted at the game."

"Like?"

"Like Maxwell's foreman, Ferdie Renfrew. He sometimes rides a motorcycle, cross-country style."

"I've seen it," said Carrick grimly. He shook his head. "It'll keep. Go on."

"Well—" Bell rubbed his chin. "Maxwell brought Renfrew up here with him from the South. Since Renfrew arrived, he's gathered a reasonable reputation as a hard man. The rest of it is that Maxwell's permanent people are locals, but he has some other hard-case drifters hanging around."

Carrick nodded. "How about Maxwell?"

"He pays what he owes, no delays. That's about all they know—or care. He doesn't mix much wi' the fishing skippers. He goes higher up the ladder."

"Like to Russian officers." Carrick poured the dregs of the coffee pot into his cup, took a sip, and grimaced at the taste. "Any Russians about tonight?"

"Some, but not many. No sign of our commander, an' the leave boat was on its way back well before midnight." Bell paused and took another long draw on his cigarette. "But something odd happened out on the *Zarakov* about ten days ago—or it looked that way. Not a single Ruskie came ashore for three days. Any boat takin' a catch alongside was treated like it had the plague—no chat, an' a couple of guards dumped aboard till it left."

Ten days back meant before the storm, almost certainly before the frogman had died—but just about the time Gibby MacNeil had written his letter to Shannon. Carrick nodded slowly.

"Then?"

"Then things drifted back to normal." Bell shrugged apologetically. "No explanations—but it happened." He eyed Carrick shrewdly. "So—how about you?"

"A few things."

Carrick told him.

"You stuck your neck out," Bell protested. "You're in command now, an' even flamin' acting captains are supposed to know better." The scowl on his face eased. "So we take another look at Targe Island?"

"Tomorrow," Carrick told him, and got to his feet. "First thing."

Bell grinned, and gave another belch.

CHAPTER 6

Wakened to darkness, cursing, some nursing hangovers, *Marlin*'s crew ate breakfast and were at their stations by dawn. A white rime of frost still clung to the fishery cruiser's rigging and superstructure as she edged her way out of harbour and steered a deliberate course through the grey early light towards Targe Island.

A little later, as the sun began to edge up on the mainland horizon, she anchored near the underwater entrance to the grotto cave. A boat was lowered and took up position as a diving tender. But that pretence was for the benefit of any passing vessel with inquisitive eyes aboard. At the same time, two of her rubber inflatables took a party of eight men ashore at one of the few landing places available.

Carrick led one group, consisting of Clapper Bell and two seamen. Ferguson had the others and had volunteered—Ferguson sometimes did, when the task didn't involve people. Once both inflatables had been concealed among the rocks, Carrick gathered the men around him.

"You know what to do." He saw some of them shivering in the cold. A wisping morning mist was still clearing from the island's steep cliffs. "Moving about will warm you enough. Mr. Ferguson's party concentrate along the shoreline, the rest of us check towards those ruins at the top. We're looking for a trace of a recent landing. Don't show yourselves more than you need." He paused. "Any questions?"

"Recall signal," prompted Ferguson.

Carrick nodded. "Two whistle blasts, repeated. Anything else?"

The men, a couple carrying pickaxe hafts, shook their heads.

"Then spread out and let's go." Carrick stood for a moment, watching Ferguson's party crunch off along the shingle. Further along, they would have to get past sheer rock leading straight down to the sea. Then he glanced at Bell and nodded.

"On your bikes," Bell told the two seamen. "An' nobody breaks a leg without permission, right?"

It was a hard, slogging, plodding, sometimes scrambling climb. There was no path to follow. Occasionally they saw traces of a rabbit run. But the only island life were the seabirds, who every now and again exploded skywards from almost underfoot. Where there was soil, there was thorned scrub.

The last of the mist was just lifting as Carrick, sweating like the others, reached the comparatively level ground at the top. The ruins of the old Highland clan chief's castle lay ahead, most of the walls almost flattened by time and the elements, only a few standing stark against the blue of the sky.

Splitting up, they began searching among the tumbled stonework. Carrick had hardly begun his area when one of the seamen shouted and beckoned.

Carrick went over. The man was barely visible, standing in what at first sight looked like a pit some four feet below ground level where two thick walls joined in a right angle. But there was stone flagging at the bottom, the original floor level.

"Over here, sir." The man pointed at the corner formed by the walls. "Like someone might have been here for a spell, eh?"

Carrick nodded, dropped down beside him, then bent to rake cold fragments of charred wood which, with a heavy staining of soot on the stone above, were all that remained of a small fire. Rain had left the charred wood damp, wind had blown away any trace of ash. But it was still where someone seeking shelter and warmth could have found one and created the other.

A fragment of white jammed between two of the cracked flagstones caught his eye. He teased the torn strip of paper out carefully, smoothed it, and stiffened. The last thing he'd expected was to find a fragment from a Russian-language newspaper.

"Any use, sir?" asked the seaman.

"Keep looking," said Carrick. He tucked the fragment in a pocket.

They worked on. A rusted beer can, a mystery from an earlier decade, was tossed aside. But in quick succession the same seaman found an emptied, flattened meat tin, not long abandoned, the metal still gleaming, and Clapper Bell, further away, located the remains of a makeshift latrine.

"Like they had someone camping out," suggested Bell, puzzled. "A lookout, maybe?"

"Looking out at what?" asked Carrick wearily.

The view from the top of Targe Island was spectacular in terms of scenery, from the sweep of mainland mountains to the distant outlines of some of the nearer Hebridean islands. Even *Marlin,* floating below, looked like a toy. But if it had any other importance, it escaped him.

The second seaman, prowling the perimeter, came back a moment later. He had discovered what appeared to be a path down to the shore.

"I'll try it," decided Carrick. He gestured to the others. "Keep looking."

He started down the faint, overgrown track. Here and there positioned blocks of stone showed it had been man-made—but maybe centuries before, when the castle had been built. Thorned scrub clawed at his duffel jacket, and he had to handhold his way across a washed-out section.

Then he heard voices. A moment later, Ferguson and one of *Marlin*'s seamen came into sight, making their way up.

"We just wondered—" began Ferguson.

"So did I." He motioned them back down the way they'd come. At the bottom, under the shadow of a giant block of rock, he stopped and turned to Ferguson. "Any luck?"

Ferguson scowled down at a rip in his trouser leg. "These are ruined. One of my people took a tumble and—"

"What did you find?" Carrick cut him short, impatiently.

"What you expected. Maybe more." Ferguson was offended. "Two patches of beach used for landing, both recently—"

"Two?" Carrick showed his surprise.

"One further along, sand and shingle disturbed where a boat was hauled in, footprints of several men." Ferguson sniffed, glad to have Carrick confused. "The other—round here."

They went round the massive boulder. On the seaward side, where a few smaller rocks sheltered a patch of wispy, salt-stained grass, Ferguson pointed.

Something bulky had been dragged across the shingle leading to the grass. On the grass itself an oval area, the size of a small inflatable boat, had been flattened.

"There's your clincher," said Ferguson. Stooping, he lifted a straggling length of dark-green bladder-wrack seaweed, still damp to the touch. One of the little bladders popped as he squeezed it. "Has to be less than a day old. They probably brought it in tangled on the prop shaft."

"Two boats." Carrick drew a deep breath. "You're sure?"

"The other one had a keel. My guess would be a large dinghy." Ferguson was implacable.

Carrick nodded. But that meant two separate groups of men, one probably Russian, the other almost certainly Maxwell's people from the *Goosewing*.

"Any path up from the shore where the other boat came in?"

"Not like this one. But anyone could make it to the top." Ferguson paused and glanced deliberately at his wristwatch. "You know we've been here an hour?"

The sun was already well above the horizon in an almost cloudless sky. The sea, gently restless, was a deep blue dappled with white-capped wavelets—and *Marlin* had a patrol sector waiting.

"Bring them in," said Carrick reluctantly.

Producing his whistle, Ferguson blew two shrill blasts, the recall signal. Then they made their way back to the hidden inflatables.

Fifteen minutes later, boats recovered and men aboard, *Marlin* got under way. Building up to an economical twenty-knot cruising speed, she passed the Sump at a respectable distance and steered a curving course out into the Minch.

Carrick waited until the mainland had begun to blur astern. Then he left the bridge and went aft to the chartroom. For the moment it was empty and he closed the door behind him. The Admiralty charts covering their patrol area were spread and waiting on the chart table. He stood for a moment, hands resting lightly on the table, looking down at the charts yet barely seeing them.

Fleet Support decided a fishery cruiser's patrol beat and left most of the rest to the discretion of her commander. But the orders given to Shannon for this patrol—orders which Carrick had inherited—were specific in terms of what lay ahead. She would make an initial prowl down towards the Shiant fishing banks. From there, openly and slowly working her way up the Outer Islands, she was to make a show of anchoring by dusk. By then, every skipper in the North Minch area, regardless of nationality, would know by the radio grapevine and expect her to stay there.

So *Marlin* would promptly make a high-speed night dash across the wide Atlantic mouth of the Minch to the rich fishing grounds near the Cape Wrath mainland. Reasonably certain of surprising a few bold trawlers on a poaching raid into forbidden waters.

It was done now and again. A style of psychological warfare in a situation any law-enforcement officer could understand. There were too few fishery cruisers, too many fishing skippers ready to gamble their luck—but the surprise swoop-and-arrest technique made at least some skippers nervous, made them think again.

For once, Carrick didn't give a damn whether it worked or not. Two boats at Targe Island, clear traces of Russian involvement, his own convinced belief that Maxwell's launch had been out at the island—how did it all come together?

He heard a light tap on the chartroom door and looked round as it opened and Clapper Bell came in.

"Got a moment, sir?" Bell's voice was casual but with an underlying seriousness.

"Several," Carrick said. "Well?"

"Something I found back on the island—on the way back to the boats." Bell reached into a pocket. "I thought I'd keep it till you were on your own." He brought out his hand, a spent brass cartridge case resting in his leathery palm. "This was on the edge of the path."

Carrick took the cartridge case, sniffed it, then examined the base. He looked at Bell again.

"Pistol ammunition, .38 calibre," said Bell. "Probably from an automatic—you can see the ejector marks. Fired reasonably recently."

Carrick nodded. There was just enough of a residual odour of burnt powder to register that Bell was probably right.

"The Ruskies don't use .38 calibre," mused Bell. He paused and raised a deliberate eyebrow. "So?"

"Maxwell's private navy?" Carrick sighed. "I don't know, Clapper. I don't damned well know. But when we get back there—"

He left the rest unsaid, but Bell understood and gave a faint, encouraging grin.

Patrol routine took over. For Carrick, that included ship's rounds, an inspection visit to each department, a chance to hear problems, to spot possible shortcomings. He ran head on into one complaint when he reached the gleaming, noisy, oil-smelling world of the engine room. Andy Shaw was still anything but happy about the starboard diesel.

"I thought you'd worked on it," said Carrick.

"But we need more time. We're coping with a sick injector." Shaw thumbed over his shoulder at the gleaming, pounding machinery. A few feet away, a couple of his engine-room squad watched closely, lip-reading the conversation through the noise. "Man, I can nurse things along—but only for a spell."

"That's all I'm asking," said Carrick.

"Is it? Nobody issues us magic wands down here. I'm warning you —if that diesel was an animal, we could be reported for cruelty."

"Don't weep on my shoulder, Andy," said Carrick with an attempt at patience. "I'm not in the mood."

"Then you're as bad as Shannon." Shaw glared at him. "All right, why not go all the way? Get yourself a whip and a squad o' damned galley slaves."

The watching men grinned.

"Maybe I will," said Carrick. "Book your oar now, Andy. You've earned it."

He escaped Shaw's gathering wrath and got back to deck level.

Time passed, the watch changed.

Ferguson was on the bridge when a signal came in on low-band radio from *Swordfish,* the fishery cruiser patrolling the next sector to the south. *Swordfish* was temporarily in trouble, with half a trawl net wrapped round her starboard shaft. The net had been dumped by a trawler she'd been chasing, a trawler last seen still heading north with indecent haste.

They picked up the trawler half an hour later, on the fifteen-mile radar scan. She was still heading north, still travelling fast, and confirmation came in a flurry of cursing protests over the fishing-band radio as she carved a way through a cluster of prawn dredgers.

Twenty minutes later, *Marlin* closed the culprit on a direct-inter-cept course. The trawler, a big, steel-hulled English vessel, turned away to make another try at escaping—then gave up as *Marlin*'s high-speed launch hammered down on her from the west.

The trawler's remaining nets were wet, her fishholds full. The boarding party who searched her ran into a brief flurry of opposition, which cooled when one of *Marlin*'s high-pressure hoses drenched some of the more recalcitrant fishermen.

Then the mood changed. The trawler crew were almost out of to-bacco. They swapped a basket of illegal fish for a carton of *Marlin*'s cigarettes. The chastened skipper, under arrest, turned on a new course which would take him into Stornoway. A petty officer and two seamen from *Marlin* were in the wheelhouse beside him, to make sure he didn't get lost on the way.

Handing over to Ferguson again, Carrick went down to the day cabin to enter a preliminary report in Shannon's log and draft a telex signal for Fleet Support. He still felt an intruder, still felt it wrong that he should be at Shannon's desk as he noted times, positions, and the other basic details which would have to be fleshed out later in some courtroom witness box.

He was left alone. Word had got round to that extent. Even the wardroom steward simply glanced in at the open door and kept moving. But, as he finished, the ship's telephone beside the desk gave an urgent buzz.

Ferguson was on the other end. He sounded unusually puzzled.

"You'd better come up, Carrick," he said without preliminaries. "We're getting some unusual traffic on the fishing band—hell knows what's going on, but they're Port Ard boats."

By the time Carrick got there, Jumbo Wills was also on the bridge. A crackle of voices was coming from the relay speaker overhead.

"Something's wrong all right," said Ferguson. "The radio room's picking up transmissions on the emergency waveband—it sounds like a couple of helicopters are being heaved in from the nearest R.A.F. base."

"Nothing for us?" demanded Carrick.

"Not yet." Ferguson shook his head.

"Jumbo." Carrick turned to Wills. "Signal our position to Search and Rescue. Tell them we're available."

Wills hurried out, and Carrick took a quick glance at the compass binnacle. They were still following patrol pattern. He nodded to the helmsman.

"Come round to sixty degrees."

"Port Ard?" Ferguson frowned as the order was acknowledged and the wheel began to spin. "Shouldn't we wait?"

"We will," said Carrick cryptically. "But in the right direction."

Marlin was heeling round, her wake shaping a long white curve astern, ensign flapping in the breeze. On deck, a few of the more experienced hands already seemed to sense something was going on and had begun glancing up towards the bridge as they worked.

"Let's get more volume on that thing." Carrick screwed up the knob on the speaker box and concentrated on the jumble of disembodied voices.

None were using call sign or procedure. They were men who knew each other, who were too busy with the job in hand.

"Harry," came one shout. "Over to starboard o' you a bit. See it? Might be."

"Aye." The other voice stayed silent. Someone else cut in with a mutter about wreckage that ended in a deafening rasp of static.

"Got it," said the second voice suddenly and clearly. "Just a dam' life jacket. Who's that coming up south of me?"

A new voice cut in. Another boat was joining an obvious search that wasn't getting far.

Jumbo Wills hurried back into the bridge a minute later, his plump, freckled face strangely pale.

"Search and Rescue say they can use us." He stopped, moistened his lips, and stared at Carrick. "It's the *Harmony,* Webb—Jamie Ross's boat. Some sort of explosion aboard and she went straight down."

"Survivors?"

"None reported yet. These"—Wills gestured vaguely at the relay speaker—"there were other boats in the area. I've got coordinates. It's about twelve miles northwest of Port Ard."

"Great." Ferguson broke the brief silence with a grunt. "We're a hell of a long way from there." His lined face wiped of emotion, he glanced at Carrick.

"Increase speed to full ahead. Come round to course zero-five-two," said Carrick. He drew a deep breath as the bridge telegraph levers were flipped. "If Andy Shaw as much as opens his mouth about his damned engines, somebody go down and kick his head in. What about air search?"

"Two helicopters on their way." Wills shook his head. "Not much sense in it, though. In weather like this—"

Carrick nodded. In a calm sea, with boats already in the area, rescue shouldn't have posed a problem.

If there had been anyone left to rescue.

It took almost two hours to reach the position where the *Harmony* had blown up, two hours with *Marlin* pounding along under a blue sky at her full thirty knots capability.

On the way, the exhaust gases gouting from the fishery cruiser's squat funnel began to show more and more traces of oily black smoke, and the first of a thin rain of greasy soot particles started to fall along the afterdeck. The sick injector on the starboard diesel was still working, but under growing protest.

On the bridge, they continued to listen to the voices on the fishing waveband. The searching boats spoke less and less, a sure sign that hopes were already fading. For as long as he could, Carrick kept a tight rein on his anxious impatience. Then, when Ferguson at last reported he had their pattern on the radar ten-mile scan, he gave in.

"Call them up," he ordered. "Find out what's going on."

Ferguson used the bridge handset. It seemed inevitable that the skipper he made contact with was Hugh Campbell of the *Cailinn*, the purse-netter on which Gibby MacNeil had died.

"Not much for you to do, *Marlin*," rasped Campbell's voice from the loudspeaker above Carrick's head. "All we've got is three dead and some wreckage—we're still looking, but there's not much hope."

"No survivors?" asked Ferguson over the handset.

"None," answered Campbell. "Not yet, an' I wouldn't count on any. I saw her blow up, *Marlin*—from a mile away. One moment she was there, the next she'd damned well gone."

"How about the helicopters?" demanded Ferguson.

"They're here. One about ready to leave wi' the dead we've got. The other says he'll stay for a bit." Campbell broke off for a moment, then came back on the air. "We've maybe got another body, *Marlin*. Back to work, eh?"

The loudspeaker was left with a hiss of static.

A little later, the bridge lookouts saw a solitary helicopter flying a regular search pattern over the sea. A few minutes more and the fishing boats on the same task were visible ahead. As *Marlin* closed the gap, the helicopter, a big R.A.F. Wessex, abandoned its pattern and flew towards them. Coming down low, it positioned itself level with the fishery cruiser's bridge. The helicopter pilot waved a greeting from his cockpit, then shook his head and gave a deliberate thumbs-down sign.

"That's it," said Carrick in a flat, controlled voice as the machine rose again, beating its way towards the mainland. He looked around him. Ferguson was busy with the bridge glasses, studying the pattern of craft ahead. Jumbo Wills and Clapper Bell were both standing near the helmsman, and an additional petty officer was waiting in the background. Slowly he shook his head. "It's over. Keep one boat ready for lowering. Secure the rest."

Some of the fishing boats had given up and had gone by the time *Marlin* arrived. All three that remained were Port Ard boats, and even they had abandoned any real pretence of continuing their search.

Marlin joined them. Engines cut back to a murmur, making little more than steerage way, the fishery cruiser circled a thin, spreading oil slick and the drifting flotsam which bobbed in and around it. Caught in her faint wash, the remains of a hatch cover heaved and bubbled air for a moment, then settled deeper. On deck, watching,

Marlin's crew stood silent as they passed the few barely identifiable fragments of wreckage which had once been the *Harmony*.

Easing close to Hugh Campbell's *Cailinn*, the fishery cruiser stopped. Fenders took the first contact as *Marlin*'s steel hull touched the side of the smaller craft. Climbing down a ladder, Carrick jumped for the fishing boat as they touched again. Campbell himself was one of the fishermen who grabbed and steadied him as he landed.

"A bad day, Chief Officer," said Campbell. He led the way to the wheelhouse, then, once inside, leaned his elbows on the tiny wooden instrument panel and frowned out through the glass in front of him towards the lazy, rippling waves. "Man, there never was much hope. But we had to try, eh?"

"Tell me about it," said Carrick.

"From the beginning?" Campbell shrugged. "We left Port Ard this morning—most of the local boats came out. None of us had much luck for long enough, then suddenly a few of us picked up a real run —layer on layer o' mackerel, a damned great shoal of the fish."

"The *Harmony* was with you?"

"Not at the start, but she joined in. Jamie had been reasonably near and heard the radio chat." Campbell's weather-beaten face tightened at the memory. "Anyway, there were half a dozen boats at work, all scoring with every shot o' the nets. Then—well, it just happened. The *Harmony* just blew up. One moment she was there, the next and she'd gone."

"No warning, no distress call?" Carrick fought to keep his voice level. All through *Marlin*'s dash to the scene he'd kept a tight grip on a personal, horrifying doubt and suspicion. One that made him feel sick to even contemplate. For the moment he had to stay with fact. "Nothing?"

"No." Slowly, Campbell shook his head. "Hell, man, Jamie himself was talking to me on the radio minutes before it."

"About what?"

"Just joking. About how every time he had his kid sister aboard they were bound to be lucky."

"Katie?" Carrick stared at him. "Katie was with him?"

"Aye." Campbell seemed to go suddenly hoarse. He cleared his throat gruffly. "You didn't know? She had a day off work or something—an' bad leg and everything, that girl loved the sea." He paused, then added softly, "Her body was the first we picked up—

then two more. Old Bert MacPherson, and a lad, Willie Campbell—
no relation o' mine, thank God."

The wheelhouse door swung open. A young deckhand came in,
gravely handed each of them a mug of dark, sweet tea, then left
again without a word. Carrick was glad of the interruption. It gave
him a moment to recover from the new shock, to steady his voice
again.

"Jamie?" he asked. "Did you find him?"

"No." Campbell took a gulp of tea and wiped his mouth with the
back of his hand. "He and another two with him—the sea has them
somewhere." He looked out through the wheelhouse glass again, then
added softly, "Aye, and will keep them until she decides we can have
them—the way it always is."

Carrick said nothing. It was part of any fisherman's philosophy,
part of the acceptance of peril they took as part of life. But that peril
seldom came with a calm sea and a cloudless sky.

"One of the helicopters took the bodies," said Campbell almost
conversationally. "They're good lads, the helicopter crews." He considered Carrick for a moment. "You tried too, I know—made
damned good time getting here. When it matters, you fishery snoops
aren't too bad."

"But not much help. Not this time." A picture of Katie Ross
crossed Carrick's mind. The way the young, fair-haired girl had
laughed at him and teased him, the way she had refused to accept her
disability as more than a minor annoyance. He chewed his lip. "Skipper, how do you reckon it happened?"

"Me?" Campbell didn't answer straightaway. In the silence of the
wheelhouse, Carrick felt and heard the creak of the *Cailinn*'s hull as
she was nuzzled by the swell. Outside, he could see some of *Marlin*'s
crew leaning over the rail of the fishery cruiser, talking to the fishermen below them.

"It could have been inboard—the fuel tank maybe." Campbell
looked as doubtful as he sounded. "Mind you, if I had to bet on it,
I'd say an old wartime mine." He scowled a quick challenge at Carrick. "Man, I saw the way she blew up. That's as likely as anything—
they bring up a mine in their nets, they don't see it till too late. Why
not? It's happened before."

"Yes." Carrick knew it had. All the long years since the end of
World War II, and it was still commonplace for a fishing boat to
howl for help because she had an old, drifting, totally lethal mine
tangled in her nets. At that, they were still lucky. A drifting mine,

broken from its mooring in some long-forgotten storm, was a rogue killer. Boats had been sunk that way. Others had simply vanished, their fate a mystery but with the same suspicion in the background.

"Still, how the hell would I know?" Campbell said. "It happened, they're dead. Does the rest matter hellish much to any family they have ashore? It won't bring them back, mister."

The wheelhouse radio squawked, the voice a low mutter. Campbell listened and nodded to himself.

"The other lads want to head home." He looked at Carrick and shrugged. "We might as well, now. We've got fish to land—and folk who'll be waiting."

Carrick left the fishing boat the way he'd come. By the time he'd reached *Marlin*'s deck, the *Cailinn* was already under way, steering a course to join the other two Port Ard boats.

"Sir." Clapper Bell was at his elbow when he turned from the rail. For once, the Glasgow-Irishman's rugged face looked strained. "Is it right about Ross's sister? Those blokes on the *Cailinn* say—"

"She's dead," said Carrick. "They found her. They didn't get Jamie."

"She wasn't much more than a kid." Bell made it a hurt, bitter protest. "A helluva nice kid. Maybe her brother was an idiot at the edges, but she was—"

"Fairly special," said Carrick.

He left Bell and went up to the bridge. They'd heard there too, and both Wills and Ferguson faced him gravely.

"How much water under us?" he asked.

"We're on the sixty-fathom line," answered Wills. He frowned, uncertain. "You're not going down? I mean—"

"Nobody's going down. Not right now," said Carrick. "I want a marker buoy at that oil slick, then bring aboard some of the bigger chunks of wreckage floating around it. Your job, Jumbo."

Wills nodded and hurried off.

"I met the girl, of course," said Ferguson. He left it at that. "Are we off patrol?"

"Yes." Carrick answered more brusquely than he meant. "We're going back to Port Ard."

Ferguson raised an eyebrow. "Going to clear it with anyone first?"

"No," said Carrick grimly. "Just send a signal telling them that's where we'll be." He fixed Ferguson with a deliberate glare. "If anyone argues—"

"We've got engine trouble," suggested Ferguson. He sniffed hard.

"Half a truth is better than a downright lie—most of the time, anyway."

It took about half an hour before they got under way again. A marker buoy floated beside the oil slick, and the sodden collection of salvaged flotsam taken aboard was locked in a 'tween-decks storeroom.

Headquarters had acknowledged their signal, nothing more. The only other message to come in had been from Stornoway radio, to report that the trawler they'd arrested that morning had arrived in port and was now officially detained.

And by then, Carrick had broken his own self-imposed rule. He had gone down to Shannon's day cabin. The door closed, he sat in one of the armchairs, let his head go back, and closed his eyes. Thinking, asking himself the same question over and over.

He'd used Ross's van, a little vehicle so customised that most people in Port Ard could identify it at a glance. He'd had it when he went out to Maxwell's cottage. All right, he'd hidden it, hidden it far enough away to feel certain it wouldn't be spotted.

But he might have been wrong. Could it have been spotted, recognised, as he made his escape? If that had happened, then John Maxwell could have decided Jamie Ross was spying on him, spying on whatever linked the happenings on Targe Island, at Port Ard, and much more into a strange, deadly chain.

Put that together, and was it any kind of coincidence that the *Harmony* had blown up about twelve hours later?

He thought it over yet again, despairingly. Because if that was what had happened, he had condemned Katie Ross, Jamie, and four totally innocent fishermen to death.

The feel of *Marlin* coming alive and moving got him on his feet. He opened the locker where Shannon kept his whisky, poured himself a drink, took the first swallow neat, then added water to the rest. Using the intercom phone above Shannon's desk, he punched buttons until he finally located Clapper Bell in the petty officers' mess.

"Come through, will you?" he asked and hung up.

He had a drink poured for Bell when he arrived.

"Thanks." Bell lifted the glass but didn't raise it to his lips. Instead, he eyed Carrick carefully. "Trouble?"

"Last night." Carrick chose his words deliberately. "You said Jamie Ross wasn't at the poker session all the time. What did you mean?"

"That he came late an' left early. He wasn't with us more than an hour." Bell frowned and waited.

"Any hint where he'd been, or where he was going?" Carrick kept his voice flat and level.

"No." Bell looked at the whisky in his glass, swirled it, and pursed his lips. "But I could maybe make a guess, if it helps."

Carrick nodded. "Anything might."

"It was a mutter I heard, between a couple of the other fishing skippers." Bell gave an enigmatic twist of a grin. "Maybe Jamie Ross used his scuba gear for more than just fun an' games."

"Meaning?"

"It's been a good season for lobsters along most of the coast—except around here. Funny thing is, it just happens now an' again."

"What happens?" Carrick grew impatient.

"One line of creels will have a good catch. The next line won't have a single lobster trapped. Like someone either hauled them up an' emptied them during the night or—"

"Or someone in scuba gear came poaching?" Carrick swallowed hard. "They suspected Ross?"

"Some of them wondered. It's been pretty small-scale, not enough to cause any kind of war—but lobsters fetch a good price." Bell cleared his throat deliberately. "What is it you're trying to put together, sir? It wouldn't be a reason why the *Harmony* blew up?"

"Yes," said Carrick quietly.

"There's good lobster fishing off Targe Island," mused Bell. His voice was empty of emotion, but his eyes were hard and cold. "He could have been out there last night and been seen—in the wrong place, at the wrong time."

"Before the poker session or after?"

Bell shrugged. "Before, I'd reckon. I hadn't thought much about it till now, but that long, fair hair of his was—well, damp-looking. Like when someone washes his hair an' just towels it dry." Suddenly, he took a long gulp of whisky from his glass and scowled. "Look, what else is wrong? Don't try to fog me—what's this really about?"

Carrick looked at him grimly. "The chance I was the reason the *Harmony* was blown up. When I was at Maxwell's place last night, I used the Rosses' van."

Bell blinked. "Didn't you reckon you weren't recognised, that the van was far enough away?"

"Maybe I was wrong."

"It was supposed to be Captain Shannon who got his brains

scrambled." Outraged, Clapper Bell swore under his breath. "Look, stop feelin' sorry for yourself. You said Jamie Ross was going to pick up that van last night from the Fisheries Office. Right?"

Carrick nodded.

"He didn't," said Bell emphatically. "It was still there when I came back from the poker session—and it was still there when we left Port Ard at that godawful uncivilised hour this morning. I saw it."

"You're sure?" Carrick felt a wave of relief sweep over him. The jumbled pieces came together in his mind in a new, totally possible way. "He'd use the dinghy with the outboard he kept at their cottage. Suppose he'd been out, came into harbour with it afterwards—yes, he'd want to sail it back home when he left the game!"

"Right." Clapper Bell gave a long sigh, finished his drink and looked significantly at the empty glass. "That's the Old Man's whisky we're drinking, isn't it?"

"Yes." Carrick pushed the bottle across. "But you've earned a refill." He managed a brief, lopsided grin, then his mouth tightened. "We're going to nail them, Clapper. Every last damned one of them, beginning with Maxwell."

"I'll drink to that," said Bell, a good four fingers of neat whisky in his glass. His expression softened for a moment. "You know, there really was something special about that girl—an' I only spoke to her once." He paused, sipped his drink, and looked at Carrick over the glass. "How about if those Russians on the *Zarakov* are involved? Does that worry you?"

"No."

"Fair enough." Bell grinned at him. "But go carefully, eh? Who the hell wants to start World War III?"

The weather began to change as they neared Port Ard. First the sky clouded over from the northwest. It became colder and a thin grey bank of sea mist began to roll in, patchy, swirling lazily, broken in places. Targe Island was a hazy shape to starboard. The mainland cliff, with its matching ruins, was obliterated at sea level, then suddenly appeared, sharp and clear from about thirty feet up.

Boats were still moving. The lookouts saw some, vague shapes that appeared out of nowhere and answered the warning whoop of *Marlin*'s siren with a cheeky Klaxon bray. Others were simply contact blips on the radar screen.

They reached harbour and berthed. From the fishery cruiser's bridge, Webb Carrick looked out at a village where even the weather seemed to be mourning.

By religion and upbringing, West Highlanders tried hard not to wear grief on their sleeves. But the signs were still there—from the lonely flag, hanging limp at half-mast on the pole at the harbour master's office, to the drawn blinds at some of the little cottages along the shore.

The harbour was still working, but with a subdued air. He saw the *Cailinn* and the other boats which had taken part in the search were already tied up at the other quayside. Small groups of fishermen stood talking, ignoring the cold and the damping mist. It would be the same in the village. Port Ard had been hurt, stunned. But its weeping would be private.

"Sir." The helmsman, who had been patiently waiting for word he could go, cleared his throat apologetically, then gestured down to where *Marlin*'s gangway was being run ashore. "Visitors."

A police car was murmuring to a halt. Sergeant Ballantyne got out of the driver's door. The first of his passengers was a stranger in civilian clothes topped by a loose, flapping anorak jacket. But as the remaining passenger emerged, Carrick stiffened.

Tall, thin, immaculate in a dark business suit, carrying a government-issue briefcase, Captain Robert Dobie stood for a moment while he made an anything but cursory consideration of *Marlin*'s length. Then, nodding to his two companions, the Marine Superintendent of the Fisheries Protection Squadron briskly led the way aboard.

Hurrying down, Carrick met his visitors on the foredeck. A flushed and flustered Jumbo Wills was already there, with an equally anxious petty officer hovering in the background.

"Unannounced, I know." Captain Dobie acknowledged Carrick's salute with a slight nod, then looked pointedly aft. "Been chimney-sweeping, Carrick? Things look pretty grubby back there."

"Injector trouble, sir." Carrick cursed the Marine Superintendent's sharp eyes. "We had other priorities."

"Naturally. That's why we're here. We'll talk in the day cabin."

"Sir." Carrick led the way, managing a sideways glance at Jumbo Wills. Wills gave a fractional nod—if the Marine Superintendent turned his visit into an inspection tour, every department aboard would be ready.

They reached the day cabin, the stranger close behind Dobie, an unusually worried-looking Sergeant Ballantyne a respectful couple of paces to the rear. Still buttoning a clean white jacket, the steward was at the door.

"Hanson, isn't it?" said Dobie. "Family well?"

"Yes, sir."

"Good. See we're not disturbed." Dobie waved him aside.

They went in. Carrick closed the cabin door and Dobie, tossing his briefcase on Shannon's desk, took the nearest chair. He waited until the others were settled, then began.

"Introductions first." He barely glanced at Ballantyne. "Carrick, you know the local police sergeant?"

Carrick nodded. Ballantyne shifted uncomfortably but said nothing.

"Right." Dobie indicated the stranger, a stockily built middle-aged man with a sad face, a small moustache and big, brown, spaniel-like eyes. "This is Detective Chief Inspector Johns—we shared a damned uncomfortable helicopter ride to get here, then Ballantyne picked us up. Johns is a Special Branch—ah—person."

"Who prefers wheels." The stranger gave a mild smile. "Adam Johns—I'm not particularly important, Chief Officer. I just get sent anywhere there's a mess."

"Like now," said Dobie. He brought out a small leather cigar case, selected a thin black cheroot, and lit it with a match. "I reckoned you'd head for Port Ard come hell or high water, Carrick. But I was glad when your signal confirmed it." He drew on the cheroot, frowning. "Well, we've got problems. More than I realised at the beginning."

"I had that feeling," said Carrick.

"And that nobody cared?" Dobie raised an eyebrow. "Chief Officer, if you expect me to encourage radio chitchat when you're practically sitting in the lap of a Russian electronic spyship, the kind that can probably monitor what you had for breakfast, you can think again. Agreed, Johns?"

"He's right." The Special Branch man nodded.

"Exactly." Dobie indicated Ballantyne. "I brought the sergeant along for two reasons—first, obviously, the local police are involved. In addition, he knows Port Ard—and local opinion about what happened to the *Harmony*."

"Most people think she hit a floating mine," said Ballantyne. He shrugged. "A few have other notions, but a floating mine is favourite."

"The rescue skippers went for that," agreed Carrick. He caught

Captain Dobie's warning glance and didn't press the point. "How are the crew's families?"

The village sergeant shook his head, his large face unhappy.

"The way you'd expect. Two of the men were married, one had children. Any dependents will be looked after, of course, the usual way."

Carrick nodded. A fishing community looked after its own, was too used to tragedy to regard it as exceptional.

"How about Mrs. Ross?"

"Hit hard. Mrs. Jordan is with her, and I heard Dr. Blair was in early on. Losing a son's bad enough, but the girl—"

He stopped. There was an awkward silence in the room, finally, deliberately broken by Dobie.

"The—ah—recovered bodies were flown inland. Postmortems at Inverness, then—well, back here for burial, I suppose." He frowned. "We'll have to wait on the others. Bad for the families, but incidental."

"To us," said Carrick softly.

"Exactly." The Marine Superintendent nodded. "Our feelings can wait." He looked at Ballantyne. "Thank you, Sergeant. Why don't you take that walk around the harbour we talked about? Spread the word that Chief Inspector Johns is just another damned government official, up to make some kind of a report."

"Sir." Obediently, but with some reluctance, Ballantyne got to his feet. At the cabin door he stopped, looked at Carrick, gave a slight shrug, then left.

"Now," said Dobie as the door closed again. "Let's get to the meat of it. Nothing wrong with our village sergeant—Johns ran him through a computer before we left. But there's no sense in burdening him—not for the moment."

"Though he may not see it that way," said Johns. His sad, spaniel eyes showed a suspicion of a twinkle. "From his record, Ballantyne is no fool. But if he wants to consider us a pair of bastards, there's no harm in it." He sat back. "Go ahead with the chat, Captain—I'll listen."

"Thank you." The Marine Superintendent was chillingly polite. Getting up, he went over to the rubber plant in the corner and deliberately flicked the ash from his cheroot into the pot. Then he turned. "Right, Carrick. I've already heard James Shannon's story—and he's alive, well, and currently creating havoc in a certain Edinburgh hospital. They've had to hide his damned trousers to keep him in. Now it's your turn. From the beginning—I want the lot."

"There's a lot of it, sir," warned Carrick.

"I take my motto from the Bible, mister. Luke eighteen, verse eleven—'God, I thank Thee that I am not as other men are.' Meaning I'm patient. Go ahead."

From the beginning took time, but Carrick recited through it while his audience listened, Dobie sometimes frowning, holding himself from interrupting, Johns sitting relaxed, as if almost asleep, but making an occasional tooth-sucking noise.

"Damn it to hell," said Dobie at the end.

"Ditto," agreed the Special Branch man. He stirred and sat more or less upright. "All right, let's buy the basics—that this old fisherman MacNeil was murdered, that your dead frogman was up to something peculiar, this character Maxwell and all the rest—including the Targe Island business. Then, because this young idiot Ross stuck his nose in too far, somebody stuffed a bomb aboard the *Harmony?*"

Carrick nodded.

"Plus a few hundred Russians on the edges. Great." Johns lapsed into silence again.

"Carrick." Captain Dobie was prowling the cabin again as he spoke. "You accept you've got damned little in the way of real evidence?"

"Except for eight dead." Carrick met his glare steadily. "And it could have been nine."

"Nine?" Dobie blinked, then understood. "Shannon—yes, of course. But what matters now is catching someone actually doing something—any damned thing. Maxwell's people or the Russians."

"Better still, both together," said Johns. "My people are already trying to run a check on Maxwell." He shrugged. "One problem is that it's as if he didn't exist—not until he appeared up here. We'll try his tame sidekick, Renfrew. He might be easier."

"And there's no obvious security situation," said Dobie. "According to the Navy, the nearest sensitive area is a good distance south of here, in the Sound of Raasay—you know about that?"

"Underwater missiles." Carrick nodded. The whole area around the sound had been closed to fishing for months. He knew the Navy had high-speed patrol boats to make sure it stayed that way.

"Seabed hydrophones, acoustic torpedoes, air-dropped Stingray missiles. No, it's not there—the Navy say there's a Soviet submarine, a Whisky class, sitting on the bottom nearby pretending to be part of the scenery. They're leaving her alone—and a squad of Intelligence boffins are having the time of their lives letting her intercept phoney information." Dobie scowled at the digression. "You feel whatever is happening here is still an active affair?"

"It has to be," said Carrick. "Someone's running too many risks." He looked at Johns. "Ashore, our main lead is Maxwell. If we kept tabs on him—"

"You've got it," said Johns. "Soon as some of my educated young thugs arrive. Captain Dobie says you're some kind of diving expert. Couldn't you drop down and take a look at what's left of the *Harmony*, find out what did happen to her?"

"She's in sixty fathoms," said Carrick. "We could get down, yes. But we'd have to locate her—and the hull must have been blasted apart, scattered."

"Exactly," said Dobie. "Stick to being a land animal, Johns. Yes, it could be done. But you're talking of a lot of time, a salvage ship, a lot more." He sniffed. "I imagine it will have to be done later. But right now? We might as well advertise there's something wrong."

The Special Branch man shrugged. "Sorry. I'm just a simple cop."

"We did bring in some wreckage we found floating," Carrick volunteered. "Get it to a laboratory and—"

"More time," said Dobie impatiently.

"The other thing we've got to do is keep tabs on our Russians," said Johns. He tried again. "How about sneaking some kind of small boat into this Loch Armach by night, to keep an eye on the ship?"

"Forget it," snapped Dobie. "The *Zarakov*'s kind of radar can pick up a floating seabird." He looked worried. "Though we need something—"

"Targe Island," suggested Carrick. "If we land a couple of men on it with a radio—"

"Better—a lot better." Dobie seized on the notion. "We could use that damned island like a mousetrap."

"If the cheese is still there," said Johns. "If it ever *was* there." He got to his feet. "I've things to do. What about you, Dobie?"

The Marine Superintendent shook his head. "I'll stay a few moments."

"Sailor talk?" Johns gave one of his sad, spaniel-eyed smiles. "Meet you at the car then—I want to find Sergeant Ballantyne. Use him as your contact, Carrick."

He left them. As the cabin door closed, Dobie gave a grunt of relief.

"Some practicalities, Carrick." Beckoning, he led the way over to Shannon's desk, opened his briefcase, and unfolded a chart. "Depending on what develops, you may need backup—our kind, another fishery cruiser." He moved a finger lightly and quickly. *"Hammerhead,* with Captain Stanton, is moving round from the Outer Isles. She'll lie just north of your patrol area—about here, around Cape Wrath."

Carrick nodded. He knew Stanton, unimaginative but totally reliable. The open Atlantic lay to the north, and trouble, coming or going, was most likely to use that route.

"South—well, *Swordfish* is working down there anyway. If things really get critical, the Navy have a frigate handy at Stornoway—they'd love to get involved." Dobie stubbed what was left of his cheroot in an ashtray. "But that only happens over my dead body. Or to be more precise, yours."

"Yes, sir."

"Quite." Dobie folded the chart and tucked it away. Then he considered Carrick pensively. "James Shannon has a high regard for your capabilities. That's one reason I'm leaving you in the middle of this despite your—well, lack of command experience." He paused. "You still haven't answered my letter about the *Barracuda,* have you?"

"No, sir." Carrick shook his head.

"Why not?"

"I thought I had till the end of the month," said Carrick warily.

"True." Dobie seemed satisfied. "Well, I won't hang around your neck here. It wouldn't look good. I'll talk to Chief Inspector Johns again, ashore, then get back to that damned helicopter. The best help I can give you is to be available but to coordinate from Headquarters." Unexpectedly, he touched Carrick on the arm. "The only advice I can give you is that you're in a situation more likely to bring kicks than medals."

Turning, Dobie picked up his briefcase. As he lifted it he knocked something from the desk to the deck. Stooping, he picked it up and raised an interested eyebrow.

"What's this?"

It was the embroidered canvas Shannon had brought from Gibby MacNeil's cottage. Carrick smiled. The steward, tidying, must have moved it to the desk.

"Gibby MacNeil made them. Captain Shannon saw it."

"Not bad." Dobie considered the delicate needlework. "In fact, very pleasant. The sailing ship is good. Ever try your hand at this?"

"No, sir."

"Soothing." Dobie examined the canvas again. "Odd design, this black pattern round the edge. Varied, yet regular."

Carrick nodded dutifully.

"Unusual design. Like little broken flagpoles, eh?" Suddenly, Dobie swore and stared. "In fact—yes, they are. You're sure MacNeil did this?"

"It looked like he'd just finished." Carrick was puzzled.

"Then take another look," snapped Dobie. He moistened his lips. "It's semaphore, man—a damned semaphore message. Little men wagging flags. That's not a pattern, it's a message."

Carrick felt sick. Standing close to Dobie, he peered at the pattern. The Marine Superintendent was right.

"I didn't think—"

"No. Your generation is all radio chat and electronics." Dobie was concentrating as he spoke. "MacNeil's generation, my generation, we didn't have it so easy." He stopped and stood scowling. "But it's a damned jumble of lettering."

"Some kind of code?"

"Has to be. There's a pattern; it's not random and I'd say the work was hurried, not as neat as the rest." Dobie straightened up. "Well, maybe we've got the answer to that. Get John Ferguson here."

"Sir?"

"Ferguson," said Dobie. "Your Junior Second, if I've got to spell it out, mister. Get him."

Carrick used the ship's telephone. A minute or so passed, then Ferguson entered. He glanced at Carrick, then turned to Dobie, his lined face stubbornly disinterested.

"Sir?"

"John." Dobie beckoned him over. "I've something for you here. Your old speciality"—he held up a hand before Ferguson could say anything—"I know. But it matters."

Silently, Ferguson examined the canvas for a moment.

"Who worked it?" he asked.

"Gibby MacNeil," Carrick told him.

Ferguson nodded, picked up a pencil and paper from the desk, then glanced at Dobie again.

"You'll wait?"

Dobie nodded.

For the next two or three minutes Ferguson scribbled, now and again checking back. A strange noise came from his lips. He was humming a tune. Finally he paused, read over what he'd done, then gave an unexpected chuckle.

"Simple—with someone like MacNeil, it had to be. It's not a code, it's a trick, one of the oldest." Ferguson tapped pencil on paper. "You write your message, push the words together without spacing, break the whole thing into four-letter groups, and stick an additional letter between each—he used Y. Schoolboy stuff, but effective."

"Then you've got it?" asked Dobie softly.

Ferguson nodded and passed over the paper. Dobie and Carrick together read the message which had been hidden in the embroidery work.

"J.S.—MAXWELL TRUCKS CARRYING HIDDEN PACK-AGES IN FISH RUNS S. AND EX-UK. RUSSES MAYBE INVOLVED. TARGE LOBSTER CREELS MATTER. THIS FOR INSURANCE AS MAXWELL MAY SUS ME. G."

"Thank you, John," said Dobie.

"Easy enough, sir. I—uh—tidied his spelling a little." Ferguson shuffled his feet. "Is that all?"

Dobie nodded. Laying down the pencil, taking a last glance at the embroidery work, Ferguson padded out.

"So now we know," said Dobie almost to himself. "Or know some of it, eh?"

"Yes." Carrick drew a deep breath and indicated the door. "But—"

"Ferguson?" Dobie shook his head. "Don't ask—one or two of us just know a little more about him and what he used to be. So forget it—that's an order." He considered the message again. "And this is what matters."

"Like being a motive for murder?"

Dobie nodded. "Among other things. The rest of it?"

"It depends what they're smuggling." Carrick paused, trying to put it together. "I'd say he only knew so much, was trying to guess more of it."

"And the lobster creels?"

"Would make sense." Carrick suddenly felt on surer ground. "Mr. A puts down a line of lobster creels—say, off Targe Island—by day. Mr. B comes along at night, lifts them, puts them back down with a package in each, ready for collection."

"No direct contact. And if Mr. *C*—your Jamie Ross—picked the wrong line of creels when he went poaching—"

It fitted, totally.

It was clever too. A refrigerated container truck from the lonely North of Scotland, a truck apparently loaded with only frozen fish, was about the last thing on wheels likely to be stopped or searched—even by the most diligent of customs officers.

"But what the hell are they moving?" muttered Dobie. "And if the *Zarakov* is involved—" He shook his head despairingly. "I'll tell Chief Inspector Johns. It won't make him any happier." He looked at Carrick. "For our side of it, you've got *Marlin*. Use her."

CHAPTER 7

What was left of a damp, mist-shrouded afternoon passed busily. *Marlin* had to refuel, which meant shifting to the bunkering jetty. Brought aboard and connected, the thick, slippery hoses began pumping their metered oil while the depot manager hung around hoping for a wardroom drink.

Carrick left Ferguson to cope with it. A small queue of people wanted his attention, with Andy Shaw first in line.

"It's that damned injector," explained Shaw. "I need working time on it."

"How long?"

"For a proper job, three hours."

"No way." Carrick shook his head firmly. "Two hours—then we're going out on engine trials."

"Eh?" Shaw stared at him.

"Two hours," repeated Carrick. "Andy, I've a reason—a damned good one."

"If you put it that way." The Chief Engineer gave a gloomy, resigned nod. "But don't look for any six-month guarantee."

Shaw left. Men from different departments took his place, with a string of minor requests or problems. Carrick shelved most of them, turned down any notion of shore leave, left Jumbo Wills to do what he could about the rest, and finally went aft to see Clapper Bell in the scuba compartment.

"I want you to take a run ashore for me, Clapper," he said without preliminaries. "You'll need a reason—Jumbo Wills has ship's mail that needs posting."

"Right." Bell set aside a piece of wire tackle he was splicing, spat on his hands, and rubbed them with a rag. "What am I really doin'?"

"Make complaining noises that I'm taking *Marlin* out for engine trials for a spell this evening. I want the word to get around." Carrick paused and eyed Bell soberly. "Then, the part that matters—

John Maxwell is interested in a line of lobster creels. I want to know exactly where they are."

"Shouldn't be too difficult." Bell nodded, unperturbed. "Anything else?"

"When you get back, get things ready for a night dive—both of us."

"Like along that lobster line?" Bell stopped and frowned. "Wait a minute—you're not diving. You've a ship to run."

Carrick waited.

"Look," said Bell patiently, "I can handle it—no problems. Why should there be?"

"If you're sure." Carrick gave in reluctantly. It meant breaking their normal safety code, but there was no alternative. The only other man aboard with scuba experience was Jumbo Wills, and he was at the beginner stage.

"I'm sure." Bell glanced at his watch. "When do I go ashore?"

They left it until *Marlin* had finished refuelling and had returned to her berth on the quayside. When she got there a small truck with Fisheries Department badges on the doors was waiting. The driver had orders to collect the pieces of wreckage recovered from the *Harmony*.

Bell went ashore as the collection of broken debris was transferred to the vehicle. The driver gave a receipt when the job was done, then drove off. His destination was many miles away, a marine test engineering laboratory at Aberdeen. If he was lucky, he'd get there before midnight.

A little later, Carrick left the ship. It would soon be dusk and the same damp, dismal mist still clung in sad wisps everywhere. He saw hardly a soul as he walked out of the harbour, and the Fisheries Office was closed and deserted.

Port Ard itself was equally quiet, still shocked and mourning its loss. Most of the little shops were closed, only a few people were out and about. Some were fishermen, and he noticed the way their mood had changed. Where before there had been occasional underlying hostility, they now went by with a quiet nod of greeting.

They knew of *Marlin*'s dash. Even though it hadn't been successful, even though it was what they would have expected, it was a reminder that in some situations they had a common cause.

When he reached the clinic, it was open. Going in, he stopped in the well-lit reception area and spoke to the nurse he'd met the previous day. She was pleasant but firm. Dr. Blair was with a patient. She didn't know how long it would be, but there was a waiting room.

It was empty. He sat down, picked up a months-old magazine, and tried to get interested in an article on the feeding habits of the African crocodile. At last the door opened and Jan Blair came in. She was wearing her white medical coat, she looked tired, but she gave him a subdued, welcoming smile.

"I'm clear now," she said with some relief. "Come on through, Webb."

She led the way to her consulting room, closed the door, and gave a sigh as she settled back behind her desk. Taking the chair opposite, Carrick said, "You've had a rough day."

"Yes." Jan Blair brought her fingertips together, as if building a small steeple, and let her chin rest on them. "Most of it feeling helpless—handing out sympathy, platitudes, and tranquillisers." She pursed her lips. "Every one of the *Harmony*'s people was local."

"I know." He hesitated. "How is Mrs. Ross?"

"Resting. Thank heaven for Alexis Jordan—she's staying with her until one of her sisters arrives." She paused. "Katie was probably her favourite. But until they find Jamie's body—"

Carrick said nothing. It was often that way. Death could be accepted, but death with that additional, tragic dimension came worse.

"Webb." Those grey eyes met his own seriously. "You were there —soon afterwards, I mean. The way it happened—was it a floating mine?"

"We've no proof of anything." He said it harshly, without intention. "Not there, anyway."

Horror showed on her face as his meaning sank in. She sat upright, biting her lip.

"Six people—"

"We've no proof," he repeated.

"But something else has happened?"

"Gibby MacNeil." He told her the rest and she shook her head, almost despairingly.

"I spoke to the pathologist by telephone. I won't say I convinced him, but he's willing to run some extra tests, consider things again, take a different approach."

"How long will it take?"

"That depends." Jan Blair paused, absently flicking back a lock of her long, fair hair. "A suspicious death widens the options, Webb.

When you get into that kind of situation, the same set of postmortem factors can be read different ways—"

"Until you check the fine print?"

She nodded. "He said he'd work late on it, call me back sometime tonight. Is *Marlin* staying in harbour?"

"Later, yes—unless something happens." He left it at that. "You'll be here?"

"I'm not planning anything else."

"Good." Carrick got to his feet. "I thought I'd go out to the Rosses' cottage." He saw her frown. "I'll be gentle. That's a promise."

Jan Blair sighed and glanced at her watch. "I'll give you a lift. I've a patient to see near there—but you'll have to make your own way back."

Carrick waited while she collected her bag, slipped on an outdoor coat, and locked her desk. Then they left.

Jan Blair's car, a small, tan-coloured Fiat, was parked across the street. It smelled faintly of antiseptic, and the remains of a chocolate bar littered the glove compartment.

She drove in a casual but careful style, saying little about whatever she was thinking. Port Ard's streetlights had come on, each a bright halo in the misty dusk, and the inevitable fish trucks were rumbling in on their empty return journeys from the south.

One was a Maxwell Transport vehicle, headlamps blazing. Carrick watched it pass, the driver slouched behind the wheel. His mouth tightened at the sight. If Gibby MacNeil's embroidered semaphore message was right, the Maxwell trucks were an all-important link in the murderous chain of happenings which had already cost the unsuspecting little village so much.

It had to be stopped. Whatever lay behind it, whatever the extent of any Russian involvement.

When they reached the Rosses' cottage, lights showed at the windows. Jan Blair stopped the Fiat at the side of the road, and Carrick thanked her as he got out. She smiled, then set the little car moving again. As the red taillights faded, Carrick walked down the pebbled lane towards the house.

Then he swore under his breath. Two cars were parked outside— Alexis Jordan's grey Volvo and John Maxwell's black B.M.W. Whatever the reason for Maxwell's visit, it wasn't going to make things any easier.

Alexis Jordan opened the front door when he knocked. She was quietly dressed, wasn't wearing makeup, and looked older than her years.

"You'd better come in," she said, her welcome lukewarm. "But don't make it a long visit. Her sister only arrived five minutes ago."

Carrick followed her into the cottage living room. A peat fire smouldered in the hearth and John Maxwell stood in front of it, warming his back. It was a bright, cheerful room, or it had been. Photographs of Katie Ross and her brother, each in a silver frame, sat on either side of the fireplace mantelpiece.

"Carrick—yes, I expected you'd be out." John Maxwell greeted him with a cool nod, his face suitably grave and his voice a careful murmur. "Bad luck, both of them being aboard—one would have been rough enough."

"Yes." Carrick glanced at Alexis Jordan, who was standing near the doorway. "How did that happen?"

"Katie was due some time off." She gave a vague, helpless gesture, her glance flickering towards Maxwell for a moment. "She tele-phoned me this morning to say she wouldn't be in. She—well, it was Jamie's idea they should have a day together. To patch up a row they'd been having."

"And I won't ask what that was about," said Maxwell. "That only makes me feel worse." He picked up his gloves from a table. "Well, I've done what I came for—told their mother how sorry I am. I'll get on my way."

He nodded to Carrick, and Alexis Jordan went with him to the front door. When she returned, she stood for a moment, saying noth-ing. Then as they heard Maxwell's car start up and draw away, she came to life again.

"How did you get out here?" she asked.

"Jan Blair gave me a lift."

She nodded slowly. "That girl has worked hard today. I—I'll tell Mrs. Ross you're here. Then I can give you a lift back if you want—I don't need to stay now her sister is here."

Alexis Jordan went out. He heard a soft murmur of voices from the rear of the cottage, then she returned, Morag Ross at her side. The older woman's face was puffy from weeping and she moved slowly, as if still caught in a nightmare she didn't totally believe. But she held her head high, with an inborn dignity.

"It was good of you to come, Mr. Carrick," she said quietly. "I appreciate it—and Mrs. Jordan told me how your ship tried to help. You'll tell your crew I'm grateful?"

"Yes, I'll be glad to." Carrick hated what he had to do next. "Your son and daughter were nice people, Mrs. Ross. I know they both loved the sea. In fact, someone was telling me Jamie was out in his dinghy again last night."

"That's true." She managed a quavering smile at the memory. "He'd go out like that, on his own, every now and again and I'd never know when he'd get back. Usually, I'd be in bed."

"Was he late last night?" Carrick kept his voice gentle.

"Well after midnight. I heard the boat come in." Her voice broke and she fought back fresh tears. "I used to worry about him, in that little boat. Yet it's still out there and—and—" She gave up.

Quickly, Alexis Jordan put a comforting arm around the woman's shoulders and scowled at Carrick, jerking her head towards the door.

"I'll be outside," he said softly. "Good-bye, Mrs. Ross."

He left the cottage. On the way out, he passed Morag Ross's sister emerging from a bedroom. She gave him a sad smile and went on towards the living room.

It was peaceful outside. The aroma of peat smoke and the scent of gorse mixed with the salt-air tang from the sea. He walked round the cottage, passing the white Ford van, and went down to the little jetty. Jamie Ross's dinghy was bobbing in the water a few feet away, secured to the jetty's framework by a slack mooring line.

Stooping, Carrick gripped the line and hauled the little boat in. It bumped alongside and he stepped aboard. At the bow, a piece of tarpaulin was tucked round something bulky. He lifted the tarpaulin, and Jamie Ross's scuba-diving outfit lay exposed in the early twilight. The rubber suit, folded carelessly, was still wet at the seams. An old towel was damp to the touch, and the gauge on the big single air cylinder showed it was more than half empty.

There was just one thing more, but it was the clincher. A thin length of line was draped over the side of the dinghy, fastened to a rowlock. When he pulled, it came up dripping water, a small metal and wire mesh cage swaying on the end. A single lobster lay inside, claws snapping angrily.

He let the cage down again, left the dinghy, and walked round to Alexis Jordan's station wagon.

She was already behind the wheel, the car's engine ticking over.

"Where were you?" she demanded as he got aboard.

"Looking around—keeping out of the way," Carrick answered vaguely. He indicated the cottage. "You did a good job there."

"I was fond of Katie. I'll miss her a lot." Alexis Jordan set the Volvo moving. As it crunched over the pebbled track and reached the road, she fumbled one-handed with a pack of cigarettes, then lit one with the dashboard lighter. "Why were you so interested in what Jamie was doing last night?"

"Was I?" asked Carrick mildly.

"Yes. One more question back there and—" she left it unfinished.

Carrick shrugged. "Their van. It wasn't collected from the harbour the way Katie planned."

"I know." She pursed her lips. "He forgot about it. Then, this morning, it meant Katie didn't have transport to come in—at least, not to get to the office on time. That was part of the reason she took the day off."

Part of the reason she had been aboard the *Harmony*. Another small piece in a tragic jigsaw of circumstance which had caused her death. Carrick thought of the other men aboard, probably equally innocent. He watched the Volvo accelerate past a couple of cyclists who were wobbling along without lights.

"How are things between you and Maxwell?" he asked quietly.

"I'd say that was *my* business." Her manner chilled.

"It could be Department business too, Alexis." He caught her quick sideways glance. "I mean it."

"We're still reasonably friendly. But—well, nothing more at the moment." Alexis Jordan kept her voice carefully neutral. "I'm seeing him tonight, but for a good reason. The village is setting up an appeal committee, to raise money for the *Harmony* crew families—we've both been asked to be members."

"I see." The bitter incongruity of it almost made Carrick grimace. "When and where?"

"The Memorial Hall, at nine o'clock." She shrugged. "Some people couldn't make it earlier. I suppose it'll last a couple of hours or so." Her hands tightened on the steering wheel. "May I ask why you're so interested?"

"No."

"Meaning you don't trust me?"

He shook his head. "Meaning I can't tell you—not yet. When I can, I will. Take it like that, Alexis—please."

"Trust." She pronounced the word almost savagely. "That's something I'm beginning to wonder about."

But she nodded.

A few minutes later, after being dropped at the harbour gates, Carrick went back aboard *Marlin*. The fishery cruiser's diesels were murmuring, Andy Shaw was leaning against a companionway door that led down to the engine room.

"Finished?" asked Carrick.

"Thanks to blood, sweat and tears." The Chief Engineer sniffed in studied disgust. "Anything you want for an encore, the odd small miracle?"

"I'll think about it," said Carrick.

Clapper Bell was waiting for him at the chartroom.

"Got what you wanted," reported Bell. "Maxwell does run a string o' lobster creels—it's a bit of a joke around the harbour, because they're out where no one else would bother. Poor lobster territory."

"Where?"

"Here." Bell turned to the chart lying beside him and tapped a stubby forefinger. "Off the southwest end of Targe Island." He grinned at Carrick. "You expected that, right?"

"It figures," said Carrick. He looked at the point marked by Bell's finger. It was moderately close to the Sump overfall, but not too close. The island's bulk sat like a barrier in terms of anyone looking out to sea from Port Ard. A hazy memory of a line of floats bobbing in the area came to his mind. "Think you can find them?"

"No problem," said Bell cheerfully.

Ten minutes after that, *Marlin* nosed her way out of harbour, through a mixture of wisping mist and heavily clouded moonlight. She was brightly lit. Her siren gave a brief, totally unnecessary whoop as she cleared the entrance.

To a casual observer, her progress over the next half hour formed an understandable pattern. At varying speeds, but with only navigation lights showing, *Marlin* carried out a series of runs in the stretch of water between the mainland and Targe Island. Each run took her a little further out from Port Ard. At last, coming down from the north, she was lost to sight behind the island.

Immediately, several things began to happen on the fishery cruiser's deck. She slowed, coming down to steerage way. One of her

small inflatable boats splashed into the moderate swell, then two of
Marlin's seamen clambered aboard and grabbed the two haversacks
which followed them down. One haversack contained a radio. Both
men had been handpicked for the job.

The inflatable drifted away. A brief flash of phosphorescence as
the seamen began to use paddles, then she vanished. *Marlin* moved
on again, at slow ahead, and a trickier moment had come.

Another, larger inflatable was ready. Beside it stood Jumbo Wills
with a petty officer and two men. Wills wore a rubber scuba suit; a
spare set of aqualung gear lay on deck beside Clapper Bell's equipment. It was a compromise. Wills would go down if Clapper Bell hit
real trouble.

On the bridge, extra lookouts in position and Ferguson frowning
over the helmsman's shoulder, Webb Carrick cursed the ragged mist
and wayward moonlight. He waited until they had passed the Sump,
then left it to Ferguson to edge the fishery cruiser in towards the island. Using the bridge glasses, he peered ahead for a moment.

"Clapper?" He spoke over his shoulder. Bell stood behind him,
clad in his diving gear, the dull red night-vision lights of the bridge
area making him look like some visiting demon.

"Has to be soon," said Bell confidently.

Carrick heard Ferguson grunt. Bell's fisherman had given what
seemed an almost foolproof way to locate the lobster line. A needle
peak of rock on the island had to be lined up with a cleft in the distant hills of the mainland. They'd done that. The rest would probably
have been simple enough in daylight, but at night, in this visibility—

"Sir." The lookout on the port wing of the bridge spoke just
loudly enough for his voice to carry. "Object almost dead ahead, fine
on the port bow."

Carrick used the bridge glasses again, and caught a glimpse of a
small float as it rose briefly in the swell. He waited, saw another beyond it, and knew there had to be more.

"We've arrived," he said over his shoulder. "On your way,
Clapper."

Once again *Marlin* came down to steerage way for a brief, tense
moment while the second inflatable splashed down and men scrambled aboard.

Then the fishery cruiser's twin diesels increased their rhythm and
she swung away, leaving the rubber boat drifting in the slapping
wavecrests.

Exactly one hour later, *Marlin* returned. Most of that time was spent in a series of genuine engine trials for Andy Shaw's benefit, testing the serviced injector unit at varying speeds.

At the end of it the engine room made reasonably happy noises. Other things seemed to be going as planned. A brief murmur of a radio signal confirmed that the two men who were to form the watching post on Targe Island had settled into position. Two telex messages, apparently routine, chattered in. *Hammerhead* and *Swordfish*, the backup support promised by Captain Dobie, were at their allotted stations.

Even the latest weather update seemed reasonable. The wind would freshen from the northwest before morning, with clouds and rain. Sea conditions would remain moderate to good.

But Carrick had little to do but wait, and felt every minute crawl past. Ferguson was on the bridge, the radar screen showed an empty sea. He remembered Shannon's restlessness at similar times but avoided his occasional remedy of a prowl around the ship—he'd heard Shannon cursed behind his back too often following that kind of surprise visit.

Eventually, he took to the day cabin and had the steward bring coffee and sandwiches. He ate with little enthusiasm, his thoughts back at that lobster line.

Sometimes a line was called a fleet. Maxwell's line was made up of twelve creels, modest in number when some professional lobster men might use up to fifty. Each surface float led down to a baited, basket-shaped creel with a cement sinker to hold it on the seabed. Made of thin strips of wood and knotted twine, centuries-old in design, a creel formed an eye-ring trap easy for a lobster to enter, difficult, almost impossible, to leave again.

Sometimes the shape or the materials varied. Scottish west-coast creels used hazel wood. It was willow in Cornwall and Brittany, chestnut in the rest of France—only Orcadians and the Dutch perversely used metal hoops, partly because they didn't have many trees around.

None of which was going to matter much to Clapper Bell. Working underwater, using a battery lantern, a thin signalling line connecting him to *Marlin*'s boat above, he was going to have to work his way along from creel to creel.

Both Ferguson and Wills had suggested hauling the creels up, then letting them sink again. But it wasn't so simple. Underwater was

faster, surer, meant no disturbance—and an absolute certainty as to
what lay below.

A job Carrick had had to delegate. He was back on the bridge
when *Marlin* swung back into the shelter of the island. A carefully
shaded light blinked briefly in the darkness ahead, and soon the
inflatable was bumping alongside.

Carrick was on the main deck to greet Bell. As *Marlin* got under
way again, on a curving course which would take her back to Port
Ard, Bell shrugged out of his aqualung harness. Still wet and dripping, he showed his teeth in a slightly puzzled grin.

"No problems?" asked Carrick.

"None—except trying to work out what they're doin' down there,"
said Bell bluntly. "Not one of those creels is baited, sir."

"No?" Carrick thumbed at a large lobster which was wriggling and
snapping at Bell's feet.

"That?" Bell blinked innocently. "It had got into one by mistake—
seemed a shame to waste it."

"What else?" asked Carrick.

"The middle six creels aren't for fishing," said Bell. "They've been
altered—each o' them has an open-and-close door. Stuff something
inside, and it's going to stay there till someone else comes along. It's
a smuggling line—no doubt about it."

"Then we got that part right," said Carrick. "What else?"

"This." Bell fumbled in a pocket of his suit. "It was caught inside
one of the altered creels."

Carrick took the find, a ragged strip of thick black waterproof
plastic. It had no markings and seemed to have been ripped from the
rest of its sheet by sheer force.

"Could be they're into the drug-smuggling game," suggested Bell.
"Except—well, how would the Ruskies fit in?"

Carrick nodded. That was the extra factor, the explosive complication that had to be discovered and defused—whatever else happened.

"Yes, could be drugs," said Chief Inspector Johns another half
hour later. The Special Branch man had come aboard as soon as
Marlin had berthed at Port Ard. Alone with Johns in the day cabin,
Carrick had brought him up to date. Nursing the glass of whisky in
his hand, Johns frowned at the roll repeater on the cabin bulkhead.
"What does that thing do?"

"Tells the captain when his ship is going to capsize," said Carrick.

"Interesting." Johns gave one of his sad-eyed smiles. "Drugs now—yes, it's possible—a nice easy way to keep an intelligence network in funds. Particularly if you're short of hard currency. It wouldn't be a first time. Weapons?" He shook his head. "Also possible, but doubtful. There are easier ways—down to the diplomatic bag or even parcel post." He shrugged. "Though with postal rates these days, that's getting expensive."

"What about Maxwell?" asked Carrick.

"Some progress." Johns sipped his drink and sighed appreciatively. "Round the edges, anyway. My people think he could match with a John Marchell, British citizen, Anglo-French by birth, who got out of Iran a few years ago before the Ayatollah moved in." He grinned. "Marchell was something vague in imports and exports. When he got back here he just vanished into the woodwork—annoying, because a few people wanted to talk to him."

"Meaning he could have been working for the Russians?"

"Maybe, maybe not," said Johns. "For anyone—or himself."

"Is that supposed to help?" asked Carrick.

"No." Johns paused and brightened. "But his foreman, Ferdie Renfrew, is easier. He's on file—ex-soldier, ex-mercenary. Wasn't quite convicted of attempted murder over here—the Crown witnesses took fright." He eyed Carrick sympathetically. "We're doing our best. I can tell you where Maxwell will be tonight."

"At the appeal fund meeting," said Carrick. "Anything else?"

"Maybe." The Special Branch man hesitated, frowning a little. "I'm not saying it makes much sense. I kicked Sergeant Ballantyne's backside a few times and put him to work, which didn't please his wife—she wanted him to hang curtains or something similar. Suppose I told you Targe Island may not be the only place with odd visitors lately?"

"The way things are, they could be little green men and I'd still listen," Carrick told him.

"Size and colour I can't talk about," said Johns. "But he has three separate reports from crofters living along the coast of seeing men coming ashore from some kind of launch, prowling around, then going away again."

"Like they were looking for something?" Carrick frowned at him. "The *Zarakov* lost their frogman—"

"I know. But these men were armed—rifles and what could be machine pistols. Not standard equipment on a mercy mission." Johns finished his drink and got to his feet. "Keep in touch, eh?"

"Wait." Carrick stopped him. "What about Maxwell?"

"We don't touch him—yet." The sad spaniel eyes considered him mildly. "Nobody's going to rush this one, Carrick."

Johns left. Going over to the cabin porthole, Carrick saw him go down the gangway and amble off into the night, towards the harbour gates. Pursing his lips, Carrick glanced at his watch. It was close on nine o'clock. Maxwell would be on his way to the Memorial Hall meeting.

Going over to the ship's phone, he buzzed the radio room. Jumbo Wills answered. The radio room was maintaining a listening watch, ready for any signal from the Targe Island team.

"Nothing yet," reported Wills in a bored voice.

"Too early—it could be nearer midnight." He had already made up his mind. "I'm going ashore. If you really need me, I'll be at the clinic."

"Ring twice and ask for the lady," said Wills gloomily. "Bullying acting captain leaves underpaid underling to hold the fort—"

"Ship," corrected Carrick and smiled to himself. "Don't let her sink till I get back."

He hung up.

The clinic seemed in darkness when he reached it, but Jan Blair's car was parked nearby. Carrick rang the night bell, waited, and after a few moments a light came on in the clinic lobby. Jan Blair opened the door.

"Webb!" Her grey eyes widened in surprise.

"I said I'd be back," he reminded. She was wearing a white shirt top, tucked into a pair of faded blue jeans. Her expression puzzled him. "If my timing's bad—"

"No." She said it earnestly and grabbed his arm. "Come in. I was going to have to come looking for you."

"Why?" He took a guess as he went in and she closed the door again. "Hold on—you've heard from your pathologist pal?"

"Yes. He phoned—I've just finished talking to him."

Carrick had to walk quickly to keep up as she led the way through the empty clinic to her small apartment at the rear. At last, in the living room, she went over to where a telephone sat on a small table. Picking up a notepad beside it, she came back.

"Captain Shannon was right," she said. "Gibby MacNeil's death wasn't any kind of accident. It was murder."

Carrick moistened his lips. "You're sure?"

"It has to be—unless he chose a very odd way to commit suicide. He was poisoned, Webb. Someone fed him a massive dose of heroin."

He stared at her. "I think I'll take the rest of this sitting down."

"All right." She waited until Carrick settled in a chair, then perched herself on the arm beside him. "Ready?"

Heroin—part of Carrick's mind was already busy linking that news with the "post box" system out at the lobster creels. He nodded and waited.

"The original autopsy report was that the cause of death was a combination of cold and asphyxia—"

"No doubts, no reservations," he murmured with a faint sarcasm. "I remember."

"It was what we expected," admitted Jan Blair. "All the signs were there, Webb."

"But?"

"We accepted too much—that we were just dealing with a drunken old fisherman who'd died in a freak accident." She bit her lip. "Pathologists don't like being told they're wrong. But when that happens, the rule is go back to the beginning again. The regional laboratory ran tests on the tissue and fluid samples they'd kept. They got a positive reaction to heroin and they calculate it was a major dose."

Carrick frowned. "By injection, you mean?"

"No, most probably it was in the whisky he drank. The same whisky didn't help in other ways—often, in an autopsy, the odour of a drug can be detected in the stomach contents. I learned that early in Hong Kong. But it can be masked—"

"Like with whisky?" He nodded. "What would you call a fatal dose of heroin?"

Jan Blair shrugged. "Heroin is a derivative of opium—of morphine, anyway. An alkaloid poison. In the case of a nonaddict, as little as a grain can be enough to kill within forty-five minutes. Gibby MacNeil must have swallowed five or six grains, maybe more."

"How much would he know about it?" asked Carrick.

"At first, little or nothing. Then, with that size dose, he might be 'high' for a few minutes—probably less. After that"—she shook her head—"very drowsy, a slide into a coma, with a chance of a partial return to consciousness, not caring about anything. Then death." She reached for his hand and held it. "I'm sorry, Webb. If you'd known earlier—"

"Who'd expect it?" He stroked her hand with his fingertips, frowning. "So someone, somewhere, fed him that doctored whisky. Would he make it to the fishing boat on his own?"

"No. Or very unlikely."

"Then he was put there. Suppose he'd been found before the ice was dumped on him? Would he have been alive?"

"There's no way of knowing." She gave a slight shrug. "Maybe. But the postmortem signs of heroin poisoning, asphyxia, and death by cold have certain similarities—for the same reason: oxygen starvation."

"Meaning they stop breathing?"

"Crudely, yes. And that's the end of the lecture."

"It mattered." He looked up at her. "Who else has been told?"

"They called me first. The police should know soon." Jan Blair gave a wry smile. "That'll be a case of polite apologies—sorry we got it wrong." She paused, puzzled. "But heroin—here! That's what I can't understand."

"There could be an easy answer, one that explains a lot more." He saw the flicker of horrified understanding in her eyes and nodded. Releasing her hand gently, he got to his feet. "There's a man called Johns who should be told about this. Can I use your phone?"

She came over and stood beside him as he dialled Sergeant Ballantyne's number. It was engaged, and he replaced the receiver with a mutter of impatience.

"What will you do now?" she asked. "About Gibby MacNeil, I mean?"

"Hope someone makes a wrong move."

She frowned. "Can I help?"

Carrick looked at her and smiled. "You've done enough."

Her frown deepened. "But—"

"No."

She was very close to him. Carrick took her gently by the shoulders and kissed her on the lips. She came closer, warm and soft against him, and they stayed that way for a long moment, sharing an open longing and a need.

Then, suddenly, a bell on the wall buzzed, paused, and buzzed again.

"Damn," said Jan Blair softly. She looked at Carrick, sighed, and shook her head. "That's the night bell for the clinic."

"And it might be for me," said Carrick ruefully. "I left word I'd be here."

"Well"—she eased out of his arms as the bell buzzed again—"I'd better find out."

He nodded reluctantly and she gave him a provocative wink before she turned and went out. Carrick grinned, then stood for a moment looking at her photograph above the fireplace. At last, almost reluctantly, he went over to the telephone and once again dialled Sergeant Ballantyne's number. Once again the engaged tone mocked him over the line and he replaced the receiver with a sour vision of Ballantyne's wife, probably sitting at the other end having an evening gossip with a friend.

"No reply?" asked a calm, chillingly unexpected voice behind him. Carrick stiffened and the warning came curtly. "Turn slowly, very slowly. We don't want anything to happen to the lady, do we?"

He obeyed.

John Maxwell stood almost casually in the doorway that led to the clinic corridor. Beside him, half a pace back, Ferdie Renfrew was holding Jan with one hand over her mouth. The other hand held a thin, sharp, fish-gutting knife against her throat. His broad, unshaven face was as impassive as granite.

"You'll behave?" asked Maxwell.

Tight-lipped, Carrick nodded.

Coming over, Maxwell quickly frisked his clothing, then, satisfied, retired a couple of paces.

"Ferdie, I'm sure the lady will stay quiet and sensible."

Shrugging, Renfrew took his hand away from Jan Blair's mouth and, instead, pulled her left arm behind her back. But the knife stayed at her throat.

"At least you're not pretending to be surprised," said Maxwell. "That helps."

"Aren't you supposed to be at a meeting?" asked Carrick bitterly.

"The appeal fund?" Maxwell brought out his cigarettes, lit one, and drew on it. "Yes. I went, stayed a few minutes, then apologised and left. Urgent business." He considered Carrick carefully. "Meaning you, Chief Officer. I hoped you'd come ashore. In fact, I was counting on it."

"Why?"

"Because I need you." Maxwell's smile was devoid of humour. "You know, too many odd things have been happening lately—little things, but worrying. People nosing about, strangers asking questions —and now more strangers arriving." He glanced over his shoulder. "Ferdie, bring the lady nearer."

Renfrew grunted and pushed Jan Blair forward. Her face was pale but her eyes were angry. A tiny trickle of blood showed at her throat, where the keen edge of the gutting knife had nicked the skin.

"I'm sorry, Webb," she said. "When I opened the door—"

"We grabbed her," said Maxwell. His manner hardened. "And now she's a very good reason why you're not going to cause me any trouble. This new man, Johns—the man I've seen talking to Sergeant Ballantyne. He's some kind of detective?"

Reluctantly, Carrick nodded.

"And how far does it all go back? To Gibby MacNeil?"

"Yes." For the moment, Carrick sensed his best course was to admit the obvious and try to hold back on what really mattered.

"The old nosing fool." Maxwell drew on his cigarette again and let the smoke out slowly. "So he did get some kind of word out."

"And you killed him," said Jan Blair.

"Yes." Maxwell gave her a curious glance, then understood. "So that's why you're here, Carrick. I thought—well, something different. But our lady doctor was involved in the autopsy—I remember. So the medical profession have changed their minds?"

"Not just here," said Carrick.

"Naturally." Maxwell accepted it calmly. "How long since you heard?" He frowned as Carrick stayed silent. "Ferdie—"

Jan Blair gave a sharp gasp of pain as Renfrew gave her arm a vicious twist.

"Tonight," admitted Carrick.

"Thank you." Maxwell smiled. "Whatever you're hoping, Carrick, you're likely to be disappointed. And I'll tell you why I need you. I've sense enough to know that it's time to—well, shut shop here. But I need tonight. The one complication I can't afford is to have *Marlin* prowling around off the coast. But that's not likely to happen if her captain—even just her acting captain—has vanished somewhere ashore. Is it?"

Carrick shrugged. "I wouldn't bank on that."

"No?" Maxwell flicked what was left of his cigarette into the fireplace. "*I* would. Ferdie, that side door out of this place—we'll use it." As he spoke, he produced an automatic pistol from one pocket, holding it casually. "Now move, both of you."

They were pushed out of the room and through the clinic to a small delivery door. It was locked, but a key was hanging on a nail. Maxwell opened the door, then led the way into a narrow lane. The old Land Rover which Carrick had seen before was parked in the shadows.

"Get in," ordered Maxwell. He saw Carrick hesitate. "Don't worry, I'm keeping both of you safe for now—in case I need you."

"Where's your own car?" asked Carrick.

"Down near the harbour—in case anyone is interested enough to keep an eye on it."

They got in, Ferdie Renfrew still menacing Jan with the knife, Maxwell taking the wheel. Moving off, the Land Rover growled out of the lane, then, headlamps sweeping an empty street, it turned in the direction of the Maxwell Transport yard.

They cruised past without slowing. Lights were burning in the yard and two big container trucks were parked near the office block.

"A pity," murmured Maxwell. He gave Carrick a sideways glance. "One way and another, things were quite good here."

"You had it made," said Carrick sarcastically. A thought had been growing steadily in his mind. "Do the Russians know you're pulling out?"

"No, I haven't been advertising." Maxwell looked startled, grated a gear change as he blinked, then almost chuckled. "You're being helpful. If that's what's been worrying your people—yes, good."

Carrick tried again. "What about Commander Vasilek? Is he in on this?"

Maxwell sighed but seemed pleased. "No. Let's say Vasilek and his friends on the *Zarakov* have their own problems. They're being a nuisance, nothing more—right, Ferdie?"

Behind them, Renfrew gave an amused grunt but said nothing.

"Put it this way," said Maxwell. He paused, working at the wheel to take the Land Rover round a tight corner. They were heading out of the village but in the opposite direction to his cottage, on a side road which had become narrow and bumpy. "You got the MacNeil postmortem report. So you know what killed him—heroin. How much heroin, Dr. Blair?"

"Several grains," said Jan. "In the whisky, I suppose."

"Yes. He thought we were feeding him booze to loosen his tongue." Maxwell chuckled, his face a dark outline in the glow of the instrument lights. "An expensive method—did you know the price of heroin has increased six hundred percent in Europe in the last eighteen months? Supply and demand, Carrick—and of course, you've probably worked out that we're in the supply business."

Carrick shrugged. "But not the Russians?"

"Not here. Other places maybe—I've heard stories."

Maxwell stopped talking. The Land Rover slowed, the headlamps gave a glimpse of a small building ahead, then the vehicle bounced and jolted as it drove over a patch of rough ground before coming to a halt.

"Out," ordered Maxwell.

As he switched off lights and engine, two figures appeared cautiously from the hut. Carrick recognised them, the same two fishermen as before. The one he'd struck down the previous night had a white adhesive dressing on his nose and was carrying a rifle. His companion had a shotgun. Opening the Land Rover doors, they waited while Carrick and Jan Blair climbed down.

"Take them in," said Maxwell. There was just time to glance around before they were pushed along. The hut was brick-built, with small windows and a flat roof, and Port Ard's lights were about a mile away.

As soon as they were inside, the door was closed. Sacking had been draped over the windows, and the hut interior was lit by a couple of hissing kerosene lamps. Two camp beds sat against one wall. The rest of the furniture amounted to an old table and a couple of chairs, a stove for heating and cooking, and an aluminium sink with a single cold-water tap.

"What is this place?" asked Carrick.

"It belongs to a hill-walking club who only come up in the summer—isolated enough to be useful. Eddie and Matt haven't complained."

The two men grinned. The stocker laid down his shotgun and picked up a coil of thin rope.

"Boss?" He raised a questioning eyebrow.

Maxwell nodded. "Gift-wrapped, Eddie."

He turned away, went over to Renfrew, and they went together into a small side room.

There was nothing gentle about the process. Each pushed into a chair, Carrick and Jan Blair had their wrists tied behind them. An additional turn of rope secured them to their chairs. Carrick was cuffed hard across the face in the process, and the treatment meted out to Jan left her tight-lipped, flushed with anger, and with her shirt almost off one shoulder.

When John Maxwell and Ferdie Renfrew emerged from the side room, Maxwell had changed into overalls and a heavy sweater. Renfrew was wearing a waterproof jacket.

"Time for us to go, Carrick," said Maxwell. He pointed toward the stockily built fisherman. "Eddie will stay and keep you company."

"That's nice," said Jan Blair sarcastically.

"We'll be back." Maxwell considered her with a frown. "I'm sorry you're here, Dr. Blair."

"That makes two of us," she told him coldly.

"And what about afterwards?" asked Carrick.

Maxwell shrugged. "When we don't need you, we'll let you go." He was lying. They both knew it.

"How long till you get back?" asked Carrick.

"A few hours—well before dawn." Maxwell paused, a hint of uncertainty in his manner. He recovered quickly. "Things haven't gone quite to schedule lately, but tonight is different."

"You hope."

Maxwell smiled. "You'd better hope too. But all we need is a clear run. The final batch from the last delivery went south this morning. Once we collect this cargo, we're on our way." He glanced at his wristwatch. "Don't try anything clever while I'm gone. Eddie has been told what to do."

Turning, he jerked his head at Renfrew and the other man and they started for the door.

"Maxwell—" Carrick waited until he looked round. "Why did you plant a bomb on the *Harmony?*"

Renfrew gave a surprised glance at Maxwell. The other men froze. But Maxwell barely hesitated.

"Because it was the easiest way to get rid of Jamie Ross," he answered unemotionally. "Good-bye, Carrick. Doctor."

He was the last to leave. As the door closed, their guard settled in a chair. He had his shotgun cradled in his lap. Outside, the Land Rover started up and growled away.

Carrick made a surreptitious try at the rope round his wrists. The man noticed and grinned.

"Forget it," he advised, tapping the shotgun idly.

Carrick shrugged and looked at Jan Blair. She shifted slightly in her chair, moving her feet.

"Cramp," she said apologetically. But her grey eyes met his, as if trying to tell him something. She drew a deep breath, then faced their guard. "Eddie—that's your name, isn't it?"

He nodded.

"Do you really think they will be back?"

He looked at her but didn't answer.

"No sense in it, is there, Webb?" She shook her head. "If they've any sense, they'll get what they want and keep going. I mean, why risk coming back here?"

"Don't mess about," said their guard. "They've got Matt with them, right? He's my mate."

"That might be his hard luck," said Jan calmly.

The man's mouth tightened for a moment, then he scowled.

"Like a gag in your mouth?" he asked curtly.

They stayed silent. After a few minutes, Eddie carried the shotgun one-handed while he rose, went over to the stove, opened it, and fed in some pieces of wood from a box on the floor. As the wood began sparking, he closed the stove door and returned to his chair.

"Eddie." Carrick took his turn. "Didn't it strike any of you that we might be watching Maxwell's boat?"

"The *Goosewing?*" The man grinned. "We're not using her, mister. The boss got hold of another boat—smaller, but good enough. She's waiting along the coast."

"Then there are the Russians," said Carrick, startled but trying to appear unperturbed. "Supposing they stuck their noses in—" He paused. "Was that what happened before, Eddie? Did their frogman pop up at the wrong place, at the wrong time?"

"I wouldn't know." The man moved uneasily.

"You weren't there?"

The man shrugged.

"And now he's left behind," said Jan in a mock-tragic voice. "Hard luck. You should start running now, Eddie."

He glared. "Shut up."

"Go to hell," she retorted, still mocking him. "If you really think you'll ever see John Maxwell again, you're the way you look—a prize idiot."

He swore crudely, lumbered to his feet, and for a few chill seconds Carrick thought he was going to use the shotgun. Instead, the man laid it on the table. Dragging a grubby cloth from his pocket, he walked towards Jan.

"I told you," he said hoarsely. "All right, a gag you need, a gag you'll get."

Until it had almost happened, Carrick didn't understand. Then, as the man made to bend over Jan Blair, he saw her tense, saw the sudden glint in her eyes—and feet tight together, she kicked with both legs, a piston-blow movement which started from the hips. Her feet slammed into their captor, taking him low, exactly in the crotch.

He screamed and staggered, clutching at himself, while the sheer force of her effort sent Jan Blair's chair tumbling backwards. As she crashed on the floor, the man sank to his knees, moaning.

Awkwardly, desperately, Carrick rose with the chair dragging behind him and shuffled over. The man saw him. Face twisted with pain, he started to crawl towards the table and the shotgun.

Carrick paused, balanced on his left foot and kicked with his right. A flat, deliberate kick, with the heel of his shoe connecting hard and low on the man's jaw, under his left ear.

He heard a click. The man jerked, his body stiffened. Then, just as suddenly, he went limp and collapsed with his head twisted at an obscene angle.

Carrick looked down at him, saw the staring, wide-open eyes, and drew a deep breath. Moistening his lips, he turned.

"Jan—"

"I'm all right." Sprawled on the floor, still tied to her chair, hair hiding part of her face, legs helplessly in the air, Jan Blair nodded vigorously. "Just get me out of this."

It wasn't easy. First Carrick had to get rid of his own chair, smashing it against a wall until the wooden framework splintered and collapsed. Then he needed something to cut the rope round his wrists. An empty beer bottle was lying under the sink. He sat down, picked it up, smashed it on the floor, fumbled for a sharp piece of glass, and began sawing. Several times he winced as the glass slipped and cut into his flesh.

But at last the rope parted. He got up, rubbing the circulation back into his wrists, blood oozing from the cuts. Then he went over and released Jan Blair.

"Thanks." She let him help her to her feet, then leaned against him for a moment, her head against his shoulder. She was shivering.

"It's all right," Carrick told her gently.

"I know, damn it," she said tremulously. Looking up, she managed a smile. "But I also know I was scared stiff." She looked past him. "What about—"

Carrick shook his head.

"Let me check." She went across, bent over the limp shape on the floor, then rose slowly and nodded. "Dead. You broke his neck." Her mouth tightened. "It could have been us."

"Yes," said Carrick.

"Right." She did what she could to make her shirt more respectable, saw him watching, and grimaced. "Habit."

Carrick gave a wisp of a grin and nodded.

"Where did you learn to kick like that? Medical school?"

"No, a lot earlier. My mother thought every girl should be prepared." She looked at him soberly. "What now?"

"We get out of here."

Carrick went through to the side room. There was a jacket hanging on a peg and he brought it back, draping it round her shoulders. Then he picked up the shotgun. Both barrels were loaded with buckshot. He tucked the gun under his arm, nodded, and she opened the door.

It was quiet outside in the darkness. The moon was behind a cloud, but here and there the sky was clear and sprinkled with stars. The lights of Port Ard glinted encouragingly near.

They took half a dozen steps away from the hut.

There was a click, a powerful spotlamp blinded them with its glare, and a voice rasped out.

"Drop that gun. Stay where you—" The warning ended in a surprised oath.

Then figures were running in towards them. Adam Johns and Clapper Bell, some strangers carrying guns who kept going and barged into the hut, and finally, bewilderingly, Alexis Jordan with Sergeant Ballantyne at her side. Carrick swallowed hard, and stood clutching Jan Blair's hand.

"What the hell kept you?" he asked wearily.

"This and that," said Johns, poker-faced. Then he paused and, like the others, grinned. "But we decided we needed you. The Russians have gone sail-about."

CHAPTER 8

For Webb Carrick, it seemed as if he moved through the next couple of minutes in a daze. The spotlamp clicked off. He and Jan Blair were led to where two police cars and Alexis Jordan's grey station wagon were waiting. Clapper Bell stayed close to his side, Alexis Jordan was only a few feet away.

Johns had gone into the hut. By the time he came over, Jan had borrowed a first-aid kit from one of the police cars and was bandaging Carrick's wrists.

Carrick looked up at him. "How did you find us?"

"*She* did." The Special Branch man indicated Alexis Jordan. He gave her an appreciative nod. "Tell them."

"John Maxwell." In the glow of the cars' lights, her face showed both strain and relief. "He was at the appeal meeting, then Renfrew came in. When they left"—she paused and shrugged—"I'm not sure why. But I got into my car and followed."

"To the clinic, then out here," said Johns. "She knew they'd collected you and the girl, so she came straight back into Port Ard and got us." He pursed his lips. "And it's a small miracle she wasn't spotted."

"I didn't use my lights." Alexis Jordan gave a short, humourless laugh. "That's some kind of offence, isn't it?"

"Usually," said Jan. She touched the older woman's arm. "Thank you."

"At least I've salvaged some of my pride," said Alexis Jordan. She turned away.

"Rough on her." Johns cleared his throat, embarrassed but trying not to waste time. "What about the dead man in there?"

"Later," suggested Carrick.

"He'll keep," agreed Johns. "All right, that's about it. Except we were already looking for you." He indicated Bell. "When Mrs. Jordan showed up, this character just tagged along." He paused. "How long since Maxwell left?"

"Ten, probably nearer fifteen minutes," said Carrick. "There's a cargo coming in—he's collecting."

"A cargo?" Johns frowned.

"Heroin."

The Special Branch man's spaniel eyes widened and he swore. "You're sure?"

Carrick nodded impatiently. "And you said Russians. Where?"

"Targe Island. But—"

"Wait." Carrick cut him short. "Clapper?"

"The lookout post," nodded Bell. "They radioed in. A whole damned boatload, sir—practically under their noses, chattering away."

"Anything else?"

"Not up till I left." Bell shook his head.

"Carrick"—Johns made it almost a plea—"look, are you saying Maxwell and the Russians are in a heroin run? My God, if you are—"

"No. The Russians are after something else." A faint tendril of an idea was stirring in Carrick's mind, but it was no time to dwell on it. "What's *Marlin* doing?"

"Probably still holding up the quay at Port Ard," said Johns. "She's your boat, not mine. Maxwell, now—if he's heading for home and that launch of his, I've got a car there, on a surveillance job. They—"

"He's using another boat."

Johns sagged, deflated. "So what do we do?"

"For a start?" Carrick paused as Jan finished the bandaging on his wrists and gave her a quick, lopsided smile of thanks. "Get back to Port Ard, take it from there."

"Yes." Johns moistened his lips. "I'll leave a couple of my lads here." He hesitated and glanced towards Alexis Jordan. "Uh—"

"We'll stay together," said Jan, understanding. "Alexis?"

"I'd like that," she said quietly.

Johns hurried towards the hut. He returned in a moment with one of his men, a lanky individual wearing jeans and a leather jacket and hugging an automatic carbine. Sergeant Ballantyne was at their heels.

"This is Jimmy," said Johns, gesturing towards his companion. "He'll come with us, Ballantyne can look after the ladies. Let's go."

Carrick signalled Clapper Bell to go with them, then he turned to Jan Blair. Their eyes met and neither of them had to say anything. She gave a small, serious nod, then went back to Alexis Jordan and Sergeant Ballantyne.

They took the lead police car and Johns drove. Carrick talked as they travelled, the others listening, Johns asking an occasional, curtly professional question while he kept the car racing towards the village. They reached the first streetlights, kept on without slowing, and skidded in through the harbour gates.

Marlin was still there, but her gangway was in and she was moving, the gap widening between her hull and the quayside. Swearing under his breath, Johns flashed his headlights and slapped a hand on the horn button as the police car bounced and rocked towards the fishery cruiser's berth.

They were seen. As they braked to a halt and jumped out, the slim grey hull began to ease back in, a white flurry of wash boiling the dark water below. Her fenders touched the stonework briefly and all four men jumped across, to be caught and steadied by seamen on her deck.

Carrick hurried to the bridge, the diesels idling below, the fishery cruiser temporarily motionless. He arrived to find both Jumbo Wills and Ferguson waiting on him, Wills looking slightly apprehensive, Ferguson's lined features cynically impassive.

"Webb, I'm sorry." Wills gestured apologetically. "We—I thought we had to do something."

"So you were going out?"

Wills nodded. "Targe Island."

"Then get on with it," Carrick told him. "What's keeping you?"

Ferguson muttered under his breath and the helmsman grinned. Looking at them, Carrick raised a questioning eyebrow.

Ferguson shrugged. "I said there's hope for him yet."

Carrick nodded. But Wills hadn't heard. He was too busy. *Marlin* was moving again.

"Targe Island—" began Ferguson.

"More signals?"

Ferguson shook his head. "Nothing since the first one. We tried calling them, but they didn't answer." He paused and shrugged. "Maybe they're having to keep their heads down."

"But we know where the landing was made?" asked Carrick, frowning.

"Yes. On the southwest side. Same area as last time," said Ferguson. He tapped a fingertip on the edge of the radar console, lips pursed. "I don't like it."

Nobody argued with him.

They darkened ship as soon as they'd cleared harbour. Building up

speed, running without lights, *Marlin* became as much part of the
night as the white wash creaming from her stern would allow. Extra
lookouts were at their stations, there was a constant watch on the
radar scan. For once, their departure didn't bring a crackle of comment on the fishing-band radio—but Port Ard's attention was inward,
on the mourning in its midst.

Carrick went below. Once in his own cabin, he changed his blood-
stained shirt and crumpled tie for a roll-neck sweater. Suddenly he
realised his hands were shaking with reaction, and, grimacing to himself, he gave in. Taking his cigarettes from their hiding place, he lit
one and sat on the edge of the bunk, smoking it slowly and deliberately, letting the vibrating beat of the diesels settle him down.

It worked. He stubbed the last of the cigarette, carefully pulled
down the cuffs of the sweater to hide the bandages on his wrists, and
went back up to the bridge.

The modest area of space looked unusually crowded in the soft
red lighting. Jumbo Wills and his bridge team were at their stations,
Ferguson had taken over the radar watch, and Clapper Bell had also
eased in, uninvited, trying to look inconspicuous beside the helmsman. A little further back, Johns and the young Special Branch man
lurked close to the bulky cabinet which housed some of the electronics for one of the navigation computers. Even Andy Shaw had
decided to join the party and stood scratching his chest through his
overalls, trying to look as though he wasn't interested.

The east side of Targe Island was dead ahead, a firm silhouette
growing more detailed by the moment.

Ferguson looked round.

"Nothing on radar," he reported, then remembered they had company. "Nothing at all, sir. No further signal."

"That's it, then." Carrick hoisted himself into the command chair
and stared ahead. Seen like this, in the faint moonlight, the island
looked like some grotesque sleeping monster. "We're going to act on
the basis of the *Zarakov*'s landing party being still ashore. So we deal
with them first."

"Eh?" Johns frowned and pushed forward a little. "Look, maybe
there's some sense in it, Carrick. But what about Maxwell?"

"Afterwards," said Carrick curtly. He was thinking of the two men
he'd left on Targe Island. For the moment, they were his first priority. "Mr. Wills—"

"Sir?" Jumbo Wills glanced round quickly.

"We'll round the point, come down to half speed and comb down the west side. But give yourself enough sea room to manoeuvre if they make a run for home, and keep us well clear of the Sump."

"Sir." Wills glanced at the helmsman, who gave a faint nod.

"What about when you find them?" demanded Johns. "Will you go in?"

"Yes."

"Suppose they start shooting? Jimmy has his carbine—what else have we got?"

"Not a lot." Carrick smiled a little. *Marlin* carried three rifles, old bolt-action military .303s, used for a variety of fairly peaceful purposes, both official and unofficial. He knew there were two handguns in Shannon's safe. "I'm hoping they won't."

"Amen," said Johns. "Well, Jimmy and I will come with you—help you slap their wrists."

"No," said Carrick. "I'm going in alone." He paused, looked straight at Clapper Bell, and corrected himself. "Except for one—uh —volunteer."

Bell grinned.

Ten minutes later, *Marlin* made a curving turn round the north tip of the island and reduced speed. Cutting her way through the lazy, chopping swell, she eased past the hidden menace of the Sump, then her engines faded until she was barely moving.

On bridge and foredeck, lookouts strained their eyes against the night darkness in a vain attempt to locate their quarry. But the black mass of rocks and sea-cliffs mocked them; only the white line of surf along the broken shore seemed to register.

"It has to be about now." Ferguson lowered his glasses as he spoke. "At least, if it's where they landed last time—"

Carrick nodded. "Try it."

A moment later, the big twenty-one-inch searchlight above the bridge flared to life, swung like a searing lance across the water, steadied, then began a slow, deliberate sweep along the shore.

Then it stopped, a large open launch pinned in its glare. The *Zarakov*'s boat was grounded on shingle, apparently deserted and empty. Then, the searchlight still holding its target, *Marlin* switched on her deck lights and *Zarakov*'s grey hull became illuminated from stem to stern, where an extra spotlamp played on the Blue Ensign which fluttered in the night wind.

A quick bustle on deck, and one of *Marlin*'s small inflatable boats splashed over the side. Clapper Bell clambered down first, yanked the outboard engine's starter cord, and it fired and sputtered busily. Carrick followed him down, gave a brief wave to the faces lining the rail above, then settled back as the boat set off.

They were barely clear when a second, smaller searchlight came to life on the fishery cruiser's upper deck, caught them in its beam, and stayed that way, following them in towards the shore.

"Reminds me of something," bellowed Bell above the outboard's noise. His teeth shone in the glare as he grinned. "Makes us like two ducks in a flamin' shooting gallery."

Carrick nodded. That was exactly how it was meant to be.

They came in a short stone's throw away from the deserted launch, cut the engine, jumped out as their boat's rubber hull grated on the shingle, then splashed through the last few inches of water, dragging the boat ashore. Aboard *Marlin*, the big twenty-one-inch switched off, leaving its smaller sister to light the scene.

"You know what to do," said Carrick softly.

"The original unperturbed British seaman," agreed Bell. "It's a hell of a way to earn a living."

Carrick left him by the boat and crunched his way over the shingle towards the *Zarakov*'s launch. Something rustled above the rocks, he caught a glimpse of a movement in the shadows, but he gave no sign and kept on, one hand touching the bulky shape of the Very flare pistol tucked into the leather belt round his waist.

He reached the launch and stood beside it for a moment, a total target in the searchlight's beam. A single shot barked from the rocks and a bullet slammed into the shingle near his feet. Ignoring it, drawing a deep breath, he climbed aboard the boat.

The engine and controls shared a small open cockpit midships. The metal fuel tank was located in front. He stopped there, looked towards the rocks, and very deliberately produced the flare pistol.

Another shot came from the same spot among the rocks, the bullet whining over his head. His mouth felt dry and he moistened his lips before he shouted.

"I'm here to talk, Fedor Vasilek. What about it? If we don't, one of two things happens." He paused, hearing his voice echoing among the rocks. "Either I put a flare through your fuel tank and your boat burns, or you shoot me and you're in even deeper trouble."

A moment passed, then there was a clatter of dislodged rock and stones. A handful of shadowy figures moved on the edge of the searchlight's beam, then one came out into the open. Vasilek, dressed in black, hesitated, then walked grimly over the shingle towards him.

He stopped a few paces away from the launch, his face tight and bitter in the light.

"Good evening," said Carrick.

Vasilek nodded. "Any more theatricals, Chief Officer?"

"They got things this far." Carrick climbed out of the launch and crossed to meet him. He heard the click of a safety catch somewhere further back, remembered the flare pistol in his hand, and tucked it back in his belt. He could see Clapper Bell sitting casually on the edge of the inflatable's hull. The Glasgow-Irishman was lighting a cigarette. He glanced at Vasilek. "So, do we talk?"

"It seems necessary." The Russian's voice was cold and yet held an underlying unease. "It also seems you expected us."

"Someone," corrected Carrick. He saw the figures behind Vasilek were easing out of the shelter of the rocks. All were armed, two carrying machine pistols. He met Vasilek's glare. "You've got two of my men."

"Yes—relatively intact."

"Good." Carrick couldn't hide his relief. "I want them. That's our start point."

"And if I refuse?" Vasilek was curt.

"Then we both have a problem," Carrick told him quietly.

"I agree." Vasilek frowned. "Perhaps—yes, perhaps more than you realise."

"Because you've found what you've been looking for—is that it?" asked Carrick.

"Yes." Vasilek said it flatly. Even in the bright, pitiless light his face was hard to read.

"Maybe I can try guessing." Carrick rubbed a hand along his chin, hearing the steady sounds of the sea, the swishing rush of shingle as each fresh wave foamed in, then retreated. It was more than a guess. It was the one possibility which might explain so much, a possibility which had strengthened in his mind each time he thought about it. "You'll listen?"

Vasilek shrugged. "Why not?"

"Then I reckon you lost something—or someone—a couple of weeks ago and you've been looking hard ever since. You wondered about Targe Island. Nobody lived there, yet you'd spotted signs of possible life around it. The problem was that it was fairly close to Port Ard, and you were still trying to keep a low profile about the situation."

"So?" Vasilek's face was impassive.

"So your so-called 'Technical Officer,' Andrei Krymov, put on his frogman suit and swam in to have a look around—he probably dropped off one of the leave boats. But he didn't come back." Carrick paused and shrugged. "Then the weather broke, we had the storm—and, afterwards, Jamie Ross found his body in that cave."

"A sad accident," said Vasilek. "Is there more to this—ah—story?"

"Some of your people were here, camped out in the ruins," said Carrick softly. "What happened to them, Vasilek? Then what really happened to your frogman?"

Vasilek moistened his lips. "Krymov drowned—"

"You can drown a man in a puddle if you hold him down," countered Carrick sharply. "What about the others—what about the crew of the *Harmony?*"

"The fishing boat, Ross's boat?" Genuine bewilderment showed in Vasilek's expression. "We knew it blew up today. But we heard—"

"That it was another accident?" asked Carrick. "Just a coincidence—five men and a girl dead?" He shook his head. "They were murdered, Vasilek. For the same reason."

A rogue gust of wind blew in from the sea, rustling the stunted scrub and grass among the rocks. Vasilek moved uneasily as it passed.

"You know this reason?"

"Drug smuggling. Your friend John Maxwell runs this end of the operation—with Port Ard as the start of a pipeline down to London and across to Europe."

The Russian stared at him. "Can you prove this?"

"Yes."

He heard the other man give a long sigh. Turning away, Vasilek looked out towards the sea and *Marlin* for a long moment, his features hard and angry in the bright, unwavering light.

"Come with me," he said suddenly.

They went back into the rocks, past the armed seamen. One of them moved to follow, but Vasilek gestured him away.

The Russian leading, Carrick close behind, they began a scrambling climb towards the top of the island. Out of the searchlight's beam, stumbling in the darkness, Carrick was panting and sweating by the time they got there. Other figures came to meet them, carrying shielded torches. An order from Vasilek, and they were led across to the black silhouette of the ruined castle.

"What the hell do they want this time?" grumbled a voice as they arrived.

Smiling slightly, Vasilek took one of the torches and shone its beam into a corner of the shadows. *Marlin*'s two seamen sat unhappily on the ground, their smashed radio beside them. Both showed signs of having been in a struggle, one had a badly swollen eye. They were handcuffed together. A guard with a rifle stood nearby.

"You're a miserable-looking pair," said Carrick conversationally. The men blinked, peered against the torchbeam, then grinned with relief.

"Come to get us out of this, sir?" asked the man with the swollen eye.

"That's the general idea," agreed Carrick. He saw the two men exchange a glance. "Something wrong with that?"

"They saw what we found," said Vasilek. "When we caught them, one tried to escape. There was a struggle, some rubble was disturbed." He touched Carrick's arm. "Over here."

Vasilek took him a few yards to the right, towards what seemed to be a collapsed section of stonework. As they reached it, Carrick's nostrils caught a sickly odour in the night air. Slowly, he glanced at the Russian.

"Yes," said Vasilek grimly. "The smell—you recognise it?"

Carrick nodded. Taking two more steps forward, Vasilek swung the torchbeam. The stonework had been cleared at one spot, exposing an old ditch. In it were the bodies of two men dressed in seamen's clothing. They showed all the signs of having been dead for several days.

"We found them when we cleared more of the rubble," said Vasilek simply. "They had been shot through the back of the head. Probably at close range."

"Who were they?" Carrick fought to sound dispassionate.

"Production workers on the *Zarakov*. They stole a dinghy one night and—yes, I think you would call it 'jumped ship.' "

"Hoping for political asylum?" asked Carrick.

"Perhaps. There are always dissidents, reactionaries." Vasilek was defensive. "Politics can be incidental. There are always fools who imagine every capitalist street is paved with gold."

Carrick forced himself to look at the bodies again.

"But why hide on an island? Why not try for Port Ard?" he demanded, puzzled.

Vasilek shrugged. "They would know we would want them back. Our captain encourages a belief that the British authorities usually return deserters. It's possible they hoped we would give up looking after a few days, that things would be easier for them after that."

"But they ran out of luck."

Vasilek nodded, beckoned wearily, and they moved a short distance away. Then he stopped.

"What do you say now?" he asked.

"That it doesn't change anything," said Carrick. "You're on British soil. You're carrying arms, you attacked two British seamen. How are you going to ease your way out of that lot? Do you think your bosses will hand you a medal?"

"No." Vasilek stuck his hands in his pockets and scowled at the night. "I have been through sufficient disillusionment already. You asked me once about my last ship. I was executive officer on a *Gorki*-class destroyer—in the Mediterranean. We were involved in an unfortunate incident with an American destroyer. There was an enquiry—"

"And you ended up on the *Zarakov*." Carrick nodded. "Then you know what I'm talking about."

"But we could do a deal," suggested Vasilek. "Your two men, unharmed, in exchange for our two dead. We leave, go back to the *Zarakov*, and the matter is closed."

"Not good enough. Sorry." Carrick gave a slight, encouraging smile. "On the other hand, if you threw in a bonus—"

"Something extra?" Vasilek was immediately suspicious. "What?"

"John Maxwell." Carrick gestured out towards the sea. "He's out there somewhere, making for a rendezvous with a boat that is coming in. It's a delivery—heroin."

Vasilek frowned. "And you want me to help. But how?"

"The *Zarakov*," Carrick told him. "Let's not play around. We both know she's more than just a factory ship. You're carrying a package of some of the best electronic monitoring equipment available."

"I would deny it, of course," said Vasilek. "Even if it was true, your NATO alliance is just as well equipped. Then there are your satellite tracking stations—"

"But you're here, on our doorstep," said Carrick patiently. He saw Vasilek's hesitation, knew he was already more than interested. "Don't ask me to prove it—I can't. But Maxwell or his men killed your friend Krymov."

Vasilek drew a deep breath. "Suppose it was possible. Then—?"

"You've got a deal. You can leave. Afterwards—well, I've a poor memory. I make a report, but the kind that won't cause more than mild diplomatic rumbles."

"I see." Vasilek slowly moistened his lips. Then he nodded. "I have a radio in the launch."

They retraced their way back down to the shore, where the searchlight's beam was still trained on the scene. Clapper Bell was still sitting on the edge of the inflatable and was whittling at a piece of driftwood with his diving knife. Two of the Russian seamen were smoking cigarettes and stubbed them quickly.

"Wait," said Vasilek.

He went over to the launch alone and climbed aboard. Several minutes passed. Then, at last, he emerged again and came back across the shingle.

"There is a small ship," he said. "She came into the north end of the Minch from the Atlantic this evening, staying clear of the normal shipping tracks." He paused and handed a slip of paper to Carrick. "Now—well, she is holding this position, has been for some time. Since this afternoon there have been three instances of radio traffic on the same unusual wavelength. Not military traffic, not normal shipping transmissions."

"Between the ship and Port Ard?"

"Apparently. The transmissions were brief, some form of private code," Vasilek said. "Perhaps a change of instructions, but my people weren't particularly interested. It was simply a case of automatic frequency scan locking on and—" He stopped short, mouth closing firmly.

"It's enough." Carrick put the slip of paper in his pocket. "You can collect your dead and leave, Fedor Vasilek."

Vasilek nodded, turned on his heel, and disappeared among the rocks. Another moment, and his men had also withdrawn from sight. Drawing a deep breath, Carrick went over to join Clapper Bell.

"Lads all right?" asked Bell.

"Bruised, that's all," Carrick told him.

"Good." Bell looked relieved. "One o' them owes me money."

They waited, then heard sounds of scrambling and muted cursing. Then *Marlin*'s two seamen appeared. One was limping. The other, the man with the swollen face and half-closed eye, was first to arrive.

"Reporting back, sir," he said with sheepish formality. "And—uh—I've a message for you, from the Russian officer." He grinned awkwardly. "He said he wished you luck."

"Thank you." Carrick turned and looked up at the black rocks

above the searchlight's cone, rocks silhouetted against the night sky.
Nothing moved.

He gestured to the waiting men and they launched the inflatable.

Five minutes later they were aboard *Marlin,* and the fishery
cruiser, darkened down again except for her navigation lights, was
under way.

"I don't like it, I don't trust it," said Chief Inspector Adam Johns.
"And that's being optimistic."

Webb Carrick smiled sympathetically but said nothing. They were
in the chartroom, the brass instruments on the tabletop vibrating and
occasionally sliding as *Marlin* drove at full speed through a low,
lumping and uncomfortable swell.

From the moment Carrick had returned aboard, Johns had dogged
his heels. Within a few minutes, everyone aboard had known some
kind of a deal had been made with the Russians—and *Marlin*'s two
released crewmen were minor heroes of the hour. Johns, like Wills
and Ferguson, knew most of the story. But the one part on which
Carrick had refused to be drawn was why *Marlin* was heading north,
on an exact course.

"Look." Determinedly, Johns tried again. "You say the *Zarakov*'s
people didn't know about Maxwell's racket. Right?"

"Yes."

"But that something this Commander Vasilek said makes you
sure—"

"More or less," said Carrick. He wasn't just protecting Vasilek.
He had strong doubts about how the average British Government
mandarin would react to the bargain he'd struck.

"Well, you made the deal," said Johns. "If you're backing a hunch
and it doesn't come off—"

He left the threat hanging like a warning of doom and scowled as
Carrick simply nodded and turned his attention to the charts again.

They were heading for the Goblin Stones, a thin line of small
rocky islets thirty miles up the coast and about two miles out from
the mainland. Legend claimed that the goblins of the north had once,
imprudently, taken their cattle out to graze among the waves—and
that a powerful sea wizard, angered, had turned goblins and cattle
alike into stone. Fact said that the Goblin Stones were a constant
peril to shipping, a danger area to be avoided, a maze of tidal overfalls, reefs and powerful currents.

"A hunch—nothing more?" Johns eyed Carrick with open suspicion, as if struggling to find another possibility he knew had to exist but couldn't locate. "Suppose I called you a liar?"

"Could you prove it?" Carrick set aside the dividers he'd been using and concentrated on the fine detail available.

"No," admitted Johns. "Maybe not." He winced as the fishery cruiser lurched briefly in a swell and spray pattered its way across the superstructure. "We won on points back there—that's more important. But now this, Maxwell—"

"Has a delivery coming in," said Carrick patiently. "It has to be big, from the risks he has taken. But he knew he had to change his plans, that he couldn't use the regular lobster line pickup, that Targe Island was finished as any kind of base."

"So he radios his delivery man, sets up a rendezvous." Johns considered the chart with a landsman's uncertainty, then injected an edge of sarcasm into his voice. "What you call a hunch says this Goblin Stones place. Why would he pick it?"

"Because nobody else would," said Carrick. "They'd avoid it like the plague."

Johns's eyes widened for a moment and his face seemed to pale. He took a quick breath.

"Forget I asked," he suggested. "I don't think I want to know."

Carrick chuckled, left him, and went through to the bridge. Slipping into the command chair, he nodded to Ferguson, then considered the problem that lay ahead. The ship's position Vasilek had given him was located on the west side of the Goblin Stones, nothing but open sea beyond it across the whole width of the Minch.

That made sense. Despite what he'd said to Johns, there was a narrow, relatively safe channel on the east side, between the Stones and the mainland. Nothing much bigger than an occasional fishing boat or private yacht was likely to use it, but Maxwell wasn't likely to risk that kind of chance, potentially disastrous encounter.

The real headache was the rendezvous point. Maxwell had to be somewhere north of them, well on his way.

Marlin had speed enough available, even if it came down to a long, punishing sea chase. That wasn't the problem.

He looked across at the radar screen, lips pursed. Radar was line-of-sight effective. Even the sensitive equipment aboard the fishery cruiser was pushed to locate something as small as a fishing boat at much more than twelve miles. But at that distance, thanks to her high superstructure, *Marlin* was equally likely to register on other radar screens.

An idea stirred in his mind. Getting down from the chair, he went over to the screen. The duty operator, a petty officer, looked round as he approached.

"Nothing yet, sir," he reported. "Five- and ten-mile scans both clear."

Nodding, Carrick gestured the man to stand aside for a moment and contemplated the flickering green picture on the tube. On ten-mile scan the mainland coast showed in detail to the east. A clutter to the northwest marked a small squall of rain which would pass in front of them.

On an impulse, he flicked the selector switch to twenty-mile scan. Only a large ship would register at that range. But again he had the mainland coastline—and, at the extreme top edge of the tube, the first solid blips which marked the start of the Goblin Stones.

"Thanks." He switched back to the ten-mile scan, nodded to the man, then turned away. Going over to the intercom phone, he called the radio room. As he'd expected, Jumbo Wills answered.

"Jumbo, get hold of Clapper Bell," he ordered. "I want both of you on the bridge." He paused, then added, "Better bring Chief Inspector Johns along too."

All three arrived quickly, Clapper Bell still cramming the last of a sandwich into his mouth. Carrick beckoned Ferguson to join them.

"You know where we're heading, what we're trying to do," he said deliberately, then surprised them with a grin. "But how soon will they pick us up on radar?"

Jumbo Wills shrugged. "Ten miles, I suppose. But—"

"But." Carrick stopped him there. "What we've got to do is get a lot closer without frightening anyone. Agreed?"

Adam Johns looked bewildered, out of his element. The others exchanged a puzzled glance but nodded.

"Right. So we play dirty," said Carrick. He pointed towards the radar screen. "The moment we have a positive contact, we come down to twelve knots. Then I want a gradual course correction, to take us into the channel between the Goblin Stones and the mainland."

Clapper Bell was beginning to understand, a slow, spreading grin on his face.

"That dodge we pulled off Barra last year?" he suggested.

"That one?" Ferguson glanced at Wills. "Remember?"

Wills nodded and also began to grin.

"What dodge?" demanded Johns, feeling shut out.

"We waved a magic wand," said Clapper Bell cheerfully. "Changed ourselves into a trawler. Sneaked right up to a Spanish boat an' grabbed her." He chuckled at the memory. "Remember her skipper? He nearly burst a flamin' blood vessel."

Johns looked around him, still unable to grasp what they meant. Carrick sighed and took pity on him.

"Twelve knots is the kind of speed a radar operator would expect from a trawler," he explained. "We'll show on his screen about the right size. If we also show on a course for the channel to the east side of the Goblin Stones, then they won't worry about us." He paused, still thinking ahead. "But we'll go on from there. Jumbo, I want the launch ready for lowering. You'll have her, with a full crew."

Pleased, Wills nodded.

"Clapper, how long would it take to rig some kind of radar reflector—temporary, good enough to confuse a radar scan at short range?"

Bell frowned. "On the launch?"

"Yes."

"Half an hour," said Bell confidently.

"Do it."

Ferguson cleared his throat. "Running lights?"

"Green over white," said Carrick softly. He'd almost forgotten. Masthead lights of green over white was the international code for a trawler at work. Plenty of trawler skippers were careless about extinguishing them when simply under way. "Let's do it in style."

"Do what?" Johns was still trying to grasp exactly what was going on.

"If we're lucky, fool Maxwell," Carrick told him.

Twenty minutes later, the sea still lumping and the wind veering a little more to the northwest, they had their first firm contact on the ten-mile scan—a small blip marking a ship apparently stationary on the west side of the Goblin Stones, about half a mile out from the chain of islets.

Marlin came down to twelve knots. A few moments later, looking over the operator's shoulder, Carrick heard the man grunt, then saw another faint contact beginning to firm, a smaller craft heading for the first ship and still perhaps two miles away from a rendezvous.

"Watch them." Carrick slapped the operator on the shoulder. "Alter course, Mr. Ferguson." He crossed to check the compass heading as he spoke. "Give me three degrees to starboard."

"Three degrees starboard." Ferguson repeated the order to the helmsman, waited, then gave a nod. "Midships." He steadied himself on a rail as *Marlin*'s deck lurched and a light blanket of wind-borne spray soaked the fishery cruiser's decks and patterned on the bridge glass. Then he glanced at Carrick. "Course zero-five-zero. And a question."

Carrick raised an eyebrow.

"What if this goes wrong?"

"Then we've got problems," admitted Carrick.

Ferguson nodded sourly and was satisfied.

The next stage amounted to gradually gathering tension. At her reduced speed, on her new course, *Marlin* seemed to be almost wallowing through the swell. The bright green and white trawler lights showed at her masthead and she also displayed the usual navigation lights.

But otherwise her decks were dark, shadowed areas busy with men. On the foredeck the big high-speed launch's engines were test-started and she was prepared for lowering. Other figures moved around bringing spars of wood and tubular lengths of metal. Sheets of tinplate were hammered; there was the occasional high-pitched whine of an electric drill.

Carrick stayed on the bridge, his main attention on the radar screen. He was aware of messengers coming and going around him. Adam Johns appeared again, still puzzled, trying to make conversation, but gave up and retired.

The picture on the radar screen was the key factor. Both blips ahead were now firm and clear, the larger still almost stationary off the Goblin Stones, the other plodding slowly towards her. By now, Carrick knew, *Marlin* would also be a clear contact on the other vessels' radar sets. He could imagine the equal tension there, the decisions that were having to be taken.

Except that *Marlin* was a contact apparently moving towards the coastal channel. Moving at the correct speed, already showing the correct lights for her deception role. A trawler, maybe a big one, but still a trawler, taking the shortcut route round the north tip of Scotland. Probably on her way back to some European home port.

The two blips ahead became one as they met. By then, *Marlin* was about two miles off the southern edge of the Goblin Stones, close enough for her lights to be visible to the night glasses guaranteed to be trained in her direction.

The radar picture didn't change. Dry-lipped, Carrick knew he had won the first round.

The next was equally important. He had already picked his spot, the first large islet in the chain, long enough and just high enough above sea level to hide *Marlin* briefly from the other radar screens.

"Stand by." He gave the warning in a flat, controlled voice as the first of the Goblin rocks showed to port, black shapes with white surf collars at sea level. The large islet showed moments later, and *Marlin* slid in behind its shelter. "Dead slow ahead, both engines." He moistened his lips as the diesels sank to a whisper. "Launch away—now."

Ferguson was out on the bridge wing. He flashed a torch, and another torch winked back from the foredeck. Immediately the derrick boom rumbled softly and the launch rose from her cradle. Swinging out, her slim hull hung swaying for a moment, then she was lowered smoothly into the water. Her crew followed quickly and she cast off, engines idling, a strange, tall, sail-like structure being raised just for'ard of her cockpit.

A light winked from her stern.

"Ready," said Ferguson.

Carrick nodded. "Give her 'go.'"

Ferguson's torch blinked twice. The launch began moving, the strange sail quivering in the darkness and topped by a green and a white light.

"Slow ahead starboard," ordered Carrick. He heard the order acknowledged, the bridge telegraph tinkle, and *Marlin*'s drifting motion in the swell alter as her starboard screw began churning. The helmsman stood impassive, a silhouette under the soft lighting, hands barely touching the wheel. Suddenly he realised Clapper Bell and Johns had arrived and were standing almost behind him. "Let her come round on her own."

He watched the launch. The little craft gathered speed, then throttled back exactly in time to clear the sheltering rock at a steady twelve knots. Ferguson came in noisily from the bridge wing a moment later.

"Take over," Carrick told him. "Hold position."

Ferguson nodded, muttered to the helmsman, then stalked over to the telegraph controls.

"Carrick." Johns paused awkwardly. "Can I talk?"

"In a minute." Carrick's eyes were still on the launch, but he was also listening. Suddenly, a low murmur, Will's voice came from the speaker overhead. Using the bridge handset, Carrick acknowledged. Then he turned. "Now."

"Right." Johns gestured in surrender. "I just want to make sure I—I—"

"Know what's going on?" suggested Bell helpfully.

Johns nodded.

"What I hope is going on," corrected Carrick. "We've stopped being a trawler. Now that's the job for our launch."

"And that crazy metal sail?"

"Should give the kind of radar blip they'd expect to pick up—close enough to it anyway, when the Goblin Stones are in between." Carrick gave the Special Branch man a wisp of a smile. "There's a channel through the Goblin Stones, about a mile ahead—too shallow for us, but Wills can manage it."

"What happens then?"

"We go for them two-handed—Wills from the north, *Marlin* coming round from this end."

"Right." At last Johns had a grasp of the situation. "So we hide here. I saw a couple of rifles going aboard that boat."

"Insurance," agreed Carrick.

"Well"—Johns paused—"you might need some firepower here. I've got Jimmy and his carbine. It's a noisy bloody thing, but he knows how to use it."

"Fetch him up," said Carrick. He indicated Clapper Bell, who grinned. "He'll have company."

Bell nodded. He had a rifle and several clips of ammunition already waiting in the chartroom.

More minutes dragged past. *Marlin* had swung round and was holding her position with a delicate balance of engines and rudder. Her launch was a small, shielded stern light just visible to the north. Then, at last, the bridge speaker crackled again.

"We're there, Mother," said Will's voice. "Over."

"Daughter." Carrick had the handset. "Dump the reflector. Go."

"Go," acknowledged Wills. The speaker fell silent.

Marlin shuddered a little in a swell, as if straining to be released. Carrick felt it as he settled into the command chair and took a final glance around. The full bridge team were at their stations, including a reserve helmsman and two messengers.

"Stand by." He saw Johns lick his lips and felt pretty much the same. *Marlin*'s bow crept round a little, then corrected. "Full ahead both."

The deck began to vibrate, the vibration became a shudder, and as the twin diesels began to roar, gobbling air, a churning wash began to build at the fishery cruiser's stern.

Three minutes later, *Marlin* rounded the southern tip of the Goblin Stones in a tight, foaming turn which had her heeling over, in a way that sent anything loose aboard crashing.

Her targets were dead ahead. The radar screen showed them still together, at about a mile's distance, a distance that was shrinking by the moment.

"Searchlight," ordered Carrick.

But he was beaten to it. As he spoke, the thin, sparking track of a rocket streaked across the sky and a brilliant white flare flooded its light on the scene.

Jumbo Wills had won by a nose. His launch was a fast-moving shape on the edge of the lighted sea. In the middle, a small ship with the lines of a deep-sea tug could be seen. She was stopped, a fishing boat less than half her size lying alongside.

Marlin's searchlight beam settled on the tug as the flare died. Another flare soared up from the launch, her own small searchlight joining in, as *Marlin* raced up from the south and Wills hammered on from the north.

With the naked eye, men could be seen running on the tug's deck. A gap appeared between her hull and the fishing boat. Her stern began to swing towards *Marlin* as she tried to get under way.

"No chance," said Clapper Bell gleefully. "We've nailed them." He turned to the lanky young Special Branch man beside him and thumped his back. "Easy—dead easy!"

The bridge glasses to his eyes, Carrick ignored the jubilation. He was watching carefully, and for the moment was leaving the ship-handling to Ferguson. The tug was the *Isabella,* Spanish-registered in Barcelona—he could read the faded lettering on the stern in the searchlight's glare. Men were still running on her deck, as if in a panic, but she was certainly under way, a frantic white wash being thrashed at her stern.

But the fishing boat was just drifting, her wheelhouse door swinging idly, no sign of life aboard. He grabbed the handset again.

"Mother to Daughter. Jumbo, forget the fishing boat. They've abandoned her. Understand?"

Wills's voice crackled an acknowledgement. The launch was coming in like a streak across the water, still sending up flares, set to make a fast, close, intimidating run to starboard of the *Isabella,* cutting through the fast-growing gap between the tug and the fishing boat.

Carrick watched, then froze as sharp pinpricks of flame pulsed from the tug's bridge and the rasp of a heavy machine gun came across the water. He swung the glasses back to the launch and swore. Her speed was falling away, her cockpit was ripped and shattered. Another moment and she was stationary in the water, rolling helplessly.

"Daughter to Mother." Wills's voice came urgently, almost sobbing, from the speaker above him. "We're shot up, Webb. All controls gone—sorry."

He snatched at the handset. "Jumbo, what about casualties? Over."

There was a pause. Then another voice answered, hesitant and uncertain.

"MacKenzie, sir. Mr. Wills was hit—an' a couple more of the lads. Not too bad, I think."

Gripping the handset tighter, Carrick moistened his lips. MacKenzie was a stoker, big and reliable.

"Do what you can for them, MacKenzie. Then just keep your heads down."

He tossed the handset aside without waiting for an acknowledgement. *Marlin* had reduced the tug's lead to less than a third of what it had been, but the way the *Isabella* was still gathering speed she was fast, fast enough to cause problems on that count alone. There was more. Three men came running aft along her deck, weapons in their hands. A moment later, a bullet punched through the bridge glass near the helmsman, leaving him cursing, blood dribbling from a small cut caused by a splinter.

"Clapper, now." He signalled to Bell, hearing other bullets ricochet off the superstructure. "Pin them."

Rifle in hand, Bell motioned the Special Branch man towards one bridge wing and pounced out on the other. They began firing back, the sharp, slow crack of Bell's rifle almost drowned by the frantic snapping of the automatic carbine.

Two of the armed men at the *Isabella*'s stern fled for cover. The third hesitated, aiming for one more shot.

Bell's rifle and the automatic carbine barked together from the bridge wings. The *Isabella* gunman pitched over backwards on her deck and lay motionless.

Someone on the fishery cruiser's main deck raised a cheer, then stopped short. They were rushing past the crippled launch. There were men waving from the shattered cockpit, urging them on. Then *Marlin*'s fierce white wake hit the fragile hull, sending it heaving.

"God," said Johns, dismayed. Then he gulped as a new white flare soared defiantly from the pitching launch, bursting directly above the *Isabella*'s bow.

"Helmsman." Carrick heard his own voice rasp across the bridge, piercing the thunder of their diesels. "We've a few revolutions in hand. Take him on his port side—but if he starts firing, don't get your head shot off."

Ferguson's eyes met his own, and the older man gave a tight-lipped nod of understanding. The machine gun mounted on the *Isabella*'s bridge seemed unable to bear directly astern. But given a chance, it would do its best to rake them.

Gradually, *Marlin* edged nearer, and the *Isabella*'s captain, as if reading his opponent's mind, waited until the fishery cruiser's bow was level with the tug's stern. Then, her whole hull shuddering, the tug made a tight, wallowing turn to starboard. As she came round and *Marlin* heeled to try to match her, the machine gun rasped again. Some of the bridge glass disintegrated and suddenly the wheel was spinning wildly, the helmsman falling back with a bullet in his shoulder.

Cursing, Ferguson and the reserve helmsman grabbed the whirling spokes, and the fishery cruiser stopped lurching and gave one massive shudder which seemed to run the whole length of her hull as she resumed her turn. Water cascaded across her decks. Gear crashed against bulkheads and smashed.

But she came round. White-faced, the wounded helmsman was helped back towards the chartroom—and it was only then that Johns gave a muffled groan and dived frantically towards the bridge wing.

Carrick jumped down to follow him. The young Special Branch man lay in a crumpled heap, the automatic carbine still clutched in his lifeless hands, a line of bullet holes stitched brutally across his chest.

"Damn them," said Johns. "Damn them to hell." He shook his head as Carrick made to help him. "No, you do your job—I'll do mine."

Nodding, knowing he was right, Carrick went back into the bridge. The tug had gained almost two cables of a lead but wasn't making a straight run to exploit it. Broad and white in the glare of the fishery

cruiser's searchlight, the *Isabella*'s wake was taking a positive curve.
Then Carrick understood why.

They were racing back the way they had come. The launch was
wallowing about half a mile ahead, still firing an occasional flare, totally helpless in the swell—and the *Isabella* was homing in on her
hull, with only one possible intention.

"Webb—" Ferguson also realised, and stared at him.

The *Isabella* was taking the one chance open to her. If she
rammed the launch, the tug's blunt, powerful bows would smash that
small hull like an eggshell. If that happened, *Marlin* would have a
stark choice—to abandon men who were shipmates, leave them to
drown as she kept on, or to give up the chase and rescue them.

Carrick bit his lip hard, felt blood trickle, but ignored it. He was
concentrating on that curving wake, realising why it was a curve,
why the *Isabella* wasn't heading straight for her target. They were
close to the Goblin Stones. The launch had drifted. The *Isabella*'s
captain was too wary of the reefs beneath the surface.

But it was close to high tide, a few feet of extra water. Enough,
with luck, to make the difference.

"Port ten degrees." He saw the reserve helmsman stiffen in surprise. "Port ten, damn you."

"Port ten, sir." Resignedly, the helmsman swung his wheel. Ferguson moistened his lips and, as *Marlin*'s bow started to swing,
Clapper Bell barged in and stood staring.

Carrick barely noticed them as he grabbed the ship's phone and
buzzed the engine room. Andy Shaw answered.

"Andy, emergency full—everything we've got." Carrick paused to
glance ahead again. "Then stand by. It'll be collision stations."

He dropped the phone on the Chief Engineer's startled protest.

It was working. They were cutting across the *Isabella*'s curve, re-
ducing the gap—a gap that began to shrink with a rush as the diesels
hammered to a new, tortured fury.

Ferguson understood. He was standing like a grim, thin skeleton,
one hand already resting lightly on the alarm Klaxon button. A quick
muttering, and Clapper Bell had taken over the helm.

They were close to rocks and reef, very close. *Marlin*'s wash broke
on some, tossing high in the air. Dark, waiting fangs seemed to be
trying to reach out to claw her hull. A grating rasp came from somewhere below, and she shook. But she didn't slow.

At last, the men on the *Isabella* understood. The machine gun on
her bridge fired a frantic burst which went wide. Three hundred

yards, no more, now separated her from the drifting launch—but her port quarter was totally exposed to the charging fury of four hundred tons of steel tipped by that high-raked bow.

The machine gun fired again. Bullets lashed along *Marlin*'s deck, then were answered by a sharp, barking rasp of automatic carbine fire as Johns, standing bolt upright on the starboard wing, aimed with a cold, calculated, totally committed anger.

"Collision stations," ordered Carrick. As the alarm Klaxon began screaming its warning throughout the fishery cruiser, he got across to Bell and grabbed for the wheel.

"Shove off," said Bell indignantly. "This one's mine—sir."

The automatic carbine was still snapping, but the *Isabella*'s machine gun had fallen silent. Carrick could see the gun's barrel, pointing skyward, the bridge framework around smashed and pitted with bullet holes.

And the tug was trying to turn away, to escape the fate rushing to meet her at well over thirty knots.

She had left it too late.

Seconds later, *Marlin* rammed the tug just for'ard of the bridge. The impact threw Carrick away from the rail he'd grabbed, sent him sprawling on the deck mats. He heard the scream of tearing metal, and *Marlin* seemed to rise out of the water for a few brief moments.

Then she settled. They were stationary. Ferguson had been thrown under the command chair and was crawling out again, swearing. Clapper Bell, both arms wrapped around the wheel, feet wide apart, was breathing heavily. The fisher cruiser was floating clear of what was left of the tug.

Getting to his feet, hardly aware of *Marlin*'s engines being silent, Carrick stared at the *Isabella*. She was already sinking, the sea rushing into a gaping, jagged hole in her side which had almost cut her in half.

The bridge phone buzzed. He staggered across and answered it.

"I suppose you know you've made a ruddy great dent in this ship," said Andy Shaw conversationally. "But I reckon we're still afloat."

"It was worth it." Carrick drew a deep breath. "Can you give me slow astern, Andy?"

"Any dam' thing you want," said Shaw. "You've got it."

The diesels muttered again, one sounding slightly ragged. Slowly, *Marlin* crept back from her victory. As she did, the *Isabella* began a slow, ponderous roll. For perhaps a minute she floated upturned in the swell. Then she went down in a hissing, gouting cauldron of bubbles.

There were men floating in the water, crying for help. Not far beyond them, close enough to show how narrow a margin had remained, the crippled launch had exhausted her flares. But a small, stabbing handlamp was winking thanks.

Johns came in from the bridge wing and threw the carbine on the deck. Then he sat down beside it, his head in his hands, drained of energy.

"Secure from collision stations," said Carrick. "Damage-control parties report. And let's get these men out of the water—all of them."

Two hours later, *Hammerhead* joined them from the north. From her captain's viewpoint, there was disappointingly little to do. But her searchlight travelled slowly along *Marlin*'s hull, rested for a long time on her crumpled bow and buckled plates, then her loudhailer rasped across the water.

"You've just lost your no-claims bonus, *Marlin*."

Carrick went out on the bridge wing and waved an acknowledgement. He was tired, very tired. The bridge had been cleaned of blood and shattered glass, the fishery cruiser's damage-control parties had at least temporarily coped with the rest.

The launch crew were back aboard. None of her three wounded were in any danger. Jumbo Wills least of all—though the bullet which had grazed his scalp was going to alter his hairline.

Only two men aboard Marlin had been wounded. Their only fatal casualty had been the young Special Branch man. His body was in a spare cabin below.

They had recovered two other bodies from the *Isabella*. One had been a crewman. The other, riddled with carbine bullets, was John Maxwell. They had five survivors, including a sullen, shattered Ferdie Renfrew.

But the rest, including the tall fisherman named Matt, had gone down with the tug.

Carrick picked up his own loudhailer and raised it to his lips.

"Stop staring like that. You're making me nervous," he told the welcome silhouette behind the searchlight. "We should be all right, but I'd be glad of company till I get home."

Hammerhead's searchlight switched off. Her loudhailer rasped again.

"You lead, *Marlin*," came the invitation. "You've earned it."

They reached Port Ard at 3 A.M. There were ambulances and police cars on the quay; a small flotilla of fishing boats acted as an extra escort for the last short distance across the bay and into harbour.

Once they'd berthed, other people took over. There were police uniforms, men in civilian suits, naval uniforms.

Captain Dobie was among them. The Marine Superintendent spoke quietly to Johns, listened to Carrick's report, and made a brief inspection of the ship. Then, without further comment, he shook Carrick by the hand and went ashore.

Gradually Carrick learned some of the rest. Partly from Sergeant Ballantyne, partly from Johns before he left.

The Maxwell Transport truck run to Europe was being traced. Two trucks, already seized, had heroin hidden among their loads of frozen fish.

"We won't get the real men behind it," said Johns quietly, standing by the gangway. He shook his head. "We never do, Carrick—not in the heroin game. But we've hurt them this time. Hurt them badly. This was a major 'back door' operation, based in North Africa." He gave a tight, grim smile. "And I guarantee you one thing. Renfew will talk—too many of my lads liked Jimmy for anything else to happen." He paused, seemed about to say something else, then shook his head. "I'll see you."

He left the ship.

It was twenty minutes later when Carrick at last went along to the day cabin. He walked in and closed the door wearily behind him.

"Well, mister," said a rumbling, icy voice. "Exactly what the hell do you think you've done to my ship? She looks like a broken-nosed parrot."

He stopped, blinked, and saw the bearded, grinning face of the man sprawled back in the nearest chair. Captain James Shannon wore a sports jacket; two full glasses of whisky sat on the table beside him.

"Here." Shannon shoved one of the glasses towards him. "You could use it—medicinal, mister."

"Sir." Carrick took the drink, drained half of it at a gulp, then realised it was neat. "I thought—"

"You had me out of the way in some damned hospital?" Shannon shook his head. "Not with this going on. I came up with Dobie in one of those damned helicopters. Incidentally, a little item of news for you. Your Russian friends are leaving. The *Zarakov* has upped

anchor and is under way. Heading home, apparently. I wonder why."
He sipped his own drink and the grin faded a little. "You did well,
mister. It's a pity I've got to lose you."

Carrick stared at him.

"The *Barracuda* command." Shannon gave a grunt of amusement.
"You thought I didn't know? Hell, I recommended you." He paused
and gave a slight frown. "You want it, don't you?"

"I'm not sure," admitted Carrick.

"Your business, not mine. There could be a complication now, I
suppose—the Department enquiry that's going to land in your lap.
Funny people, Department. Don't like us bending their ships." Shannon cleared his throat with something close to embarrassment. "Anyway, you've still time to decide. No pressures from me, either way."

"Yes, sir." Carrick nodded.

"Right." Shannon brightened again. "I damned nearly forgot—
must be that bash on the head. I've a message for you, from a certain
female doctor." His grin came back into place. "Don't ask me to
repeat exactly what she said. But I reckon it means don't bother to
knock, the door's on the latch and she's waiting."

Carrick felt the tiredness melt away from him. He finished his
drink and set down the glass.

"It's good to see you back," he said quietly.

"Back?" Shannon blinked. "Hell, mister, I'm just visiting. I've
been ordered to take a month's leave—that should be long enough to
allow some dockyard to mend my ship." He settled deeper in the
chair. "I'll just finish my drink, then be on my way. Ferguson can
look after things till you get back, eh? Good night, mister."

"Good night, sir," said Carrick.

He had an appointment ashore.